ALSO BY MARISSA VANSKIKE

How It Had To Be

BRONSWOOD

a novel

MARISSA VANSKIKE

This book is a work of fiction. Any references to historical events, real people, or real places are used fictitiously. Other names, characters, places, and events are products of the author's imagination, and any resemblance to actual events or places or persons living, or dead is entirely coincidental.

Copyright © 2023 by Marissa Vanskike

All rights reserved, including the right to reproduce this book or portions thereof in any form whatsoever. No part of this book may be stored in a retrieval system, or transmitted in any form or by any means, electronic, mechanical, photocopying, recording, or otherwise without express written permission of the publisher.

Cover image by Ksnyd_10/Shutterstock.com

ISBN: 9798852785343

FOR EVERY PARENT WHO WOULD SCORCH THE EARTH
FOR THEIR CHILDREN.

HAILEY, FRANK, AND RAEGAN. I LOVE YOU INFINITY. IF YOU REMEMBER NOTHING ELSE IN THIS LIFE, SAVE FOR THAT, I WILL CONSIDER MY JOB, THE HONOR THAT IS BEING YOUR MOTHER, WELL DONE.

BRONSWOOD

THIS BOOK INCLUDES CONTENT THAT SOME READERS MAY FIND DISTRESSING, INCLUDING DOMESTIC VIOLENCE AND DANGER TO CHILDREN. READER DISCRETION IS ADVISED.

Chapter 1

"I am so sorry I'm late," Heather sighs, her words mixing into her exhale. "Nick called this morning, and I couldn't get him off the phone." Heather jogs over to the table and plops into the seat across from Zola, cringing just slightly as she settles into the chair.

Zola sucks on her teeth before rearranging her face. She has never been a fan of Heather's husband, and her annoyance at the mention of Nick's name is easy to spot. Heather brushes a piece of chestnut hair away from her face, pretending she hasn't noticed Zola's reaction. "Ugh, sorry I'm a mess. It's been a morning." She shifts in her seat to hook her purse on the back of her chair.

Zola slides a mug across the table. A chai tea soy latte, extra hot. Heather's favorite. "Actually, I was just wondering how you can still look so put together with everything you've been dealing with."

Heather has always taken pride in her appearance. Ever since she left her ex-husband three years ago, she has reveled in the freedom she has to dress in a way that displays her confidence. That Nick appreciates when she looks nice doesn't hurt, either.

Nevertheless, Heather knows how self-conscious Zola can

get about her dull complexion and petite stature, so she hurries to brush off the compliment.

"Oh, please. You look incredible. I still can't get over this new hair color. I love this shade of brunette on you. It really brings out the caramel skin tone that I know you're hiding under all that dehydration." Heather teases her friend as she takes a tentative sip to check the temperature of her tea before shooting a smile at Zola. "You truly are the sweetest friend a gal could ask for. This must be what Heaven tastes like."

True to form, Zola changes the subject without so much as a blink of acknowledgment for the semi-compliment Heather paid her. "How are you holding up with all the work you're doing for the school gala this year?"

Heather's response is automatic. "Oh, I'm doing fine. I have plenty of things stored in the basement that I've been gathering over the last few years. I just hope they pass Harriet's inspection." Heather chuckles, trying not to imagine the scrutiny bound to rain down from the head of the PTA.

Zola snorts. "Right. Good luck with that."

"You could help me, you know," Heather says, ignoring the snide remark. When Zola rolls her eyes, Heather pushes a little further. "Come on. It would be a great way for you to get involved at the school. You're always telling me you still don't feel like you've found your place in this crowd." Heather sips her tea. "Besides, you and Beck have a special connection to this event."

Zola sighs and drums her fingernails on the table. "I don't know. Maybe." When Heather's head cocks to the side, perturbed, Zola concedes. "I'll think about it."

Bronswood is the most prestigious elementary school in the state. Its annual gala is the fundraising event of the year. Built with red brick and slate grey stone, the school has stood strong for nearly a century. Its presence looms over the entire town. Its events seep into every aspect of the town's social life. Until recently, Bronswood's attendees were comprised exclusively of prominent public figures from Northern California's most affluent families. Pillars of the Windwood community.

Heather casts a disbelieving look and lays a palm firmly on the table, aiming it in Zola's direction. "Beck was selected at last year's gala as the first child to receive a *full* tuition scholarship. That's an enormous deal. And that is entirely because you have done such an amazing job raising him. By yourself, in case you forgot." Heather leans back in her chair and sips her tea, taking in the way the warm, creamy vanilla scent mingles with the spiciness of the cloves.

Zola takes a deep gulp of her coffee. "It's not like it would help any. If these women haven't accepted me into their little club by now, they never will. It's obvious they don't like me. I'll always be just the new single mom with a scholarship kid." Zola looks down at the table as she lowers her voice. "No one will ever accept me the way you do."

There's no denying that the school mothers are divided into cliques, so Heather doesn't try. Instead, she nudges her knee against Zola's under the table to get her attention. "If the PTA momsters can't see how truly wonderful you are, that's their loss. They're the ones missing out."

Zola offers a timid smile.

"But you really do need to put yourself out there. It would be good for you to get involved and show them you aren't so standoffish." Heather likes Zola. She cares about her. But, Heather is desperate to fit in with the PTA royalty now that Charlie is in his second year at Bronswood. And she wants Zola to fit in too, because if Heather is being honest, she could use a safety net when the PTA moms become unbearable. But it's so much easier for Heather to tell herself that she pushes Zola for her friend's own good rather than admitting the truth. Heather is afraid of what it looks like for her if she spends so much time with a mom who just doesn't seem to belong.

"I am not standoffish." Zola defends herself. "You've got to admit those women are intimidating. I can't, for the life of me, fathom how you infiltrated them so quickly."

"Well, you know how Nick feels about making a good appearance." Heather doesn't look at Zola when she speaks, and she bites her lip as she deliberately turns the focus back to her friend. "How's work going? The boutique's new website looks great!"

Zola blushes. "Thanks! I'm pretty proud of that one. To tell the truth, I don't love designing websites. Of course, I'd much rather be creating cover art for books and music. But hopefully it will help get me a foot in the door down the road." Zola smiles and adds a cheerful final note. "Anyhow, I'm grateful for the flexible work schedule with Beck starting at Bronswood and all."

Heather offers a weak smile, trying not to think about her pitiful lack of sleep in the last few days. She hurries to correct her expression, but she knows better than to think Zola would miss the break in her facade.

"What about you? Are you getting enough sleep? I know you don't sleep well when Nick is away on business."

Heather indulges Zola with a nod, but says nothing. Zola clicks her tongue. "I have no idea why…" Zola sits up straighter, taking her mug in her hand. "You get the entire bed to yourself. You should spread out like a skydiver and watch all the true crime shows you want."

Heather giggles before wiping her face clean and replacing it with a somber expression. "I'm fine. He's only gone for three nights this time. Plus, he gets home on Friday, so it's only two more nights." She shifts nervously in her chair and leans in closer to Zola.

"Honestly, I'm more concerned about Paul. Ever since I saw him again at the funeral in September, he's been contacting me and demanding to see the kids more. I just don't know what to do about it." Heather twists her wedding ring around her finger. "On one hand, he's Charlie and Theo's father. He has a right to see them, doesn't he? But then again, the way he was at the end…"

Heather's voice trails off as she tries to distract herself from vivid memories of alcohol-tainted breath and knuckle-shaped bruises. This time, Zola doesn't save her from the silence, and Heather collects herself before she continues. "The idea of leaving my kids alone with him frightens me. It's the reason I ran in the middle of the night." Heather casts her eyes down at her cup.

"What does Nick think? Surely he must have an opin—."

"Nick doesn't know." Heather cuts Zola off before she can think better of it. She steadies her voice before continuing, "I haven't told him yet. I just know that he would completely freak out if he knew that Paul and I had even spoken again." Heather scrambles to add, "Because he knows our history, of course. He just wants to protect me and the kids." Heather hates herself for lying to Zola. She pauses before continuing. "I'm going to tell him. I will. I just can't tell him until I know what I'm going to do about it."

Zola nods, and Heather can feel Zola's eyes scrutinizing her. "You're the only one I can talk to about this," Heather says quietly. "I can't talk to any of the other women. All of their husbands are friends with Nick. They'd tell him for sure."

"It's ok, Heather. I understand. And you know I won't tell a soul. You can trust me with anything." Zola lays a hand on top of Heather's only to rip it away when the bell over the cafe door jingles, announcing the arrival of Bronswood's most elite mothers. Unaffectionately dubbed by Zola as the PTA Triplets, the trio is as close to school royalty as any mothers could be. The Triplets are privy to every piece of gossip, every school announcement, and every family's secrets long before the rest of the Bronswood population.

Liv Osborne, Harriet Porter, and Shay Stafford breeze through the door, and a sea of varying shades of blonde floats over to the counter, moving as one entity, and pausing when Liv spots Heather and spins on her heels.

Liv makes her way to where Heather and Zola sit. "Heather! What are you doing here? I didn't know you brunched at The Cafe." Harriet and Shay beam at Heather, offering a tiny wave of their hands before turning to Zola to give a curt, but polite, nod of acknowledgement.

Heather's eyes connect with Zola's briefly before she sees her friend retreat behind a curtain of tawny brown hair. Heather looks up to face the trio of ladies, who each look remarkably similar to the others. With slightly different hues of blonde hair in varying lengths and similar trendy designer outfits, the PTA Triplets differ mainly in the eyes. Each of them has a unique eye color, but the resemblance between the three of them is striking. It took Heather quite a long time to match the correct name to its correct face at a moment's notice. "Oh yes, Zola and I brunch here often. Usually Thursdays after drop-off. I'm surprised we haven't run into each other before."

Liv exchanges a smug look and a sharp smile with Harriet and Shay. "Well, we are a bit early today since we were able to cover everything on the PTA agenda in record time."

Shay leans forward, and her bangles chime as she drops a hand to the table next to Heather. "Can I just say, Heather, how thrilled we are that you are helping our little Harriet Potter with the gala decor this year?" Heather glances at Zola, who seems to be pretending not to notice the fact that Heather is being praised for participating. Heather feels a tug of irritation at her friend's reaction but brushes it away.

"Harriet Potter?" Heather asks.

Liv takes over. "Oh yes. We call her that because she seems to produce the most magical events out of thin air. We just don't know how she does it," Liv gushes.

Shay continues talking to Heather. "Maybe someone can finally reign her in and make her understand we don't actually need twelve different specialty cocktails and ninety-nine golden roses in the centerpieces." Shay pokes Harriet with her elbow.

Harriet huffs. "That was specifically to honor the twelve headmistresses of Bronswood and to celebrate the ninety-ninth Bronswood Gala." Harriet rolls her eyes dramatically, as if it were the most obvious thing in the world, and Liv stifles a laugh.

"I still can't believe that I'm working alongside the mastermind behind last year's gala. I'm in awe of your ability to stitch together such a beautiful party." Heather knows she might have gone a bit overboard with her praise when Zola chokes on her drink mid-sip.

Liv shoots Zola a stern look, but Harriet doesn't seem to have noticed.

Shay leans in, close to the table. "Honestly, Heather. It only took us a year and a half to get you on board. But Nick says you're worth the wait," she teases.

Heather's cheeks warm. "I know. Nick wanted me to jump in straight away when Charlie started at Bronswood last year, but I just wanted to get settled first. Really get an understanding of where I fit." Heather looks up at Harriet. "But, I'm so happy I'm here now, learning from such an impeccable event planner."

Harriet beams as she nudges Heather's arm. "Well, if only I looked half as polished as you while doing it. I love that shirt on you. Where did you get it?"

Heather looks down, tugging nervously at the cuff of the crisp, fitted white button-down. The women don't appear to have noticed when Heather looks up, but a glance at Zola tells Heather that she was watching her stretch the sleeve further down her wrist. Heather paints a smile on her lips and looks up at Harriet. "You're too sweet. It's from Bloomingdales, and it's actually a bodysuit as well. Nick picked it out for me."

"So chic," Harriet chirps.

Liv nods her agreement. "That is just the sweetest thing. Ugh, you two are so adorable." She looks at Shay. "Isn't that the cutest thing? I wish our husbands were so thoughtful." Shay and Harriet bob their heads and offer their respective "mm hmms."

Heather flushes and chuckles awkwardly. She drops her eyes to her lap. "Yes, it can be a very sweet gesture."

Liv looks down at her watch and gasps. "Look at the time. Girls?" She looks to her almost-clones. "We really must be going if we are going to get a bite before our meeting with the headmistress." Liv flaps a hand in Heather's direction. "It was fabulous running into you." She gives a tight, close-lipped smile to Zola, as if her etiquette wins out over her desire.

Heather and Zola watch as the group floats up to the counter to place their order. It doesn't escape Heather's notice that each of them leaves with an unsweetened tea in hand and not a single nibble of actual food.

Zola turns her attention back to Heather, nodding toward Heather's wrist. "Are you sure you're alright?" Zola asks in a near whisper.

Heather fidgets with her wedding ring before screwing her smile into place. "I'm fine. I promise. Nick will be home in a couple of days. I always feel a little more settled knowing he's home." The look on Zola's face can only be interpreted as disappointment. Or worse, perhaps pity.

Zola just nods, and the pair gathers their bags and make their way toward the door.

The frigid air catches them both off guard, and Heather pulls her jacket tighter around her. It should start to warm up by now, but the air only seems to grow colder. Heather looks up at the pale grey sky and wonders if they are in for a long winter.

Zola turns to Heather. "Same time on Monday?"

Heather nods. "I wouldn't miss it."

Zola pulls Heather into a tight hug, catching her off guard. Heather smiles before turning to walk to her car. She stops when a strange shiver races down her spine. She turns to look back at Zola, but Zola is already gone.

I've seen that look before, Heather, though you hide it well. Or maybe it's that no one really looks at you. Is that it? They never see you, but I do. You're beautiful even when you're sad. You changed last Fall. But I like it. You seem stronger now. I wasn't ready before, but I'm ready now. I'm going to be here for you.

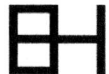

Chapter 2

Heather stares out the window the following morning as she chops the herbs she cut fresh from her garden. The note found pinned by the rubber band around the morning paper burns a hole in the pocket of her robe. It's for her, but she doesn't know who wrote it, or what it means. She considered showing it to Nick, but she decided against it, unsure how to explain anything about it. The note makes her uneasy, but she'll think about it later.

Instead, she tucked it away and walked out into the backyard. Though she usually finds calm in tending to her garden and cooking, her focus remains elsewhere this morning. Her ex-husband, Paul, tried to contact her again the prior evening, asking if she'd be willing to talk about a new visitation schedule with the children. She'd been so confident she was doing the right thing by them, until she saw Paul at his cousin's wake last September, his cheeks hallow and pallid. She can't understand how such an evil man can sound so earnest. And without meaning to, her mind drifts back to the night she escaped him.

IT WAS A PARTICULARLY bad evening. Paul had gone out with some coworkers after an important meeting with a potential client. Heather never knew if Paul went out to celebrate or to drown his failure. The answer to that question might have saved Heather that night.

As a mother of two small children with no help from her partner, Heather lived in a perpetual state of exhaustion, constantly struggling to manage both the needs of a new baby and the boundless energy of a school-age boy at the same time. No matter the effort required, on nights when her then-husband went out drinking, Heather was careful to have everything and everyone in their exact right places when Paul showed up. She knew from experience that preparing for the worst was far better than hoping for the best.

Heather was at home, exhausted from trying to round up her son for a bath after dinner and put him to bed so she could prepare for whatever was going to stumble through the front door that night.

She was scrambling to have everything and everyone in their exact right places when Paul showed up.

Theodora was only a few weeks old then, wailing and hungry again. Charlie was five and had recently discovered some fantastic hiding spots in their modest home. Places Heather never knew existed until she found him contorted inside.

Charlie must have uncovered a new location because he was nowhere to be found. Heather was beginning to panic as Theodora continued to scream her indignation at being left this long without food. Heather needed to find Charlie before Paul came home. As the hours ticked by, she could only imagine how much of Paul's composure might remain.

"Charlie! Where are you? It's time to come out now." Heather's voice was shaking.

Nothing.

"Charlie, please! Mommy is getting worried."

Silence, save for Theodora's sobs.

It was now well past Charlie's bedtime and Heather still hadn't been able to tend to Theodora. Heather's bones rattled around inside of her from the stress of being torn in half, desperately needing to both find her son and to feed her daughter. To calm the shaking that racked her body, she ran to Theodora's crib and swooped the baby up to feed her while continuing to tear the house apart looking for Charlie.

Twenty minutes later, Theodora had finally calmed with a full belly. Heather had only just set the bottle in the sink and flung Theo over her shoulder to burp her when a pair of headlights pulled into the driveway, blinding her as they whipped past the kitchen window.

Heather wanted to move, but her feet were stuck where they stood.

The front door creaked as it opened and Heather snapped into life. She patted Theodora firmly between the shoulder blades and was rewarded with a loud belch. Heather shuffled into view of the front door with a huge smile on her face.

"Honey, you're home. We're so happy to see you." Heather oozed with what she hoped sounded like affection.

Paul trudged over to her, and Heather waited anxiously to see what kind of mood he was in. "We lost the account." His voice was flat, revealing nothing. Paul slowly leaned in towards Heather, sending a shiver down her spine. His cheeks were red, his eyes glassy and vacant. He plucked a light kiss on her cheek and stroked the other cheek with the pad of his thumb as he pulled back to turn his attention to Theodora. "And what have my girls been up to tonight?" He slurred his coo at his daughter's face. He smelled like a distillery.

It was a miracle that he made it home without killing himself or someone else. Heather decided that night there must not be a God. How could God spare Paul's life, time and time again, while Heather remained trapped beneath Paul's fists?

Heather's instinct called her to empathize with Paul's disappointment, but experience told her it was dangerous to draw any more attention to his shortcomings. She pretended not to have heard about the lost account. "Well, I just finished feeding Theo, and I was getting ready to heat up a plate for you. Are you hungry?"

"Sounds great, babe. I'm starving. I'm just going to go say goodnight to Charlie."

Heather's heart sank. He was seconds away from discovering that Charlie wasn't in his bed where he should be. Not only that, but that Heather had no idea where Charlie was. "Let me just put Theo in her crib." Heather hung her head as she moved towards the nursery to lay Theo down. She kissed Theo on her head and whispered in her ear. "It's ok, baby. It'll be ok. Mommy will be right back to get you."

Heather had only just closed Theo's door behind her when she heard Paul's footsteps thundering down the hall, barreling towards her. "Where is he? Where's my son?" The pictures on the walls rattled under the boom of Paul's voice.

Heather backed up as quickly as she could, spun around on her heals and ran. Paul caught her just as she turned into the laundry room. She was grateful she'd made it this far since this was the room furthest from the kids' rooms. Sharp pain seared down her arm as he grabbed her by the wrist and whipped her around to face him.

She scrambled to explain. To give him anything that might placate his sudden rage. "He's just playing hide and seek. Y-y-you know how he loves—." She never saw the first hit coming. He always kept her on her toes that way. The left side of her face was on fire and her vision blurred. "Stop, please don't—." Another blow to the other side of her head. Paul rarely hit her in a place she couldn't cover up. On the rare occasions he did, Heather had to feign illness for a week before she could be seen in public again.

"WHERE IS HE? I WANT TO SEE MY SON!"

"He's hiding. He wanted to show you—." Heather choked the words out between sobs. Paul lunged toward her, and Heather stumbled backwards, which only infuriated him more.

"You lost our son? You have one job, Heather. Jesus Christ, you can't even do that right!" The backs of his knuckles connected with her nose and her head spun around, cracking against the tile beneath their feet as she plummeted to the floor. She thought right then, *this is it*.

When her vision finally sharpened once more, she saw them. A pair of tiny, frightened eyes peeking out from between the two laundry baskets sitting on the floor beneath the shelving. A tiny hand covering a tiny mouth. She could see him shaking. A puddle of urine seeped out from behind one basket. Heather scraped the dull, brown hair from her face and saw Paul's head fall back as he blew out a puff of air. Heather fought to bring a hand to her mouth before Paul looked down at her, and she carefully pressed her index finger to her lips, ordering Charlie to keep quiet. She prayed for any god who would at least protect her son.

Paul seemed to have tunnel vision for Heather, and she was grateful for it. He gave a hard, swift kick to her stomach and muttered *stupid bitch* under his breath before he left her there to scrape herself off the floor.

Paul didn't know that it would be the last time he ever touched her. When he passed out, Heather dragged herself to the phone and grabbed the magazine off of the side table. Her doctor had shoved it into her purse at her last physical and Heather knew that if she called the number for the gardener inside the front cover, help would follow. The police came and arrested Paul that night while

Heather quickly packed a bag for herself and her children. She fled to her best friend's house with her five-year-old son and her infant daughter, vowing no man would ever touch her that way again.

HEATHER SNAPS OUT OF the memory when she slices the pad of her finger with the chef's knife in her hand. She lifts her hand into the air as the blood trickles down her arm, splattering on the white marble island top. Instinct kicks in, sending Heather dashing to the sink to dunk her cut under cold water. As she submerges her hand, the water turns red. She stares at the bloody stream, following its path down the drain, marveling at the way it knows exactly where to go and how to get there. Wondering if she's on the right path now and how she would know since she hadn't realized she was on the wrong one before.

Not long after the night she escaped, Heather met her second husband, Nick Hartford, at a business mixer hosted by her stepfather's law firm. Heather had brought her best friend with her for support, and in truth, she hadn't even noticed Nick until her friend jabbed a finger into her ribs. "Do you think he prefers blondes or brunettes?" her friend whispered. As Heather turned, she realized that the dashing man across the room was staring right at her.

"What are you talking about?" Heather asked, trying and failing to tear her eyes away.

"Oh, come on. He is clearly interested in you. And you deserve to have some fun. Or have you forgotten how? If you don't go talk to him, I will." Heather turned her head just in time to catch her best friend tucking a lock of platinum blonde hair behind her ear and giving a devilish wink.

Heather knew she was in no position to be talking to another man. Her divorce was freshly final, and she was still shaken by her relationship with Paul. She didn't trust herself to be a great judge of men's character, but she was also lonely. She couldn't remember who she was without a husband to tell her, and the feeling was unsettling.

Heather considered what her friend was telling her. She deserved to be happy, didn't she? She certainly couldn't deny that Nick was devastatingly handsome with rakish good looks. Moreover, Heather was very much in need of a stable income. She watched as Nick ran a hand through ash blonde hair that settled right back into perfect waves. What could be the harm in talking to him? At worst, it would go nowhere. At best, he could be a fresh start and a chance to lock in some security.

They eloped six short months later.

Snapping back to the present, Heather wraps her finger in gauze and tape and returns to her breakfast. She's weighing out a cup of blueberries when Nick sneaks up behind her, startling her when he wraps his arms around her waist. He returned home early last night, surprising her with a bouquet. Nick sheepishly admitted that he hasn't a clue about which flowers make a good bouquet the way Heather does, but that these were pretty, and they reminded Nick of her. Heather has been on edge ever since. A feeling she attributes to last night's text from Paul. She reminds herself that there's no need to worry, as she had deleted the text and turned off her phone before Nick woke up. But the anxiety remains, poking at her like a tiny needle.

Heather moves to record the weight of the blueberries, Nick still wrapped around her like a blanket. Nick cranes his neck and releases one hand to scoot the food log closer to his view. He reads over it and flips through the last couple of entries. He gives a small nod of approval and releases her with a soft kiss on her cheek.

"Looks like you've been a bit light on water the last couple of days," he remarks. "You're always complaining about retaining water weight. Drinking more will help. Besides, you know how I hate hearing you talk about yourself like that." He tuts and the corner of his mouth ticks down at the thought. "You're beautiful," he whispers in her ear.

"Of course. I'll add a few extra glasses in today." Heather continues to weigh out a small amount of granola and records that, along with the plain Greek yogurt she's already put in her bowl.

Nick smiles at her before picking up his briefcase from the chair next to him. "Good. I've got to get to the office. We have an early meeting and I'm pitching the next big ad campaign for Nexin later this afternoon." He moves back around the kitchen island to where Heather is standing and he reaches for her. Heather sucks in a breath and waits. He kisses her firmly on the lips and when he pulls away, he tells her, "I've laid your clothes out for you on the bed."

Heather's skin prickles. She screws her smile into place, telling him how much she appreciates the gesture. "You are so good to me. Have a wonderful day, love. I'll see you when you get home." Heather never wishes Nick luck on a marketing pitch anymore. The first time she did, Nick had been insulted because it implied Heather believed his skill alone wasn't enough to land the account he was after. "Chinese tonight?"

"Sounds perfect. I love your chow mein. Use the light soy sauce. No need for extra salt." He turns to leave. "You should wear your hair down today. I love it when you wear your hair down. Plus, it will complement the neckline on the top I laid out for you."

As soon as Nick leaves and Heather hears the garage door close, she turns to the journal on the counter, rips the day's page out and stuffs it down the garbage disposal, angry at the effort it took to maintain her figure in her late-thirties. Angry with herself for continuing to try. She flicks the switch on and lets it run long enough to pulverize that page along with several others. Heather chucks what's left of the journal in the trash and walks over to the far drawer in the kitchen island. She sighs as she pulls it open and slides a new journal out from the stack inside and tries again, knowing full well that if she can't stay fit and desirable, that Nick could easily find someone who would. Heather tries to slam the drawer closed but only becomes more frustrated at the anti-slam mechanisms Nick made sure were installed when he remodeled the room.

Heather writes a new food journal entry with the yogurt and berries she just ate. Before she puts her pen down, she adds a large ice water with lemon. She finishes her breakfast and decides she's still hungry, so she toasts herself a bagel and slathers it in cream cheese. She doesn't add the bagel to her journal, though, reasoning that her outburst had probably already burnt enough calories to cancel it out. It basically didn't count.

After disposing of any evidence, Heather wipes the counter clean and takes out the trash. She walks back inside and throws her hair into a messy top knot before climbing the stairs to get herself, Charlie, and Theodora ready for the day.

Chapter 3

Heather steps into the enormous primary bedroom. Before Heather had ever entered the picture, Nick had torn down the wall shared by the bedroom next to it and created one room, twice the average size. Heather smiles ever so slightly when she walks across the room to the bed and sees the clothing Nick laid out for her. Before her lay a pair of dark wash boot cut denim pants, a white high-neck sleeveless bodysuit, and the beige blazer Nick loves so much. A classic look. Despite Zola's indignation at the fact that Nick regularly chooses Heather's clothing, Heather appreciates the mornings when she has one less thing to think about. And if such a small thing can make her husband happy, Heather can't see why it's such a crime. She wonders if it's simply some leftover baggage from Zola's own divorce that is being projected onto her.

Heather makes her way to her vanity and begins to curl her thick, shoulder-length locks. While the curls set, she sweeps her fringe to the side, securing it with a hair pin. She applies just enough makeup to make it look like she's hardly wearing any at all. It's been years, and she still isn't used to her bangs. She cut them after she divorced Paul. The release was as liberating as she'd hoped it would be, taking control of something as small as her own hair for once in her life. But she left the fringe long enough to hide behind. Just in case.

Once Heather is satisfied with her appearance, she strolls back to the bed to pick up the outfit Nick chose for her to wear today.

She slips into the bodysuit first and then slides into her jeans, which taper around her lower body just right. When she stands up, she can't help tugging at the material around her neck as she imagines it tightening, suffocating her. Curse Zola for planting the idea that this is anything other than thoughtful. Heather chokes down the feeling and adjusts the pants which feel just a bit too snug today. She considers for a moment that she'll forgo the blazer. Almost succumbing to the small rebellion snaking up her spine, she glances at herself in the mirror and catches the finger shaped bruises forming around her bicep.

Heather flashes back to the feel of Nick's hands around her arms, pulling her close to him. She wouldn't dare let anyone get the wrong impression.

Unsure whether her momentary need to rebel was targeted at Nick's selection of clothing, or at Zola's subtle poking at Heather's relationship, Heather compromises. She throws the blazer over her arms, but skips the statement necklace she'd been tempted to clasp around her neck. Nick isn't a fan of flashy jewelry unless Heather is on his arm at a party. When he takes her out, he likes her to turn everyone's head while keeping her own eyes trained on him.

Heather takes a deep breath and spins around to slip her feet into the black ankle boots next to the bed. She's already running behind schedule this morning.

As she walks down the hall to her son's room, she quietly pushes his door open to find Charlie sitting cross-legged in the middle of his floor building with the new Lego set Nick brought home for him. He was always thinking about the kids when he was away. Heather's heart swells at the sight, overwhelmed at the way Nick treats the kids as though they're his own.

"Good morning, my love. Did you sleep well?" Heather coos, running her fingers through her son's bedhead.

"Uh huh," Charlie responds without looking up.

"We need to get you ready for school, and then I'll make you some breakfast. Which color polo would you like today? Navy or White?"

Heather has been working on giving Charlie more responsibility and autonomy over the little things he can control, though by now she's learned to limit his choices. She smiles as she remembers Charlie's mission years ago to repurpose a long-sleeve shirt as a set of pants.

"Dad already put clothes out for me."

Heather notes the way Charlie refers to Nick as *Dad*. Ever since Nick told Charlie that he could call him "Dad" if he wanted to, Charlie has been trying it out. It's becoming more natural and Heather loves it for him. Charlie and Theodora deserve a dad like Nick. It should be Nick instead of Paul.

"Alright then, I'll give you a few minutes to get dressed and then I want you downstairs for breakfast. I'll go get your sister ready." Charlie grunts a response that could have meant "sure, mom," just as easily as it could have meant "I don't have the slightest idea what you just said."

Heather makes her way to Theodora's room and finds her still fast asleep, snuggled up under a mountain of stuffed animals. A smile spreads across Heather's face. She hates that she is going to have to wake Theo up. She gathers up an outfit for Theo before quietly making her way to her bed. Heather kneels down and rubs her daughter's back as she softly sings her name until Theo's eyelids flutter open. After a couple of minutes, Theo rolls over and stretches her arms out for Heather, who pulls her slowly out of bed and gives her a hug while Theo gets steady on her feet.

    Heather dresses Theo and heads down to the kitchen, relieved when she finds Charlie dressed and seated at the kitchen island with a bowl of cereal in front of him. Heather often reflects on how Charlie is such an easy child. He always has been. Heather can't understand how she deserves him. Not after how long she stayed with Paul. She should have protected her children from witnessing what Paul did to her. It seems clear now, in hindsight. She can't, for the life of her, recall why it felt so impossible to leave him. Everyone told her it wasn't her fault, but that never assuaged Heather's guilt. And certainly not the shame. Surely there should be a heavy price to pay for subjecting your children to that kind of pain. Perhaps that was still coming. She shakes the thought away, reciting the prompts that her counselor gave her years ago. *I did nothing to cause this. The blame lies with my abuser, not with me. I am worthy of love as I am. My home should be a place of warmth and safety.*

    Heather approaches and rubs a gentle circle between Charlie's shoulder blades before plucking a kiss on his cheek. "Honey, I told you I'd make you some breakfast."

    Charlie doesn't pull away from the affection, but he doesn't return it either. "I know. But I wanted cereal and I can make it myself."

    Heather smiles and nods her approval and plunks Theo down in the chair next to him. Theo reaches for Charlie's cereal, so Heather pours Theo a bowl of her own.

    By the time they make it out the door, it's 8:05am. In the world of Bronswood, just those five miniscule minutes can add an additional twenty-five minutes to your wait time in the drop off line. You cannot simply drop your kid off on the curb and leave, of course. As an added security measure, the school requires students to remain with their guardian until school doors are open to ensure the student arrives to class safely. If you are late to the car line, you wait around longer until it's your turn to unload your child and watch them walk to class. Alternatively, Heather can park in the lot and walk Charlie to the doors. But she would still be waiting around and then there's the whole deal of loading and unloading Theodora and trying to exit the lot with the car line flowing through. Most parents are not kind enough to allow you to pull out in front of them. It's quite the ordeal.

Heather is fidgeting in her seat as she approaches the school. She is supposed to meet Harriet back at her house promptly at 9:00am, but now she will have to ask Harriet to wait for her. Not a great start to her day.

Heather sighs a breath of relief as she pulls into the drop off line. It's oddly empty, causing her to second guess the time. She must have misjudged it. When she confirms she is indeed on time, she shrugs and pulls up behind the black SUV in front of her. It's Shay Stafford.

Heather gets out of the car and knocks on the glass of the driver's side window. Shay jumps and when she sees who it is, she rolls down the window, giggling.

"Sorry, I didn't mean to startle you." Heather chuckles.

"No biggie. I was just checking that I had everything before hopping out to walk Jeanie to class." When Heather tilts her head at Shay, Shay waves a nonchalant hand in the air. "Oh, a perk of being on the PTA. I don't have to wait in the drop off line until the doors open. I just walk Jeanie in whenever I arrive and off I go." Shay smirks. "Go grab Charlie. You guys can walk with us."

Shay Stafford, otherwise known as PTA Triplet Three, is stunning and pristine. She is never less than overly put together. Her makeup looks as though it was airbrushed onto her face, which is never creased thanks to her penchant for Botox. Shay's emerald green eyes sparkle against platinum blonde locks and tanned skin.

She's married to Tom Stafford, a private investigator. Though her daughter, Jeanie, is in Charlie's grade, their teachers couldn't be more different.

"Really?" Heather can't believe her luck. "That would be great. We got a late start this morning, and I thought for sure I was going to be late to meet Harriet. I have some things at my house that she may want for the gala. She's coming over this morning to look through them."

Shay's eyes widen at the thought. "Oh, well, we can't have that." Shay waves Heather away and Heather jogs back to unload Charlie and Theo.

As they make their way down the stone walkway, Heather's curiosity gets the best of her. Charlie and Jeanie are chatting in front of them and Heather is dragging Theo along next to her. She turns to Shay. "Do you know where everyone is?"

Shay's brows pinch together as much as possible. "What do you mean?"

Heather points over her shoulder. "The drop off line. It's usually filling up by the time I get settled. Today, I'm running late and it's practically empty." After a year and a half of play dates and waiting in car lines, Heather has gotten to know more than a few of the families and can recognize that more than a few are missing.

"Really?" Shay seems genuinely unsure of what Heather means.

"Yes. You don't notice the difference? Just last week Liv was complaining about the line blocking her way out because people were double parking along the curb."

Shay seems to consider this. "Huh. I guess it does seem a little sparse today. I hadn't really thought about it. It's so rare that I'm still here at this time."

Heather is glancing over her shoulder, noting the cars she recognizes and waiting for the line to fill up. But the line remains unchanged from when she arrived. "Where are the Landers? They're always right behind me. And the Morrows. I don't see them either. Come to think of it, I haven't seen the Haply twins or the Engler kids yet this week. Is there a bug going around?"

Heather catches Shay bite her bottom lip. "Oh, you haven't heard! Well, Caleb Landers was transferred to the London branch of the Calvarious Architecture Firm, effective immediately. And I heard through the vine that Marian Morrow caught her husband in bed with the au pair and left him in the middle of the night! Can you even imagine?" Shay tosses a blonde lock behind her shoulder and sips the hot tea in her hand. "I'd die. How mortifying."

Heather realizes that while the PTA royalty might be friendly toward her, she must still be on the outskirts of Bronswood's inner circles if this is the first time she's hearing about gossip of this caliber. "And the Haply's and Engler's?"

Shay glances around before speaking again. "I'm not sure about them. Probably just a random virus or something. Tis the season, you know? Nothing to worry about, I'm sure."

Heather nods and looks up when she notices Charlie leaning in to show Jeanie something he's holding. It's his favorite Lego figurine: a small, green Lego Hulk wearing painted purple shorts and an angry face. Charlie must have slipped him into his pocket before he came downstairs. Heather smiles and makes a mental note to make sure he still has it at the end of the day. If not, she'll pull out one of the spares she keeps on hand. There is no sorrow to match that of a child who's lost their prized possession.

As they approach the brick stairs at the end of the walkway, Heather still marvels at the towering building before her. The school is a historical landmark now, known for its devotion to maintaining as many of its original features and structures as possible, all dating back to the early 1800s. If Heather is being perfectly honest, the building gives her the chills. But it is unequivocally the most sought after elementary school in the state. When Nick told her that the headmistress opened a space for Charlie last year and the astronomical tuition wasn't an issue, she couldn't say no.

Before they reach the stairs, Heather's phone dings in her pocket. She pulls it out to see who it is.

PAUL: COME ON HEATHER. I JUST WANT TO TALK. I WANT TO SEE MY KIDS. THIS DOESN'T HAVE TO GET UGLY.

Heather quickly deletes the text and puts her phone back in her pocket. She glances up to see Headmistress Rosler standing at the entrance, as she does every morning, waiting to greet the children before school starts. Charlie and Jeanie look up and offer a chipper "good morning, Headmistress" to the imposing woman before them.

Ms. Rosler nods, her mouth pursed into a tightlipped smile. "Charlie. Jeanie." She extends her arm, granting the children passage into the building before she turns her attention to Heather and Shay. "Good morning, ladies."

"Good morning, Headmistress," they say in unison.

The children turn to tell their mothers goodbye, and Heather drops to one knee to wrap Charlie in a smothering hug before he runs down the hallway to class. Theo chirps bye-bye to her brother. Glancing sideways, Heather sees Jeanie inching closer to her mother. Shay doesn't appear to notice and Jeanie simply turns to go to class.

Heather watches until Charlie's navy blue polo disappears into the fourth door on the right. When Heather and Shay turn to leave, Headmistress Rosler's voice catches them. "Ms. Stafford. If you have a minute to spare, I'd love to speak with you in my office."

Shay looks at Heather apologetically, and Heather shakes her head, "Of course, go on. I need to run if I'm going to meet Harriet on time." Headmistress Rosler gives a curt nod to Heather. "Have a lovely day, Headmistress," Heather says.

"And you as well."

Heather scoops up Theo and turns to make her way back down the path to her car. She's distracted once more at how light the car lanes are, considering how close it is to the first bell when her eyes land on Zola's powder blue minivan sitting just a few spaces behind her own. Zola has an odd look on her face and Heather wonders if she's upset that Heather was with Shay, skirting the drop off line.

Heather smiles and waves at Zola. Zola waves back, but doesn't offer a smile.

Heather trots over to the driver's side of Zola's car. "Hi!" Heather knows she sounds overly chipper, but she can't stand the idea that Zola might think that she ditched her for a woman who doesn't seem to like Zola. "I'm so sorry, I can't stay. I'm meeting Harriet at the house to get some decorations for the gala and I was running late so Shay offered to let me tag along and drop Charlie straight away before the bell so I wouldn't be any later." Heather is vomiting her explanation all over Zola when Zola finally snaps her own chipper expression in place.

"That's so nice of her. Well, don't let me keep you. Go meet Harriet. After all that, I'd hate for you to be late on my account." Zola shoos Heather away.

"Alright, alright. I'm going. See you at pickup?"

"I'll be there."

Heather races to her car and loads Theo into her car seat before pulling away from the curb. Her phone buzzes in her pocket and Heather ignores it, assuming it's Paul again. She does not have time to get into it with him right now.

You seem flustered today, Heather. Is it Nick? I know he's home now. I wonder if he told you that he would be home early, or did he surprise you? He's different lately, isn't he? Don't worry, Heather. I'll take care of everything. I'm still here.

EH

Chapter 4

Heather arrives at her house to find Harriet's SUV already parked in the middle of the driveway. She can't help her reflexive irritation. Harriet has blocked Heather's entry to the garage. Nick hates when Heather leaves the car parked outside. Only people who use their garage for storage leave their cars parked outside. It's tacky. And besides, the sun damages the paint on the roof. Heather shoves Nick's voice out of her head, reasoning that they will need to load the gala supplies into Harriet's car. It makes sense to have it as near to the house as possible.

Besides, Nick isn't home right now.

Heather chalks her anxiety up to the note she found tucked into the door handle of her car at school this morning. It's the second note she's received and it's clear she's being watched. She's unsure what is more alarming: the fact that this person seems to know a lot about her private life, or the sense of foreboding Heather feels reading their words. She wonders if she should take the notes to the police. If they could do anything at all without any clues as to who might be behind the cryptic messages or what they might want.

Heather gets out of her car with Theo, launching into an apology before she can even close the car door. "I'm so sorry we're late. Have you been waiting long?"

Heather flies into an explanation about their morning, and Harriet puts her hands up to stop Heather. "Heather, please. It's fine. I haven't been here but a moment. I was just on the phone with the hubby. No big."

"How is Lance doing? Nick said he missed the last boys' night."

Harriet rolls her eyes, which look even lighter than usual against her cream-colored scarf. "Busier than ever. With Nick's upcoming campaigns for this new tech company, everyone and their dog wants a piece. All the guys know that with Nick steering Nexin's marketing, they are going to explode. Lance has been drowning in new accounts brought to him by the senior VPs."

Heather nods, feigning interest. "Not a bad problem to have, right?"

"Not at all. Lance isn't complaining. Swimming in a sea of green and all of that…" Harriet trails off before she shifts topics. "I always forget how stunning your home is. It's been too long since I've been over here!"

She's right. The house is gorgeous. Heather fell in love with the Tudor-style home instantly. It doesn't look like the average Tudor. Nick had both the exterior and interior modernized, and it stands out from the rest of the neighborhood. He kept the core features in place with its steeply pitched roof, several gables at different heights, and tall, narrow windows. However, Nick had the brick exterior replaced with a combination of off-white stucco and stone accent walls in varying shades of grey. He added a cedar awning above the porch and matching wood-paneled garage doors. Copper replaced each of the metal accents to finish the home with polish and flare.

Heather catches herself reminiscing about the first time she laid eyes on this house and the life she imagined she'd have for herself and her children inside its walls. Her memory fades away as disquietude blooms inside her chest. She shoves the feeling aside, telling herself that everything is perfect now. Heather has to believe it's true. She has to believe it will last. She snaps out of it to find Harriet examining some bushes that line the walkway to the front porch. Heather planted them herself. Rows of fountain grass whose foxtails have died off from the cold and beautiful English lavender hanging on for dear life until spring arrives.

But it's the large, pink blooms that hold Harriet's attention. "I can't believe you have anything blooming at all when it's so cold out. What are these?"

"Rhododendren Moupinense. But most call them 'Christmas Cheer'. I picked them because they bloom in the winter. When everything else fades away, I wanted something bright to bring life back to the yard while we wait for the cold to pass."

Harriet nods thoughtfully. "They're beautiful. Who knew you had such a green thumb? I can't even keep a succulent alive and they hardly need any attention at all."

"I find gardening relaxing. And the payoff is just so gratifying. You should see the backyard. That's my little oasis." Heather chuckles and makes for the garage entrance into the house.

"I'd love to!"

Heather pauses and scoops Theo up in her arms. "Really? Would you like a tour before we get to work?"

Harriet smiles and immediately nods in response. "Lead the way."

Chapter 5

Stepping into the backyard is like being transported into another world. While everything outside of Heather's bubble is cold, muted, and covered in frost, her backyard is a vivid splash of color, bursting with life.

When they first moved in, Nick used to come out into the backyard to play with the kids. But then, as time passed, he became increasingly busy, traveling more, and the kids stopped asking him to come outside. It became a place of refuge and retreat for Heather and her children; a place where Heather can pause to breathe and relax.

"Wow," Harriet fawns. "Heather, this is truly incredible." Harriet walks around the yard examining the different plants and flowers.

"Thank you." Harriet's interest sparks a new hope in Heather that she is finally being taken into the fold. Few women that Heather has met here are interested in talking about plants. Then again, few women are ever invited to her house. She sets Theo down and watches her run laps on the grass. "I designed it so that there would be colors blooming all year round. I scattered plants that bloom in the different seasons all over the yard."

Heather waits, then adds tentatively, "The winter blooms are my favorite."

Harriet leans in to get a closer look at the yellow winter aconite. "Why is that? I mean, sure, these little guys stand out because they're bright and sunny. But, I kind of love the dark colors and vibe of the others. So unique."

Heather considers her answer. "I love the deep, moody palette too. But really, I admire the heartiness of the plants. Their ability not only to weather such a cold, dismal climate, but to thrive in it." Heather watches as Harriet moves to the snowdrops.

One of the dark purple flowers catches Harriet's attention. "What is this beauty?"

"Atropa Belladonna. Or Nightshade." Heather is smiling, but her heart leaps into her throat when Harriet reaches out to touch the plant. "Don't!"

Harriet startles, retracting her hand, and Heather hurries to apologize. "I'm sorry. You have to be careful with that one. It's toxic to humans and animals."

Harriet's eyes grow wide. "Why do you have it? Doesn't that make you nervous with the kids?"

"Charlie is old enough that he understands not to touch it. And I never leave Theo out here unattended. It's a good deterrent for unwanted critters who like to get into my herb garden."

Harriet doesn't respond and Heather wonders if there is more that she wants to say. On a whim, Heather decides to tell Harriet the truth. Maybe Harriet will understand.

"Honestly, though, I love their secrets. The bells look innocent. But if you mess with them, you discover they have a dangerous edge underneath that sweet exterior."

Harriet turns to Heather with a knowing grin. "I think these just became my new favorite."

Heather nods. "You might like the black tulips too. And you can touch them." With a wink, she adds, "They're also called Queen of the Night."

"Love that! God, I should just have you make the gala centerpieces."

Heather gasps. "Really?"

"I mean, I hired the florist long ago, but you should at the very least consult on them. What would you include that's here in your yard right now?"

Heather senses the weight of this test; she's desperate to pass and earn a place among these women. She looks around, assessing her stock. "Queen of the Night, with the Snowdrops, some Winterberries, and Hellabores."

Harriet beams, following along, and Heather feels her heart swell. "I love it. I think they'd look stunning together with some greens and gold brushed branches mixed in. And they'd go beautifully with the classic theme."

"I'd be happy to throw together a rough sample piece if you think it would be helpful," Heather offers.

Harriet claps her hands together. "You are a saint! I would love that! Do you think you can do that in the next day or so? I'm meeting with the florist on Sunday."

"Absolutely! No problem. I'll drop it off at the school tomorrow. Do you need anything else?"

Harriet shakes her head. "Just the decor."

"Right. Shall we?" Heather nods her head towards the back door.

The women walk into the kitchen through the back sliding door and set their purses down on the counter. "I have the basic things that you asked for," Heather says. "Do you have a list of everything else you're looking for? I don't know if I have all of it, but there's so much miscellaneous stuff from the parties I hosted for Nick's clients before he became VP of marketing last year."

"Why didn't you tell me when we met that you've been an event planner? I could have used you long ago." Harriet teases.

Heather flushes. "I wouldn't call myself an event planner. I've certainly never put together anything as beautiful, or large, as you have."

"Well, that will get remedied at the gala this year." Harriet pulls a small notepad out of her purse and flips open to the bookmarked page. "I do have a list of things I'm looking for, but if we can sort through everything you have, maybe something else will catch my eye."

"Sounds good. This way." Heather makes her way to the door at the top of the staircase. "Everything is down in the basement."

Harriet gasps. "You have a basement? Wow, I didn't think we had those in Windwood."

"Most homes in California don't. I think it has to do with the earthquakes. Nick had his structurally reinforced to protect the house." A chill zips down Heather's spine as she takes Theodora's hand and leads the way down the steps. The basement is her least favorite room in the house. A cold, lightless box with no windows and nonexistent acoustics.

When they reach the bottom of the stairs, something taps Heather's shoulder. She spins around to find Harriet stepping back with her hands up in surrender.

"Whoa, sorry. I didn't mean to startle you. You weren't answering my questions." Harriet's voice is gentle, as if careful not to scare Heather any further. "You ok?"

Heather shakes her head. "Yeah. I am. Where's Theo?"

Panic bubbles up in Heather's throat when she doesn't remember letting go of Theo's hand.

Harriet points to a spot on the floor behind Heather. "She's right here."

Heather sighs her relief. "Sorry. I've just never really been all that comfortable down here," Heather says, looking around. "I think I have basementophobia or something."

"Achluophobia," Harriet corrects. When Heather looks at her, confused, she continues. "Or maybe nyctophobia, or kenophobia, or cleithrophobia?"

"What?"

"There's no such thing as basementophobia. People who are afraid of basements are usually afraid of something more basic, and the basement just triggers it. Fear of darkness, or the unknown, or emptiness… Being trapped."

Heather swallows a lump in her throat. "Huh. That's interesting. How do you know all that?"

Harriet shrugs. "I know all kinds of random trivia." She looks around the room, which is flanked on all sides by rows of neatly organized shelves full of boxes. "So, where are the decorations?"

Heather makes her way to the far wall. "A bunch of these boxes have things you might like." Heather pulls a box down. "This one has the black and cream-colored table clothes. I believe I have ten rounds and five rectangles in each color." Heather drops the second box on the ground with a loud thud when Harriet squeals.

"Oh my god, what is that tiny little door over there?"

Heather looks to find Harriet squatting down to examine the small, white square door, approximately three feet by three feet with a padlock on the outside. Heather stares at the door, trying to process Harriet's question. Trying to remember what she knows about the tiny space on the other side. Her eyes gloss over.

"What's inside?"

Heather finally tears her eyes away and sees Harriet looking at her like she had grown a third arm. Heather realizes she didn't answer Harriet's question and scrambles to rearrange her face. "There's nothing in there. It's really not big enough inside to fit anything important. I think it used to be an access way to underneath the house at one time, but it's sealed up now."

Harriet looks down into the box just in front of her. "This is great," she beams. "I love these cracked gold globes! We could hang these over the tables."

Heather relaxes and pulls down three other boxes for Harriet to sort through.

When they finish gathering the supplies that Harriet selects for the gala, they make a few trips to bring the boxes upstairs. Heather holds her breath as she locks the basement door behind her, and she checks the knob is secure before helping Harriet load the boxes into the SUV.

Harriet closes the trunk of her vehicle and thanks Heather again for all of her help. "I'll see you at the next gala meeting? We'll be discussing the layout, menu, and handing out setup and tear down assignments."

"I wouldn't miss it," Heather says as she watches Theo roll around on the lawn.

Harriet climbs into the driver's seat. "Good! See you soon. Ta!"

Heather's smile vanishes the second Harriet's SUV is out of sight, and she turns to swing Theo up into her arms.

She nuzzles her daughter's nose. "Theodora, if you ever catch me saying *ta*, shoot me." Theo giggles at the silly voice and Heather decides they've both earned a snack.

She freezes as she turns to face the front of the house.

Without breaking her gaze, Heather slides her cellphone out of her pocket. Her hands are shaking and she curses beneath her breath as the phone slips through her fingers. Heather focuses on keeping Theodora steady as she squats down to retrieve it. Snapping her head back up, she uses one hand to dial Harriet's number.

"Harriet, did you close the front door behind you after you went inside to grab your purse?" She wonders if Harriet can hear the tremble in her voice.

"Of course! Remember? You flinched because I swung it closed a bit too hard." Harriet giggles on the other end of the phone. "Why?"

"Oh, no reason." Heather swallows to steady herself as she flounders for an explanation. "I went back inside through the garage, and I was just being lazy. Thanks."

Heather doesn't wait for an answer, and she clicks to end the call. Her first instinct is to dial Nick's number, but she changes her mind when she remembers he has an important meeting this afternoon. She puts the phone back in her pocket.

Heather keeps her eyes locked on the grass under her feet as her arms tighten around Theodora's tiny body.

She's imagining things. Of course, she is.

But when Heather finally lifts her eyes once more, the front door is still wide open.

Chapter 6

Heather's heart races as she straps an angry Theodora into her car seat and locks the car doors, securing her daughter inside. The alarm chirps, mixing with Theodora's wails. She takes a few steps away so she can hear and she dials 9-1-1 while walking quietly towards the front door.

"9-1-1, what's your emergency?"
"My name is Heather Hartford and I think there is an intruder in my home."
"What is your address, Heather?"
"1739 North Kensington Road."
"Do you see the intruder in the home?"
"No, I haven't seen them, but the front door is open."
"And where are you, Heather?"
"I'm outside with my daughter."
"Are you armed?"
"No, I'm not armed."

"Ok. And you're certain you didn't leave the door open?"

"I'm certain. Can you please get here as soon as you can?"

"Stay with me Heather, officers are on the way."

Heather makes it to the front door and hangs up the phone. She's heard stories of stalled dispatch, and her mother once told her that if she really needs help, to give police the important information and then hang up the call.

She looks inside as much as she can from outside the door, and she calls out, "Hello? Is someone inside?"

Silence.

She takes a few steps closer and cranes her neck around the door frame to try again. "Hello? Who's in there?"

Something rustles in the bushes to her right, sending Heather flying back to her car. She jumps into the driver's seat and races around the block as fast as she can. She loops back around and parks across the street, a few houses down, lengthening her neck to survey the scene. As she watches, Heather has to remind herself, out loud, to breathe. She tries not to blink as she waits for either the intruder to appear or for the police to arrive.

Heather tears her eyes from the scene just long enough to check the clock.

Two minutes pass.

Then three more.

Another two minutes.

She begins to wonder if the police are coming at all. Then, finally, a siren blares from somewhere, and blue and red lights flash in her rearview mirror. She races to meet the police officers. She pauses briefly, considering whether to lock the car, but decides against it. They're safe now.

"Officers! Thank you for coming. I know I closed the front

door and then when I finished helping my friend, I looked back and it was wide open…"

The officer in front of her is older, round, and regarding her with a look of boredom. "Ma'am, you live here?"

"Yes, yes. I made the call. My name is Heather Hartford." Heather is breathless even though she's been sitting in her car.

"Alright, alright, ma'am. Just try to calm down. We'll go inside and have a look around. Wait here." Heather nods her compliance and waits.

She has no idea how much time has passed when she hears Theodora screaming. Heather freezes. Something is wrong. Theodora is in the car, but it sounds like her daughter is right next to her. She swivels to find the back door of her car open. And someone is reaching inside.

"Hey! What the hell are you doing? Get away from my daughter!"

Heather doesn't remember reaching her vehicle.

One second, she's waiting on her lawn for an update from the officers inside. The next, she is yanking on the back of a stranger's collar, hitting him as hard as she can, screaming in his ear. "Get the hell away from her!"

"Heather! Heather!" She knows that voice. Someone pulls her off of her victim. "Heather, stop it right now. What the hell is going on?"

She spins around to find herself face to face with Nick, who is apologizing profusely to the body on the ground. Heather recognizes her neighbor. The person whose home she's parked in front of. It's Geoff Lindon.

"I'm sorry, Heather. I saw Theo screaming in the car and I didn't see you." Geoff sputters an apology. "I didn't know how long she'd been in there or where you were." He holds a hand over his right eye, and Nick helps him to his feet. "I saw the police car in front of your house and I was just trying to help."

Heather's mind is racing. She swallows a sob. "Geoff, I'm so sorry. I didn't recognize you." Her eyes flicker back and forth between her neighbor and her husband. "I'm a little out of sorts, and I saw someone reaching in the car for Theo." Heather covers her mouth to keep her chin from quivering.

Nick apologizes again to Geoff, who is handling this whole thing with more compassion than Heather could even dream of. "Hey, no sweat. Serves me right for poking a mama bear, huh?" He chuckles dryly and hobbles back up his driveway.

Heather watches Geoff disappear through his front door before turning back around.

Nick scoops Theo out of her car seat and puts an arm around Heather's shoulders, pulling her back over to their house where an officer is just stepping outside.

Several of their neighbors have come outside, likely having heard the commotion.

"Officer, I'm Nick Hartford. This is my house. I got a call that there was an intruder?"

"We've done a sweep of the premises and we found no signs of a break in. No signs of forced entry. Nothing unusual inside the house."

Heather's jaw drops. "But the front door…"

"It's likely that the door was left open by mistake, or perhaps it didn't latch fully when it was closed. An honest mistake. We'll have you fill out a report, however, so that if it turns out you find something unusual when you get settled, the invasion is already on record."

Nick's arm falls from Heather's shoulder. He passes Theo to Heather and reaches for the clipboard. "Thank you, Officer Jenkins, for your diligence and for your patience." Nick glances sideways at Heather. "I'm sorry my wife called you out for nothing."

Officer Jenkins's gaze flickers back and forth between them. "No harm done. It's always better to be on the cautious side. You just never know."

NICK AND HEATHER SPEND a few moments with the officers, completing the necessary paperwork, and then they walk into the house together. Nick closes the front door behind them, making sure it latches closed before he locks the deadbolt.

Heather carries Theo to her room and kneels down to send her inside. "Theo, sweetheart, go play. Mommy will be right back." She stays crouched while she watches Theo toddle over to her dollhouse.

Heather stands up and turns to walk the short way back to Nick, her head hanging. She lifts her face to find Nick staring at her. "Have you lost your goddamn mind?" His voice is quiet, but Heather can feel the rage simmering beneath his question.

Heather stays glued in place. Her instinct tells her it's best to keep her mouth shut. To ride out his anger without interruption.

"You remember that I had a huge pitch today, don't you?" Nick paces in the entryway. "It was humiliating. Right there, in the middle of the meeting, Fallon comes barging in to tell me the police are on the phone, and that it's an emergency. Someone broke into my home." Nick's face is scarlet, and he loosens the knot in his tie. "Then, I show up here to find you pummeling Geoff after having abandoned our daughter in the car! And everyone is watching the whole goddamn thing. I mean, thank God I work only fifteen minutes away. Who knows what condition I'd have found Geoff in if I hadn't showed up when I did?"

Heather opens her mouth to speak but closes it again when

he turns his back to her, pressing the heels of his palms to his eyes. When Nick speaks again, his voice is measured, as if he's exerting a great effort to scale back from fury to mere anger. "You realize that we have to live here with these people, right? And how this looks for me?"

Heather moves to wrap her arms around him at the same moment he chooses to spin around to face her again, his arm flung out wide. The back of Nick's hand connects with the side of Heather's face, and she stumbles backwards.

She touches the tips of her fingers tentatively to her cheek and stares at him, trying to process what had just happened—what cannot be happening, again.

Nick's eyes are wide with shock. "Jesus, Heather. I am so sorry. Are you alright? I didn't mean to…"

Heather steadies herself. "I'm fine. Really."

Nick steps forward and pulls her into his chest. "I'm sorry. Forgive me." His words are a warm breeze through her hair.

She pulls away, creating a small margin of space between them. Dazed and shocked, she still feels a tug to calm him. To make him ok. She shakes her head, brushing off the incident. "It's alright." Heather isn't sure what else she should say.

Nick backs away from her, like he's afraid to touch her again. "It's not alright. I don't know what got into me." He makes his way over to the glass bar cart in the living room and pours himself a finger of scotch. Nick tosses it back and pours himself another. He hasn't looked back at Heather yet and Heather watches him slowly make his way back over to her.

He reaches for her hand before lifting his eyes to meet hers and Heather can see that they are teary and rimmed with pink regret. "I shouldn't have yelled at you. And I didn't mean to hit you. I didn't see you there." He presses a light kiss to the bruise on her cheek, and her heart breaks for him. She knows he wasn't trying to hurt her. "I've been under so much pressure to land this account and then I got called out to find you and Theodora scared, and all the police. I just lost it. That's not your fault, and I am so sorry."

"I know you are." It's all Heather can muster.

He lifts his fingers to touch Heather's face. "I'll get you some ice for this. Stay here with Theo. I'll go pick up Charlie."

Heather's eyelid twitches. She sucks in a breath and sets her shoulders squarely in place as she adjusts her posture. "No, that's alright. You stay. I need a minute. To get some air." Nick nods and leaves her standing in the entryway while he retreats to the kitchen.

She waits for Nick to return with a small bag of ice, and she silently makes her way to the primary bathroom to assess the damage.

The mirror reveals purple bruising and swelling from his knuckles. Heather can see the maroon splotch where Nick's wedding ring struck her skin. She holds the ice pack to her cheek to soothe the sting. When she feels like it's helped as much as it can, she sets to applying makeup to cover the rest.

She takes a deep breath and steels herself. She has to go get Charlie from school.

Chapter 7

Heather pulls up to the school and puts her car in Park to wait for the bell to ring. She's grateful that none of her friends are here yet. She has just a few more minutes before she'll have to face them. Heather wears her largest sunglasses, and though they don't cover all the swelling, she hopes they will distract attention away with their sheer size.

Her heart hammers against the inside of her ribs when she sees Zola's van pull up behind hers. Zola gets out of her car and waves at Heather's side mirror. Heather sticks a hand out of the window before getting out to wait for Charlie.

Zola gasps when she sees Heather's face. Even with the sunglasses on, Zola isn't fooled, and Heather hurries to offer an awkward chuckle. "It's not that bad. Just the mark of a giant klutz." Zola's eyes tick down in the corner. Heather can't tell if her friend is about to shout or break into tears, and at the moment, she's keen to avoid either option. "Seriously! I was playing on the floor with Theo and I went to go fix a snack and tripped on her little tricycle. I crashed right into the edge of the nightstand. Hurt like a son-of-a…"

Heather doesn't even know why she feels like she needs to lie about what happened. It was an accident. But her new friends don't know everything about her past relationship with Paul. This is her fresh start and she won't let her past trauma creep in. Notwithstanding that, needing to convince everyone else that it was an accident just feels too much like stepping into the past.

Zola says nothing as she drapes her arm around Heather's shoulder.

Heather's face sags when she spies Liv approaching.

"Heather!! Hi!" Liv is strutting, closing the gap between them. Her sandy blonde hair falls in perfect waves to her shoulders. "So great to run into you!"

Liv Osborn is the PTA Queen and the very definition of polished. She has deep brown eyes set against a peaches-and-cream complexion. She's been a mother of Bronswood children the longest. Her daughter, Mila, graduated from Bronswood three years ago and now attends the best private middle school in the state. Her son, Henry, is in fourth grade and the star violinist in the Bronswood orchestra. She's married to Philip Osborn, an unbeatable corporate attorney who represents some of the largest corporations in the country.

Heather shrugs away the compliment, giving Zola a one-sided smile. "Hey, Liv. Are you here to pick up Henry? Doesn't he stay for band practice on Fridays?"

"You just remember everything!" Liv marvels. "He does, but I have to meet with the headmistress to go over a few remaining details for the gala." Liv removes her sunglasses and gets a good look at Heather's face. Her jaw falls open. "Heather, my god. What happened?"

Heather waves the question away and tells her the same story she told Zola just moments ago.

Liv bursts out giggling. "Oh god. I'm sorry, that's not funny. This is exactly why I make sure the nanny has the toys picked up at all times. I can't imagine leaving the house if I got banged up that badly from a silly kid's toy."

Heather's face betrays no amusement and Liv switches to a serious tone. "But you've done a lovely job with the makeup. I'm sure that will be all cleared up in no time. Would you like me to refer you to the agency where we found our nanny? They're the best in the state." Liv reaches a hand out and rests it on Heather's forearm. "I'd be happy to put in a good word."

Heather lays a gentle hand on Liv's shoulder. "You're sweet to offer. But that's alright. I love playing with my kids."

Liv nods, as if appraising the shocking information Heather just confessed. "Good for you, Mommy of the Year. Well, you know where to find me if your circumstances change." Liv glances at her watch. "Look at the time. I've got to run inside to meet the headmistress. Great chatting, ladies."

Heather waves while Zola shuffles a shoe on the sidewalk.

Heather's eyes connect with Zola, but her friend stays silent. "I know, I know. Don't say it. I just want to stand here and be grateful that I have a friend like you to balance out the PTA Triplets."

Zola nods and drapes an arm around Heather's shoulders. Heather lets her head fall to the side, meeting Zola's halfway and they stand there quietly. Just for a moment.

The bell rings and children pour out of the great wooden doors. A teacher flanks either side of the doorway, watching kids scamper off to find their parents.

Beck comes running down the path, his brown curls bouncing around, and leaps into Zola's arms. They hug for a moment before

Zola sets him down and traces her thumbs across the freckles underneath his eyes.

Heather hates to disrupt their moment. "Beck, where's Charlie? You two always walk out together."

Beck shrugs. "He was right behind me when we were getting our backpacks. I waited for him in the hallway, but I didn't see him after that. I thought he came out already."

Heather's pulse quickens. She stands on her tiptoes to look through the herd. She looks around as she waits. The crowd thins at the doorway, indicating the last of the kids. Panic expands in her chest. She wades through the sea of children, trying her best not to step on any tiny feet but not really noticing when she does.

She's nearing the entrance.

No more kids are coming out of the doors.

Heather is at the bottom of the stairs when Charlie's teacher, Miss Kilgore, appears in the doorway. "Mrs. Hartford. Good. Follow me, please. There's been an incident with Charlie."

Heather's legs wobble down the hallway as she follows Miss Kilgore into her son's classroom. Charlie is on the floor, sobbing hysterically, crawling under desks on all fours. "I can't go! I have to find it!"

Heather races over to him and collapses, folding her son into her arms, breathing in the smell of his hair as she calms him. "It's ok, baby. It's ok. What can't you find?"

"The Hulk." He sniffles. "I can't leave him. He's my favorite."

"I know, sweetheart." Heather rubs his back. "Surely he's here somewhere."

"Dad gave him to me." He chokes out the words between sobs.

Heather watches the day playback in her mind when Nick came home from a business trip, and presented the small Lego set with superhero figures to Charlie, knowing how much he loved to build with Legos. That was early on, before Charlie had settled into their new life with Nick. Nick explained The Hulk was his favorite as a child. The Hulk became Charlie's favorite that day, too.

"Ok, stand up. Let's look together."

Heather and Charlie stand, and Heather realizes that three teachers are looking on silently. "Could we just have a moment to look around?"

"Of course," replies Miss Kilgore. She doesn't look happy about it, but after a moment of hesitation, she ushers the other teachers out into the hallway.

For a few minutes, Heather and Charlie search all over the room, and Heather makes sure that her son is distracted as she peeks inside other students' desks in case someone picked him up.

No luck.

She clenches her fists and berates herself for not thinking to bring the substitute figurine.

After almost ten minutes, Heather decides her best bet is to go home and let the teachers get back to their afternoon responsibilities. It will mean a tantrum today, but she knows Charlie will recover when she conveniently finds Hulk in Charlie's backpack the next day. She doesn't let herself think about how Nick will react to Heather walking into the house with a screaming child in tow.

Heather turns to Charlie and opens her mouth to speak when she spies it.

A tiny green pair of legs is peeking out from underneath the art cabinet on the opposite side of the room. She walks over to pick up the figurine, and she confirms it is, in fact, The Hulk before calling out to Charlie. She holds it up triumphantly as her son races over to clobber her with a happy hug. If she's honest with herself, Heather is almost as relieved as Charlie is.

Heather wraps her arm around Charlie's shoulders and

escorts him out of the room, nodding appreciatively to Miss Kilgore on the way out.

They turn the corner and nearly collide with Headmistress Rosler, who is standing just outside the door.

"Headmistress! I'm so sorry. I didn't realize you were there."

The woman appears unruffled. "Ms. Hartford, are you aware that we have a policy to prevent this sort of thing from happening? There are no toys allowed in school without explicit permission given in advance."

"Of course. I apologize. I wasn't aware that my son had a stowaway in his backpack today. It won't happen again, Headmistress."

Headmistress Rosler nods. "I'm sure that it won't." She pulls her lips into a tight smile as she turns to Charlie. "See you on Monday."

They make their way down the hall together, and Heather leans in, close to Charlie, to whisper. "Maybe Hulk can stay home from now on? Or at least, in the car where I can keep an eye on him. Make sure he doesn't wander off."

Charlie nods as he turns Hulk over in his hands, never taking his eyes off him.

Heather pulls the car into the garage when they arrive home, and Charlie unbuckles his seatbelt. "Charlie, I want to chat with you before you go inside. Ni... your dad had a hard day at work. Be a good boy and head straight to your room, ok? I'll meet you there to do your homework in a few minutes."

"Okay, Mom."

Heather gets out of the car, and Charlie follows. She pauses, deeply saddened at how much Charlie seems to understand at his age. Her hand rests on the doorknob that leads into the kitchen as she takes a deep breath. Heather stands tall, pushes the door open and the two of them walk inside the house together. Heather forgets to cradle the door as it closes, and flinches when it slams closed behind them.

Makeup never covers up everything. It's one thing to wonder what goes on behind closed doors. But to see the proof up close, that's a different beast entirely. Try not to rattle him again, Heather. It can get so much worse before it gets better. I'm still here.

EH

Chapter 8

Heather can't figure out exactly why she feels so uneasy. Another note appeared yesterday. Someone knew what happened between her and Nick earlier that day. Before that, Heather had decided she'd show Nick the notes to see what he thought she should do. But then everything fell apart in the blink of an eye. Her past and present accidentally collided, and her faith in Nick wavered.

But, then last night was calm, all things considered. Nick perked up by dinnertime and they all enjoyed a mellow evening together, watching the latest Disney hit, *Up*. Charlie and Theodora sat on the couch, sandwiched by Heather on one side and Nick on the other. Heather made a big bowl of popcorn for them to share and dumped some M&M's in it. Even Nick picked at the bowl without complaint. Everything seemed to return to normal, and Nick slipped easily into the kids' bedtime routine.

It was the sort of night that Heather wishes she could put on repeat.

But tonight is different. Tonight is for business. Twice each quarter, Nick gets together with his close group of friends for a night of cards, snacks, and general man stuff. Whatever that is.

Heather floats around the house, getting everything cleaned and organized. Lucky for her, Zola offered to watch the kids for as long as she needs today. Normally, Heather has a hard time entrusting her kids to anyone else's care. But today, she accepted. Nick told her it would mean a lot to him if she would stay close tonight and help him out with hosting the guys, insisting he's no good at that sort of thing.

Heather suspects that Nick simply doesn't want to lift a finger, but it's just as well. She's happy to put on her game face and make him look good, especially after their spat yesterday. And it's far easier for Heather to play hostess if she doesn't have to worry about the kids. So, she packed up a bag for each of them with everything they might need, including jammies and toothbrushes. Zola told her she'd let them watch a movie until they fell asleep, and Heather could pick them up whenever her guests leave. One night of wrecked sleep won't be the end of the world.

Heather busies herself setting up the living room. Nick had already pushed the furniture to the sides of the room and set up a card table in the center. Heather dusts the surfaces and ensures that the bar cart is well stocked since Nick made it a point to tell her that the men coming over enjoy a good drink.

When she's done, she glides into the kitchen, scoops her favorite apron from the drawer, and begins to prepare the menu.

Nick requested some standard poker night snacks, but Heather can't do just the basics. She plans to elevate the dishes to really impress his friends. After all, it's the first time she's hosted them in her home. And on the off chance that they tell their wives about their boys' nights, she needs to send them home with a glowing report.

Heather goes to work cleaning and chopping fruits and

vegetables that will be displayed charcuterie style with a tart yogurt dip and freshly made hummus. Next, she moves to assemble the nacho bar. She pulls a stack of glass bowls from the island cabinets and fills each one with its own custom nacho option. She has everything they could need. Olives, her homemade guacamole, jalapeños, Pico de Gallo, scallions, diced artichoke hearts, and more. She even swaps out sour cream for plain Greek yogurt, which is healthier and packed with protein to keep her guests satisfied. After each bowl is cling wrapped and refrigerated, she prepares the cheesesteak dip that will accompany the sourdough loaf she baked that morning.

When all of her dishes are ready, Heather does one more double check before she heads upstairs to get showered and dressed. Nick's friends will be arriving soon. She tries not to think of this as an exam, but she really can't help it. Heather knows the grade will be there at the end of the night, whether she likes it or not.

The doorbell rings promptly at six o'clock, and Heather swings the door open to find Tom Stafford and Philip Osborn waiting to be let in. Shay's and Liv's husbands look like they could be different people in their casual clothing tonight. Heather isn't used to seeing them out of their expensive bespoke suits. She isn't used to seeing them much at all. She knew this group had money. But before getting to know them, she hadn't realized that even private investigators like Tom could be wealthy enough to afford such luxury custom clothing.

"Tom! Philip! Come in." Heather ushers them inside and wonders if she should give them a casual hug to welcome them. After an uncomfortable amount of time passes, she decides it would be awkward now. Instead, she guides them to the right, around the half wall, to where Nick is waiting in the living room.

"Phil! Tom! Good to see you." Nick meets them halfway and thrusts out a hand for them to shake.

Heather gives them a minute to exchange pleasantries before offering to get them a drink.

"What do you have?" Philip asks.

Nick laughs. "We've got everything. And Heather makes a great cocktail."

"I'll have an old-fashioned," Tom says.

Philip requests a Tom Collins, with an emphasis on the *Tom*. He releases a hearty chuckle and tosses a wink in his friend's direction. His joke is met with an exaggerated eye roll from Tom as Philip looks far too satisfied with himself.

Heather turns to Nick, silently asking him what he'd like to drink. "That sounds great, babe. I'll have a Tom Collins too." Heather walks over to the bar cart to prepare their drinks, grateful that she made time to thumb through an old recipe book, refreshing her mixology knowledge before tonight. She hands Nick his drink just as the doorbell rings again.

Stephen Ambrose has arrived. Unlike the other men, Stephen steps inside and wraps Heather in a warm, one-armed embrace. He takes a step back and holds out a bottle of white wine. "Just a little thank you for hosting tonight. I know it's probably not what you'd like to be doing on a Saturday night." His peridot eyes sparkle against his rich sepia skin.

"I'm happy to have you. And thank you. This is so thoughtful." Heather escorts him to where the other men are. She's always liked Stephen best of the group. He's the only regular poker night attendee who isn't a PTA husband. He's a Bronswood widower. His wife passed away a few years ago from a rare aortic aneurysm, leaving him a single father to eight-year-old Simone, a classmate of Charlie's, and eleven-year-old Jordan, who just entered middle school. While the two PTA Husbands, Tom and Philip, rarely speak to those outside of their inner circle, Stephen is charismatic and seems genuinely interested in other people. He's known to be aggressive when it comes to his clients' investment portfolios, but he's always been kind to Heather.

A new round of greetings is exchanged, and Heather offers Stephen a drink. "I'll just take a beer if you've got it, please."

"Any particular kind?" Heather asks.

"Surprise me," Stephen replies, giving Heather a friendly wink. Heather listens to their chatter as she retrieves a beer from the refrigerator. Nick is filling them in on his Nexin campaign and Heather hears someone ask Stephen how the market is handling the excitement over the surge in solar energy use. The doorbell rings for the third time, and she hurries over to give Stephen his beverage. He's the only one who thanks her, and she leaves to welcome their last guest.

It's their neighbor across the street, Geoff Lindon. Heather is expecting him. Nick extended the invitation to him this morning to make amends after the whole pummeling debacle from yesterday. Heather agreed, knowing it's a good, tactical move, but it doesn't ease her embarrassment at facing him again.

"Geoff, thanks for coming." Heather tilts her head to one side. "Listen, I am so sorry, again, for what happened yesterday. I was frightened and…"

Geoff cuts her off. "Heather, really. There's no need to apologize. It was completely understandable." He smiles as he continues, "You've got a mean right hook. I sure hope Nick doesn't step out of line." He laughs and Heather smiles, cringing inside. Geoff surely doesn't mean anything by his comment. He's a nice guy, and he doesn't know Heather's history. She forgives his word choice, assuming he only meant to lighten the mood.

Another round of greetings, and Geoff joins Stephen in a beer. Heather leaves to fill his order, mentally adding *server* to her growing list of job descriptions, just as Nick launches into the story of what she did to Geoff yesterday.

She returns with Geoff's beer, and he throws his hand up in mock surrender. "Hey, I'm just grateful she didn't kill me. Don't step between a mom and her kids. Am I right?"

"Some appetizers are ready in the kitchen if you boys would like a little snack before you get started." Heather watches as they migrate to the kitchen to dig into her cheesesteak dip and sourdough bread. She soaks in the compliments and clears the table when they leave to begin their game.

The rest of the evening runs smoothly. Heather's food is a hit, and Nick appears pleased with her periodic interruptions to refill drinks and offer the next round of snacks, each appropriately timed, with one of the men needing a break from losing too many hands in a row.

It's nearly eleven o'clock when the game wraps up. Heather had checked in with Zola several times to make sure all was well with her kids, and Zola assured her they were all having a great time. Heather stopped checking after Zola informed her all the kids had fallen asleep while watching *Ice Age*.

The men break into separate discussions about work and other things. Nick is chatting with Philip and Geoff near the bar cart. Stephen is engrossed in a conversation with Tom next to the fireplace. Heather walks over to Nick to see if he needs anything else before she cleans up. "Everything was perfect. Thanks, babe." He leans in, wrapping her in his arms. He lowers his voice next to her ear. "You did great."

Heather smiles, relishing her triumph. As she pulls away, her eyes flick up over Nick's shoulder, connecting with Stephen's. He's looking at her with a grin on his face, and he raises his bottle in her direction.

Back in the kitchen, Heather can't stop grinning as she wraps up the uneaten food into containers that she'll send home with the men. She wipes down the counter and then moves to retrieve the charcuterie board from the dining table. As she sets the board down on the island, her hands begin to tremble.

She feels the eyes on her before she sees them. When she raises her head, she finds Stephen leaning against the entryway, watching her.

"Oh, Stephen. I didn't hear you come in." She chuckles awkwardly.

"Sorry, didn't mean to startle you. I just came in to see if there was anything I can help you with." He shoots her a bright smile.

Heather watches as the overhead lights cast a golden glow onto his chiseled cheekbones. She wonders if he's dated anyone since his wife passed away. Heather can't imagine that he's still available due to a lack of interest. He's kind and intelligent. There's no denying how attractive he is. Heather considers whether Stephen and Zola might be a good match, and decides she'll introduce them.

"That's so nice. But I'm just about done here." Heather expects him to walk away. To rejoin the other men. But he stays where he is, contemplating her. As if he's considering what he wants to say.

He takes a few steps closer. "What happened to your cheek?"

"My cheek?" Heather watches as he approaches, closing in on her. She wants to retreat, unsure of what he wants, but she stays put.

Stephen stretches out a hand and points to where Nick hit her. "It looks bruised. Puffy." He drops his head and their eyes meet. Heather can't understand why he looks so concerned about her, and it's making her uncomfortable.

Her hand comes up to touch her face. "This? That's nothing. A clumsy moment. I tripped over a toy. The nightstand caught my fall."

His eyes soften, and he lowers his hand. "It doesn't look like nothing."

"Well, it is. Just an accident." Heather stands there in silence, not knowing what to say. "An embarrassing accident."

"Alright then." Stephen reaches across her to the platter of fruits and vegetables and grabs a sliver of strawberry. "Take care of yourself, Heather." He pops the fruit into his mouth, his eyes never leaving her face, and turns around to leave. He pauses at the entryway and spins around to face her once more. "Everything was brilliant tonight. Thanks again, Heather. Have a good night." He flashes her a half smile and leaves.

A few minutes later, she hears the men saying their goodbyes, and hears the front door latch closed, announcing their departure. Nick finds her in the kitchen. He pulls her in for a kiss, and Heather tastes the citrus bite of Tom Colins on his tongue.

"It's late. Do you want me to go pick up the kids? You did so much tonight."

Heather almost considers taking Nick up on his offer. She only holds back because he's had more than a couple of drinks and she hasn't had a single one. "No, that's alright. But, thank you. You go get ready for bed. I'll get them." Heather sends him upstairs and grabs her car keys and purse, excited to have her kids in her arms. It never feels quite right when they aren't home.

Chapter 9

The beep of the coffee maker breaks the quiet in the house on Monday morning. It's the third night in a row that sleep has evaded Heather. She lied to Zola when she said that she sleeps horribly when Nick is away. Heather sleeps best when he's gone, settling into a deep slumber unencumbered by hyper-vigilance. She's always chalked it up to a side effect of so many nights only half-sleeping next to Paul. And after what happened on Friday, insomnia wracks her body once again, her mind unable to let its guard down even though Nick has returned to his even-mannered temperament. Besides, he seems to be on his best behavior, continuing to make up for what Heather keeps telling herself was an *unfortunate incident*.

Despite her incessant rationalizations, Heather is still rattled at his becoming less predictable. She hates that she feels anxious around him now.

Heather thinks about the incident, replaying it over in her head, and she wonders how she might have changed the outcome.

When she tries again for the fifth time and gets nowhere, she throws back the blanket and trots down to the kitchen.

Ten minutes later, Heather's hands are buried in the dough that will become her favorite blueberry discard morning cake with a lemon drizzle. It's quick enough to whip up in the morning so that the kids have an indulgent treat. Besides, it's soothing for Heather to be in the kitchen. It's hard for her to make a mistake in the kitchen, and Nick loves when she cooks for the family. His picture-perfect housewife, dedicated to a life of service to him and to the children. Nick will do anything to keep up appearances.

Heather slowly works the dough. Her hands move back and forth, incorporating the blueberries and folding them into the cake base. She's already decided that after Nick leaves for work, she'll sneak a sliver for herself. Heather considers how thin it will need to be that Nick doesn't suspect that she's eaten it, because it certainly won't be recorded in her food journal. She's supposed to be on a diet, after all. She needs to fit into her dress for the gala.

Heather prepares the pan and pops the loaf into the oven before moving onto the lemon drizzle.

She glances up to check the time and startles. Heather moves swiftly around the kitchen. The sounds of her preparing breakfast bring the only signs of life to the downstairs. Nick will be back from his morning run any minute and she wants to have his protein shake ready and her food journal waiting. Heather never knows when he will inspect it, and she craves his approval each time that he does. Paul never approved of anything she did.

Heather thinks about Paul's text message to her on Friday morning. She hasn't heard from him again since then and she's grown increasingly worried that the next message will arrive at the worst possible time. Heather imagines what Nick would do if he found out.

The snap of the bell pepper she's chopping becomes her fingers breaking. The crack of the eggshells becomes her head connecting with the table. The tearing of the spinach is her skin ripping open under his fists. She finally snaps out of it when she presses the button on the blender and it whirs to life with Nick's protein shake inside. She can't let herself imagine what that sound might become for her. Breathing hard, Heather reminds herself that it's not Nick she's thinking about. It's Paul.

Nick isn't Paul.

Heather sets Nick's shake in the refrigerator and finishes cooking her egg white omelet. She's only just turned to jot down the meal in her journal when she hears the front door close. Nick appears in the kitchen a moment later, shimmering underneath a layer of sweat.

Heather beams. "How was your run, babe?"

"It was alright. I only had time to squeeze in a quick seven miler this morning, but it's better than nothing, right?" Heather thinks Nick doesn't mean to sound like an asshole when he makes comments like this. It's just who he is. Holding himself, and others, to unreasonably high standards. Always preening like a peacock.

Heather swallows her annoyance. "Seven miles is amazing. Most people aren't running even one regularly." Nick flashes a bright smile at her, and Heather notes the faux modesty behind it. "Your protein shake is waiting for you in the refrigerator."

He walks over to open the door. "Thanks, honey." He takes a big pull before setting the shake down on the counter.

Nick slides up behind Heather and wraps an arm around her waist. She flinches as his palm rests on her belly, praying that by some miracle, he won't notice that it's a new journal laying open in front of him. Of course he does.

"Did you start a new journal?" He asks as he flips through

the pages. "What happened to the other one? There was plenty of space left."

Heather forces a chuckle. "You won't believe how stupid I am. I was going to put it back in the drawer and it slipped out of my hands and into the sink while the water was on. It was ruined, so I threw it out."

Nick says nothing for a moment. Then, suddenly, he kisses her firmly on the cheek. The same one he hit just days ago. "You know, I don't like to hear you call yourself names." Heather winces under the pressure against her bruise.

Nick unwinds himself from around Heather's torso and returns to his shake. He finishes the rest in silence and Heather can't stand it. Silence has never been good for her. She can't predict what silence means. She prefers for Nick to be talking. Heather is far better at interpreting tones and body language.

"I'll be meeting Zola for brunch this morning after I take Charlie to school and Theo to her Gymboree class." Nick gives her a pointed look and moves his eyes down to her stomach, which admittedly, has gotten soft during her mini rebellions. "I'm not planning to eat anything. I'll just have some hot tea."

Nick shrugs his approval. "I don't understand why you like that woman so much."

Heather tilts her head.

"She's such a mousey little thing, following you around like a puppy dog."

Zola had come over for a surprise visit the day before. Heather had just begun creating a new sample floral arrangement for Harriet, which she'd forgotten to do amid Friday's chaos. Harriet kindly ignored Heather's memory lapse, but Heather made certain she had an arrangement to her later that day.

Zola did follow Heather around while Heather gathered the

stems she wanted from the garden, but that was to be expected. Zola had come to visit Heather. Did Nick expect her to wait alone in the kitchen? Or do the more awkward thing and stay inside to talk to him?

In a last-minute decision, Heather added one more stem variety to the arrangement. She'd let Harriet think that her favorite flower was the Nightshade, but when Zola asked about the choice of blooms, Heather confessed that the pale pink camellias are the flowers she loves most. They symbolize love, adoration, and longing. Heather feels connected to camellias in a way that she never does with the other flora in her garden, and she's always been able to count on camellias to reflect what her heart desires most.

When Zola questioned Heather's last-minute audible, Heather said it was a risk she was willing to take.

It had paid off. When Heather sent a photo of the bouquet to Harriet's phone, Harriet loved the contrast of the light camellias against the dark, deep purples of the rest of the arrangement, adding an elegant extra dimension to the centerpieces. The florist was called on the spot to make the appropriate changes.

Heather says nothing at Nick's jab and he continues. "It's nothing personal." Nick holds his hands up. "But the guys at the club said their wives can't stand her because she has no spine and she doesn't even try to make friends. Or put herself together, for that matter."

"Isn't that all the more reason to be kind and help her out?" Heather chooses her next words carefully. "She's a really sweet woman when you get to know her, and she's been a really good friend to me. It feels like I've known her my whole life." Heather takes a sip of lemon water. "Plus, she's raising Beck all by herself. I'm trying to help her get along with the other women. I think they would like her if they gave her half a chance."

Heather walks over to Nick and puts her arms around him from behind. Something she learned to do with Paul so that she would have some warning if he whips around. She rests her head sweetly on his back before she appeals to his ego. "You have so much influence with those other men. Maybe you could put in a good word for my friend? Maybe when Stephen is around."

Nick's head whips upright at the mention of his name. "Stephen? Why would it matter if he was there?"

Heather chooses her next words carefully at Nick's reaction. "Well, at your poker night, I was thinking—."

Nick cuts her off. "You were thinking about Stephen?"

Heather leans away just enough to see a muscle twitch in his jaw and she hurries to finish her thought. "I was thinking about setting him up with Zola."

"With Zola?"

"Yes. They are both single parents and they are both so sweet. I think they have a lot in common."

"I didn't realize you were so fond of Stephen. I know he's fond of you… Is that what you guys were talking about together in the kitchen? How great he'd be with Zola?" Nick takes a deep drink of his shake before setting his cup carefully down on the countertop.

Heather squeezes the backs of his arms, massaging him as she considers how to answer him. "Honey, all I meant was that I want Zola to feel comfortable around our friends. I like her. And you can get the husbands on your side." She rubs tiny circles between his shoulder blades. "They'll accept her if you do."

Nick seems to think about this for a minute. He turns around slowly and faces Heather. "Anything for my wife." He tips Heather's chin up to his face. "I'll try. But I can't make any promises."

"Thank you so much. You're so good to me."

Nick cradles her face on either side and Heather blinks back the sting in her cheek before Nick lays a soft kiss on her mouth. He releases her and goes to set his cup in the sink. He starts to leave, presumably to shower, but he pauses and turns back to Heather. "You know, I think it's great. That you have such a close friend." He smiles warmly at Heather, but Heather feels a chill creep into her bones. "It's really great, babe."

When Nick leaves the kitchen, Heather releases a breath she hadn't meant to hold and returns to her breakfast while she waits for the oven timer to tell her the breakfast cake is ready.

When Nick leaves for work, Heather finally goes upstairs to see Nick has an outfit laid out for her today. Another outfit that Nick loves. A camel-colored harem pant jumpsuit, with a black cardigan and black ankle booties. Heather goes to her closet to consider an alternate option.

Her eyes fall on the dress Nick bought for her months ago. A size two, low-cut, off the shoulder black silk gown for the Bronswood Gala coming up. It's a stunning piece, and it doesn't escape Heather's thoughts how chic and sexy she'll look when she's on Nick's arm wearing that dress. A welcome change of pace from the classy but basic outfits that Nick likes her to wear when they're apart.

After a few minutes of deliberation, Heather decides to wear the outfit Nick set aside for her, and she heads to her vanity to get ready. She examines her face. The discoloration is improving, if you can call turning from a shade of deep purple to a mixture of yellow and green an improvement. She quickly determines she'll need to wear her hair down, so she flicks her curling iron on and gets to work.

Nick has, again, laid out outfits for both of the children, and Heather knows he's intending it to be a sweet gesture, lightening her load in small ways. Perhaps even a bit so he can ensure the whole family is dressed appropriately, keeping up appearances. Regardless, it makes quick work for Heather, and she gathers the kids and heads out to tackle the drop off line and meet Zola.

Heather, I want you to know how sorry I am for what I have to do next. I need you to know how hard it is for me to do this to you. I can't imagine you'll be able to forgive me. Please try. I'm still here, Heather.

Chapter 10

Heather pulls into the car line in front of the school ten minutes early, secretly hoping that one of the PTA elite will invite her to walk Charlie in to school early again instead of waiting for the bell with all the other parents. When she doesn't see any of The Triplets, she decides it's probably best since she's meeting Zola shortly after dropping Charlie off.

Heather searches the cars in front of her for Zola's minivan but doesn't see it. She checks her side mirror. No Zola. She must be running late.

Her nerves are shot, screaming with dread at the thought of the most recent message she's received. Heather fires off a quick text to make sure Zola is alright and that they are still on for coffee. The bell rings and she still hasn't received a response, setting Heather further on edge.

Everything seems fine as Heather and her children approach the great wooden doors where Headmistress Rosler stands, Charlie tugs Heather's hand. "I don't want to go to school. I don't feel good."

Heather wonders if Charlie's anxiety is simply mirroring

her own. "I'm sure you're still upset about what happened on Friday. That was hard on you. But there's nothing to worry about, sweetheart." Heather strokes her son's cheek gently with her thumb. "Today is just like any other day. I'll be right here waiting to pick you up after school."

"No, Mom. My teacher doesn't like me." Charlie's eyes are pleading with her. He tugs the collar of his navy blue polo shirt.

This is new. Heather's never heard her son mention an issue with his teacher before. "What are you talking about? Miss Kilgore adores you." Charlie's brow furrows at Heather's question, but he's looking at Headmistress Rosler.

"Did you hear what I said? Your teacher loves you. She's always told me what an excellent student you are. A fantastic listener."

Heather can't tell if Charlie is listening. He's not looking at her, staring straight ahead towards the stairs. His lip is quivering, but he doesn't cry.

Heather has never been able to best the quivering lip. Kneeling on the sidewalk, she turns Charlie around so that he's facing her. "I'll tell you what. You go in there, and just give it your best. And if you still aren't feeling well, then you can ask to go to the office and call me to come pick you up. Is that a deal?"

Charlie responds with a weak nod and hugs her a little tighter than normal. Heather watches as he climbs the stairs past Headmistress Rosler, wondering what is really going on with him today.

Headmistress Rosler tilts her head. "Good morning, Charlie. You've been sure to leave any toys at home today?"

Charlie nods a tiny yes while looking at the ground, then he shuffles past her and down the hallway. Heather makes sure her son is out of earshot before she addresses the formidable woman. "I assure you, we had a discussion about the school policy, and it won't happen again."

"Very good." The headmistress straightens her posture, and Heather's mind wanders, curious if she ever trained in the military before taking this post at Bronswood. A military skill set would come in quite handy here. The discipline. The calm under pressure. The decisiveness. The order. Heather considers this for a moment before she catches sight of Charlie wandering into a classroom on his left, rather than the room to his right that he's entered since the beginning of the school year. Heather shrugs, presuming that maybe Charlie saw a friend he wanted to say *hello* to, before she realizes that the broad-shouldered woman is still speaking to her.

"I'm sorry, Headmistress," Heather fumbles over her words, trying to recall something, anything, that was said while she was deep in thought. No luck. "Could you repeat your question, please? I was trying to remember if I left my kitchen sink running." A poor excuse, but she hopes it's good enough.

Headmistress Rosler scowls at her, and Heather is certain that she's about to be reprimanded yet again. Instead, the headmistress clicks her tongue and says, "I was asking if the PTA can expect to see you in the recreation center this afternoon for Gala preparations, Ms. Hartford?"

"Of course. I'll be there." The headmistress gives a curt nod and turns back to the throng of incoming children, while Heather trudges back to her car, packing Theodora on her hip like a heavy sack of groceries.

She checks her phone again and sees that Zola still hasn't replied. Heather scans the car line for Zola's van, but there's still no sign of her. For one fleeting moment, she considers checking to see if Beck is already in class, but she quickly determines it's not worth the withering look it's sure to elicit from the headmistress. Perplexed, she pulls away from the curb and makes her way over to The Cafe. Maybe Zola left her phone at home.

When Heather arrives at The Cafe, she still hasn't heard from

Zola. She heads to the counter and orders a hot chai soy latte for herself and a flat white for Zola. She considers adding on a large blueberry muffin. They look especially delicious this morning. But after running her hand across her stomach and feeling the weight of Nick's eyes on her this morning, she decides better of it and orders blueberry mini muffins for Theodora instead. She buckles her daughter into a booster seat and returns to the counter for the beverages. She takes a seat at her favorite table next to the windows, and waits for her friend to arrive.

But that moment never comes.

Several text messages and phone calls later, Heather checks the time and realizes that she has to leave in order to make it back to the school to help with the gala decorations.

After sitting there long enough to finish her tea, and then Zola's coffee, not wanting great coffee to go to waste, Heather gathers the empty cups on her table and places them in the tub on the counter.

Her mind begins to spin out of control. Is Zola still angry with her for leaving Zola at the curb while she cut the drop off line with Shay? That was days ago, and Heather saw Zola over the weekend and everything seemed fine. Did something happen with Beck and Zola doesn't feel like she can talk about it with Heather? Did one of the PTA Triplets say something to Zola? Is Zola sick? Did she get into an accident? Why isn't she answering her phone?

Heather leaves the same way she arrived. With only Theodora for company. She takes one last look around, a vice tightening around her chest, and she wonders where in the hell Zola could be.

Chapter 11

By the time Heather arrives at the school gymnasium, the other volunteers are already getting started with the centennial Gala setup. She sees Shay standing in the center of the room, and two men move circular tables from place to place as Shay points at different spots. A group of women are huddled together at the far end of the room, nodding fervently as one woman spreads her arms wide, saying something as she gestures to the area. Other women are pulling strands of lights from a box and untangling the cords. A few other men are bringing in stacks of chairs, and off to one side, Heather spies Liv with a clipboard in hand, standing with Harriet near a long row of rectangular tables along one wall. Liv is chatting with someone dressed in a chef's jacket, whom Heather presumes to be the caterer.

Sensing she's running behind, Heather hurries to one side of the room and sets Theodora down on a nearby bench. She surveys the room before she pulls out Theodora's afternoon snack and portable DVD player loaded with her favorite movie, *Cinderella*.

"Alright, sweetheart. Mommy will be right over there." Heather points to the other side of the room. "Stay right here and I'll check on you soon."

Theo's already managed to start the movie and gives no sign she's heard Heather at all.

Heather inhales deeply to steady herself before she migrates over to where Liv is still chatting with Harriet, making sure that her daughter is still within eyesight.

When Heather catches Liv's eye, Liv leans in to whisper something in Harriet's ear before turning back cheerfully to Heather. "Hey, there! You made it."

"Wasn't the meeting supposed to start at 10:30?" Heather asks.

"Oh, yes. That was what we printed on the itinerary, but that really means a quarter after, so that the work starts getting done at 10:30."

"I'm sorry. I didn't realize…"

Harriet waves a hand to cut Heather off. "Don't worry about it. It's no big. Now you know." Harriet smiles.

"Besides," Liv chimes in, "you told us last week that it was your day to brunch with Lola."

"Zola." Heather corrects.

Liv doesn't seem to notice that she said the wrong name. "How was it this morning? Eat anything fabulous?" Liv turns to Harriet. "I'm on the Gala Diet, of course." She ticks off the things she's avoiding on her fingers. "No carbs, no sugar, no food." Liv giggles like she's never heard anything so funny before.

Heather laughs politely. "Well, no, I didn't eat, actually. And Zola stood me up. That's really unlike her. I'm a little worried."

Harriet steals a look at Liv, whose periwinkle eyes flicker and shoot back at Harriet slightly, the corners of her mouth turning downward.

"What's that look?" Heather catches Harriet's eye. Then Liv's. "Do you two know where she is? Have you seen her?"

They shake their heads and Harriet replies, "No. I sure haven't."

Heather slips back into her list of reasons Zola may be avoiding her and makes a mental note to reach out to Zola again, asking if something happened with the other moms. "So you guys haven't seen her? Or talked to—."

Liv turns back to Heather and puts a hand on her arm. "Oh, don't worry. I'm sure your friend will turn up. She probably just had car trouble or something."

Heather considers pushing the subject harder, but stays on the topic of the gala, knowing neither of these women is even the slightest bit concerned. "So, bosses, put me to work." She looks back and forth between Liv and Harriet, unsure of who she should report to. Harriet seems to be in charge, but Liv is the president of the PTA.

Liv taps her clipboard with a pen. "Oh, yes. Well, technically, Headmistress put me in charge, overseeing everything as president." She turns to Harriet. "But we all know this is the Harriet Potter Show. So, I'll let you two ladies get to it while I go chat with the caterers to finalize the menu."

Liv flutters off with a big smile, her sandy blonde hair swaying in perfect waves behind her.

Harriet nods her head, motioning for Heather to walk around the room with her.

As they walk, Heather can't ignore the feeling that Harriet seems nervous. Heather watches as she fidgets with her clipboard. "Let's start with the room layout." Harriet says as she points around the room in sequence. "Each table will have a large floral centerpiece, and dinner settings, of course." She pauses to look at Heather as if ensuring that Heather is paying attention. "And in the center, we should have framed lists of all auction items with their corresponding numbers and instructions on where to bid."

Heather nods along and waits for Harriet to continue talking before sneaking a glance at Theodora, who is sitting exactly where Heather left her. Heather turns her focus back to Harriet, who is still talking about the guest tables. "We should have each of the cracked golden globes hanging above the tables. We have just enough. And what do you think about draping one hundred floating orbs across the dance floor? I just can't decide if bringing the outdoor look inside is tacky or brilliant."

Heather stops Harriet from walking. "I think it's a lovely idea. And it will look beautiful surrounded by the white busts for the headmistresses. You'll set one auction item in front of each bust, right?"

When Harriet doesn't respond, Heather tries again. "Harriet? Are you alright? You seem awfully anxious."

"What? Oh. Yes, I'm fine. It's just that…" Harriet takes a deep breath. "This gala has to be perfect. This is the centennial celebration. The annual gala is important enough on its own. It's the biggest fundraiser the school does all year. But the 100th? Nothing can go wrong."

In the year and a half that Heather has been at Bronswood trying to befriend the PTA Triplets, she's never known Harriet to be so concerned about doing well. She gets the sense that more is bothering Harriet, but she still doesn't feel close enough to pry. She takes a stab at comfort and confidence instead. "It's going to be fine, Harriet. It will be perfect! Everyone knows what you can do with event curation. With you in charge, I'm not worried in the least." Heather means it and hopes that Harriet can hear the sincerity in her voice. She knows, too well, the pressure of being perfect. The endless pressure to avoid any mistakes that may end up following you later on.

The corners of Harriet's mouth tick downward. Heather thinks she looks sad. "Thanks, Heather. I really appreciate that. I know you haven't been here as long as some of the other moms, but it really has been lovely to get to know you." Harriet smiles, and it looks as though it takes a great deal of effort to produce the expression against the veil of gloom that hangs over her right now. "And Charlie, of course. He is such a sweet boy."

"He's a keeper. That's for sure." Heather agrees, not even feeling like she's biased. It's simply the truth. Her son is a gentle and kind soul and she'll do anything not to let the world strip that away from him. "Here." Heather reaches out and motions for the clipboard. "Why don't you go get some water and I'll run through the list and see what other supplies I might have now that you know what you want?"

Harriet looks as though she might argue, but she sighs and relinquishes the clipboard. "Alright, but just for a moment."

Heather wanders around the room, trying to visualize the description Harriet gave her. She takes her phone out to make a few notes before she looks for Harriet. There must be fifty people here, bustling around to prepare for an event that is a full week away. But Heather can't find Harriet, Liv, or Shay.

Suddenly nervous, Heather jogs over to check on Theo, and she can't hide her relief when she finds her daughter still transfixed by the DVD player in her lap. Deciding that she could use a brief break, Heather calls out to another mother she recognizes from Charlie's class.

"Rebecca, would you mind watching Theodora while I run to the restroom?"

"Of course not. No trouble at all."

Heather flashes her a grateful smile. "Thanks so much. I won't be long."

When she's safely inside a bathroom stall, Heather stays

standing for a moment as she tries to slow her pounding heart. The preparations are going fine, and Theo is perfectly content. But Heather can't stop thinking about Zola. Zola wouldn't just stand her up like that. She's sure of it.

For a moment, Heather allows herself to venture down the rabbit hole of wondering where Zola is and why she hasn't been responding. If something happened to her, Heather was the only one who would stand a chance of noticing. With the notable exception of Beck, who will be utterly distraught if his mother doesn't show up after school. That is, if he's even in class today.

Fighting a fresh wave of nausea, Heather closes her eyes and concentrates on breathing.

In. Out.

Zola is fine. There's a simple explanation.

In. Out.

She wills it to be true, and Heather decides that she'll wait to make sure Beck is safe with his mother at pick up that afternoon.

Heather is just about to leave the stall she's in when she hears a group burst into the bathroom talking excitedly. Without thinking about it, she silently sits back down on the toilet and draws her feet up to her chest. She glances up to make sure the stall is still locked. Heather chides herself for acting like a middle schooler when she recognizes Shay's voice.

"I'm surprised she showed up today, to be honest. With her mousey little friend bailing on her and all that." Heather recognizes Shay's voice and prays she hears someone else's name. Anyone else's but hers.

"Well, what else is she going to do? Heather is a lot more like us than she is like that doormat," Liv replies. "I totally expected her to be here."

They are definitely talking about her.

Harriet chimes in. "Yeah, I didn't think she had what it takes to be a Bronswood mother until you saw her at pickup on Friday with that shiner. That took some guts. No amount of makeup could hide that thing. I can still see it."

"That's true," Shay concedes. "But do you honestly believe that she tripped over a toy? Sounds like a classic coverup to me. Maybe she talked back to her hubby, right? That'd be pretty ballsy."

"Oh, come on. Nick loves Heather. He's got a temper, but he's not that guy."

A noise bubbles up in Heather's throat and her hand flies up to her mouth to keep it from escaping. Hearing Liv's confidence in Nick brings her fresh doubt to the surface, and it startles her to know that she's not so certain that she agrees with Liv anymore.

Liv's voice trails off, and Heather leans sideways to sneak a peek at the women through the crack of the stall door. Liv applies a fresh coat of pale pink lipstick and studies her reflection as Liv purses her lips together. Harriet is fiddling with a ring on her right hand. It's a gorgeous piece that Heather has never seen her without. Even without a clear view, Heather can picture it. A yellow gold band with a single brilliant round deco emerald in the middle.

Shay is fluffing her platinum blonde curls in the mirror. "Oh my god, Harriet. Can you believe that Lola even asked to try on your ring? Was she serious?"

"Right?" Liv takes a step back to assess herself in the mirror. "As if you'd take it off for a scholarship mom. With sausage fingers, no less. Can you imagine what your mother would say?" Liv laughs, and Heather cringes at the cruel remark.

Heather continues to watch them in the mirror through her tiny gap. Harriet's face looks sad. "You know her name is Zola. And she was just trying to be friendly. She said it reminded her of a ring her mom kept in a jewelry box. I just told her it belonged to my grandmother and I never take it off. It wasn't a big deal."

Heather knows the ring is special to Harriet, though just over a year ago, Harriet had slipped the ring onto Heather's finger to let Heather take a closer look as Harriet described how her grandmother had a tiny engraving made inside with the names of each of her grandchildren.

"Just the same, maybe she's finally got the message now." Shay fluffs her hair once more before nodding towards the door. "We'd better get back out there, ladies. Someone has to keep these moms in line."

The Triplets gather their things and leave; the door sweeping closed behind them. Heather waits for a few moments before leaving the stall. She wasn't sure what all of that was about or when Zola had even asked after Harriet's ring. But she does know now where she and Zola stand with these women. She has a feeling she'll need to tread more carefully going forward.

When Heather steps back inside the gymnasium, Harriet catches her eye immediately and flags Heather down. "Heather, there you are. I've been looking everywhere for you. Where were you?"

Heather puts on her poker face. "Oh, I just needed to use the restroom."

Harriet's smile slips, but only for a moment. "I see. Well, no big. I just wanted to check to see if you got everything you needed."

"I sure did. More than I expected, really." Heather laces sweet, honey-flavored daggers into her words. "I'll head home and see what else I can dig up for you before I pick up Charlie. If that's alright with you, *boss*."

Harriet is a portrait of unruffled feathers. "Absolutely. See you in a few hours."

Heather walks over to collect Theodora, who has fallen asleep on the bench, and heads to her car. She spends the entire drive home preparing herself to go down to the basement alone.

This place isn't all it's cracked up to be. Surely you must see it by now. I've seen more than enough, and soon, everyone else will, too. There's work to do. Don't worry, Heather. I'm going to help you. I'm still here. But I have to warn you. This is the part that is going to hurt the most.

Chapter 12

When they get home, Heather takes her time situating Theodora in her room before starting her search of the basement for the remaining supplies. There is a piece of her that is dying for her daughter to come with her, so she isn't alone downstairs. But Heather knows she wouldn't be able to focus at all with tiny hands venturing into forbidden boxes, so she resolves to leave Theo in the company of her dolls and building blocks.

Heather crouches down to meet Theo's eyes. "When mommy is finished, I'll make us some lunch. Is that a deal?"

Theo's tiny voice chimes sweetly in Heather's ears. "Das a deal, mama."

When she's convinced that Theodora is happily distracted, Heather lumbers to the basement door, and she takes in a large gulp of air before pulling the knob and finding the light switch.

When Heather makes it to the bottom of the staircase, the room is eerily calm. She looks around to find that all is in order. Each box is tucked away neatly on its shelf, larger items are all in their proper place. Heather frowns. She doesn't remember putting everything away after Harriet's visit, and she wonders if Nick came down to clean up after the fact. But Nick has never been one to pick up house chores. Heather supposes it's possible that she cleaned up and was just so distracted that she doesn't remember.

Heather pulls out the list she made on her phone and gets to work. She gets lucky with the first few boxes, successfully identifying cracked gold lanterns and oversized ribbons that match the descriptions on Harriet's list. The next box is a dud, a fact that Heather wouldn't mind except for the smell that escapes from inside.

"Oh God. It smells like something died in there," she says to no one in particular. Not stopping to wonder at what could cause the unfortunate stench, Heather hurries to seal the edges and buries it beneath a hodgepodge of holiday decorations. Whatever is inside will be a chore for another day.

Heather's stomach grumbles, and she wonders how long she's been downstairs. She picks up her phone to check the time, thinking surely it must have been a while given how hungry she feels. She's surprised to find only twenty minutes have gone by. Regardless, Theodora may be getting hungry too, Heather thinks. She decides to take a break. After lunch, she will set her daughter up with a coloring book down here with her so she can finish up before they have to pick up Charlie from school.

Heather slides her phone into her back pocket and stands up. With the boxes organized, the room is enormous and the silence looms over it. Given the kinds of outbursts that Heather has been subjected to at the hands of the men in her life, the silence ought to provide a bit of solace.

Instead, Heather is always unsettled by the silence, fearing what will eventually disrupt it.

She turns towards the stairs, eager to escape the eerie calm, but stops when she hears a scratching noise.

"Theo?"

Nothing.

Heather waits for a moment, listening. When the noise doesn't come again, she decides she must have imagined it.

She takes another step. There it is again.

"Theodora, sweetie, if you came downstairs, it's time to come out now."

Nothing.

"Mommy is going upstairs to make lunch. No more games."

Still, nothing.

Heather scans the room, slowly. There really is nowhere to hide in this room. After what happened that last night with Paul, Heather made sure of it when she organized the basement. A body, even a tiny one like Theo's, would be exposed in any corner or crevice of this space. Any spot except for one.

Heather's eyes trace slowly across the wall that leads to the tiny, locked cubby. She has to force herself to look at it. When she finally gets there, she sees something she missed earlier.

The lock on the door is sitting on the ground, and the door is propped open just slightly.

"Theo, are you in there?"

Heather takes a few steps forward.

"Theo, honey, did you go into the tiny room?"

A few more steps.

"Theo, answer mommy."

Heather's hand is on the latch, and she listens for any noise. She counts to three in her head and flings the door open to peer inside.

Empty.

Heather slams the door closed, and she thrusts the lock back into place. She forces herself to check the latch before sprinting for the stairs. She's halfway up the staircase when she trips and flails for the railing, narrowly avoiding a nasty fall. She doesn't stop to catch her breath as she throws open the basement door and barrels towards her daughter's room.

"Theo?"

No answer.

Heather's vision begins to tunnel. She's sure she's about to pass out, but she begs her muscles to obey as she runs and skids to a stop at the end of the hallway. She swallows hard before peering inside Theo's room.

"Theo!"

Her daughter is sitting cross-legged on the floor in front of her dollhouse, a doll in each hand. Just as Heather left her.

Theo turns her head. "Hi, mama." She waves five chubby fingers at Heather.

"Hi, sweetie. Have you been in here the whole time?"

"Uh huh. Mommy, you do workout?"

Heather is still catching her breath, and she puts a hand to her forehead where she feels a light sheen. She's losing her grip. That's it. She's completely losing it. "Oh, no, sweetie. I was just moving heavy boxes. Ready for lunch?"

Theodora nods and hops to her feet, skipping as well as any nearly three-year-old can all the way to the kitchen.

HEATHER'S HEART HAS FINALLY slowed to its regular rhythm by the time she returns to the school to drop off the additional items for the gala. She still hasn't heard anything from Zola, and resolves to watch for Beck at after-school pick up. Wanting to avoid distraction, Heather peaks into the gymnasium before she enters, relieved to find that the Triplets are nowhere to be seen. She prays that it's a sign that her day is turning around.

After she drops off the boxes, Heather walks with Theodora to the front of the school to wait for Charlie. She's happy to have an excuse to avoid the car line today, and she leans heavily against the brick building as Theo occupies herself. Heather digs through her bag in search of a tube of Chapstick. Her eyes glimpse an unfamiliar piece of paper which she drags out of her purse.

Her pulse races at the ominous words and the symbol she's become familiar with. She looks around her in all directions, as if the writer may be nearby, though she has no idea how long this has been in her bag or when someone could have slipped it inside.

Her heart bangs wildly against her ribs. Heather knows she'll feel better when she has both of her children in her arms, and when she knows Zola is alright.

Just a few more minutes.

Theo is dancing around, spinning in circles, when the bell finally rings. Heather grabs her daughter's hand and pulls her in close as the kids come flooding out of the doors.

Children pass by, one by one and in talkative clusters. A few minutes pass and Charlie still hasn't emerged. Neither has Beck, and Heather is disappointed to realize that she hasn't seen Zola's minivan.

The crowd begins to thin, and when one final child exits, the teachers on either side of the doorstep inside. The formidable double doors begin to swing closed.

Heather's pulse picks up speed. Her heart threatens to punch through her chest as she scoops Theo up and races to the doors. "Wait! Wait! My son is still in there! Please, wait!"

The doors come to an abrupt halt, and one teacher whom Heather doesn't recognize steps out. "I'm sorry. There are no more children inside. Who is your son?"

Heather is winded. "Charlie. Charlie Hartford. He hasn't come out yet."

The teacher wrinkles her brow. "Ms. Hartford? But you've already picked up Charlie today."

An icey chill snakes down her spine. Heather feels like she is floating away, untethered from the ground. "No, I dropped him off this morning and I haven't been back except to drop off gala decorations in the school gymnasium." Heather can feel the heat radiating from her face as her panic spreads. "Where is Charlie?"

The woman in front of Heather looks apologetic. "I'm so sorry. You must be confused." The teacher tilts her head to one side, bringing a palm to her chest. "I am the one who pulled Charlie from class and brought him to the office to be signed out. Headmistress told me she would walk him out to you herself."

Heather can't process what the teacher is telling her. She needs to see her son. She moves to go inside, but the teacher steps in front of her. "I'm sorry. We don't allow parents to roam the building after school hours. It's against policy. For safety."

It takes every ounce of composure that Heather can muster, but Heather looks down, eyeing the woman's name badge. "Miss Wardell, my son is inside." Heather's poise slips and her voice rises against her effort. "I want my son! Where is he?" The panic rages inside Heather, threatening to tear her apart. Her mind darts from one explanation to the next, none of them making any sense.

Did Nick come to sign him out? No. Miss Wardell said Heather picked him up.

Did someone else pick him up, claiming to be Heather? Or that Heather was with them? No. The school wouldn't release Charlie to someone who wasn't authorized to pick him up.

Is it possible that Heather had already picked him up? And somehow has no recollection of it? No. No, that isn't possible.

Heather would never forget picking up her child. She would know.

"Please. I want to see my son." Heather repeats, begging.

"Ms. Hartford, you've already picked him up. Perhaps you're confused about which day of the week it is." Heather looks at Miss

Wardell, stunned by her nerve. "I get confused once in a while, too. It can be very alarming."

Heather shakes her head violently, steadying Theo against her hip. "That is impossible. If I picked him up, then why am I here now, empty-handed?" She moves again to go inside. But, once more, Miss Wardell blocks her path. Heather narrows her eyes at her. "If you don't move out of my way, I'm going to have to move you myself." Heather doesn't want Theo to see her resort to violence, but she won't think twice about it. She'll do whatever she needs to get to her son.

Heather's voice is razor sharp, but Miss Wardell shakes her head, remaining unmoved. "I'm sorry, I can't do that."

Heather snaps, shoving the tiny woman back with her hand, and moves past her, shielding Theo with her shoulder. She races to Charlie's classroom. Fourth door on the right. But when Heather makes it inside, the room is empty.

The classroom looks as if it's never been used at all. Not a single desk or table. Not a single piece of children's artwork on the walls. Not even an old eraser on the chalkboard tray, which looks as clean as the day it was installed.

Heather's world begins to tip over as she hears footsteps approaching behind her. She grasps for a lifeline. "What the hell is this?" Heather doesn't care that Theo can hear her. "Where is Charlie? I want to speak to Miss Kilgore. Now! Where is his teacher?"

Miss Wardell speaks, but Heather can't bring herself to turn to look at her. "Miss Kilgore? There is no Miss Kilgore here. Nor has there ever been."

Heather's jaw falls open. "That can't be true. I've spoken to her several times this year. You're lying." Heather takes a large step towards the woman, who raises a firm palm to stop Heather from coming any closer.

A soft voice offers an explanation from somewhere behind Heather. "Ms. Hartford, Charlie's teacher is Ms. Crawford. It's always been Ms. Crawford." A hand reaches out and touches Heather's shoulder. It's ripped away when Heather spins around to look at the petite woman talking to her. "Would you like to sit down? You don't look well."

"What? No. No! I would not like to sit down. I want my son! Give me my son!" Heather storms around the classroom as if Charlie might pop up any second and yell *surprise*. She hears a woman's voice yelling for security, and then calling for the headmistress. Heather searches frantically, hearing voices but not understanding any of the words. She sets Theodora down as she rips open every cabinet door along the wall. But all the cabinets are empty.

With nowhere else to look, Heather spins around and collapses to her knees. A pit opens up beneath her, and suddenly she is falling. The room around her goes dark. Heather doesn't remember hitting the floor.

Chapter 13

"Heather? Heather, honey. Open your eyes."

Heather's eyes blink open to find Nick looking down at her, a halo of bright light flooding her eyes from behind him.

"Jesus, Heather. You scared me. Can you sit up?" Nick helps Heather prop herself upright as she takes in her surroundings, remembering her frantic search for Charlie in the empty classroom.

Charlie.

"Where is he? Where is Charlie?" Heather tries to stand up, but Nick holds her firmly in place. "And Theo!"

"Slow down, Heather. Theo is right here." Nick points to the side of the room where Theo sits in the lap of a teacher whom Heather doesn't recognize. "You need—."

Heather cuts him off. "What are you doing here? Did they bring Charlie out yet?"

Nick looks at her, one hand cupping her cheek. "The school called me when someone saw you yelling at one of the teachers during pickup. I came as quickly as I could and found you passed out on the floor."

Heather fixes her eyes on his, willing him to really hear her. "Nick, someone has Charlie. They won't give him back. They are saying—."

"I know, Heather. They told me everything. You already picked him up earlier today."

"No, I didn't! I wouldn't be here now if I had!"

Nick levels his brow at Heather. "Calm down." It sounds like a warning, but Heather can't bring herself to heed it. Not when her son is missing.

"I will not—," Heather's voice catches in her throat as tears fill her eyes. "Nick, I didn't pick Charlie up. Someone knows where he is. I don't know what I'll do if..."

Nick stands and helps Heather to her feet. He pulls her into his arms to steady her. "There's a recording. I've seen the video showing that you picked him up earlier today." Nick sighs like he's exhausted. Or maybe disappointed. "Let's get you some water and then we'll go to the office and sort this out. Whatever it is."

Heather nods, not knowing what to do. Nick picks Theodora up, drops a gentle kiss on her cheek as she lowers her head to his shoulder. He carries her out of the room, and Heather trails behind them as a hollow feeling blooms inside her chest.

HEATHER WATCHES THE SCREEN in front of her, dazed, her entire body numb. She hardly recognizes herself. But there is no denying that the woman she's watching pick up Charlie is her.

Nick is saying something to her, but it sounds as if he's underwater. Her eyes are transfixed by the video footage that's been pulled from the school surveillance system.

The time stamp on the video shows today's date, 1:10pm. But for all that appears to be in order, Heather knows this is all wrong. She wasn't at the front of the school picking Charlie up at 1:10pm. She was home, gathering supplies to help Harriet. Or maybe she was still in the gymnasium?

Why can't she remember any of this?

Someone is shaking her shoulder, breaking her trance. "Heather? Babe? Did you hear me?"

Heather turns to see Nick staring at her. His eyes are wide with concern. He's speaking softly, as if she's fragile and may break any minute. "No, I'm sorry. I didn't hear you."

"I asked you how you could possibly forget that you already picked Charlie up. I'm watching you right here on this tape. So, what did you do with him? Where is our son?"

Heather's skin crawls, suddenly sick at the thought of Nick claiming any ownership of Charlie. Nick has always treated the kids as if they were his own. It was one of the things that made Heather fall in love with him. But his accusation that Heather might have misplaced her own child and the insinuation that she's lost her mind trump any affection she holds for Nick.

Heather looks to Headmistress Rosler, who is seated behind the desk, and then back to Nick. "I'm not crazy. I see how this looks, but I am telling you, I did *not* pick Charlie up today. Something is very wrong here and I want my son!" Heather slams her fists down on the desktop, rattling the frames and trinkets that sit on top. The picture frame nearest her clatters when it topples over, snapping Heather out of her fury for the briefest moment. She automatically picks up the photo to set it upright, manners prevailing out of habit. It's a photo of a much younger Headmistress Rosler with a group of about ten children, boys on one side, girls on the other. Heather scans the photo, and she hears the headmistress speaking to her.

"My first group of students when I began teaching here."

Rosler's words spark something in Heather. "His teacher. I want to speak to Charlie's teacher. Now!"

Heather is about to set the photo down when one boy catches her eye. He's the only child not smiling at the photographer. His tiny face is familiar. His eyes remind her of someone.

Heather gently places the picture back on the desk when the headmistress's voice breaks her focus once more. "I've already called Miss Crawford to the office—."

"That isn't Charlie's teacher." Heather sucks her cheeks in, trying to keep her head from exploding as she interrupts. "Every morning, I drop him off, and I watch as he goes to Miss Kilgore's class, fourth door on the right."

"Mrs. Hartford. Your son has been taught by Miss Crawford since school began in August. And the classroom in question has been vacant for the last year to undergo remodeling and upgrades."

"You're lying!" Both of Heather's fists connect with the desk again. Her hands tremble with rage, and she tries her best to steady them.

Headmistress Rosler doesn't flinch, and she narrows her gaze decidedly at Nick. "Perhaps you should take your wife home to rest. She is clearly under a lot of stress. Understandably so." She stands up slowly and folds one hand into the other. "I'm sure Charlie will turn up once she's had some time to calm down. Is it possible that he is home now, waiting for your return?"

Heather squeezes her eyes shut, begging herself to remember whether she left him at home. She knows she would never do that. But it would be so much simpler if she had. "No. He is not at home. Because I never picked him up." Heather's lips are tight as she squeezes the words past them. "Someone has my son right now, and I want some answers."

Headmistress Rosler continues to speak to Nick as if Heather isn't there. "Is it possible that he was at home and has run off? I know we are all worried for Charlie's safety right now, but between you and me, Charlie was quite upset about coming to school this morning and seemed… displeased with his mother for making him attend."

Heather can't believe what she's hearing. "That's not true! Charlie was upset, yes, but it wasn't like that. It—."

Headmistress continues, talking over Heather. "Perhaps he's gone off to play at a friend's house after his mother picked him up?" Heather watches Nick stand up to leave. The sound of his chair scraping across the floor sets her teeth on edge. Headmistress Rosler joins Nick and places a hand on his arm. "I'd be happy to make some calls around to the parents of Charlie's friends if you think it would help."

"That would be wonderful."

Heather stands up forcefully, sending her chair toppling backwards. She's heard enough. "Like hell you will! My son disappeared on your watch." Heather takes a step towards the headmistress and lowers her voice. "I'm calling the police."

Headmistress Rosler's face betrays no emotion, and Heather feels a grip like a vice around her arm as she's dragged out of the room and into the large hallway. "Nick, stop it. You're hurting me!" Heather's arm is searing at the shoulder, ready to burst out of the socket.

"Lower your voice," Nick says, seething. "Your outbursts aren't helping anything. Go to the car. We're going home to figure out what you've done with Charlie."

Heather is stunned. "What I did? You don't honestly think I had anything to do with Charlie going missing. My own son?"

Nick ignores her and lifts Theo into his arms. Theodora lays her head on his shoulder, chipping a piece of Heather's heart away. Or what's left of it.

Heather trails a few steps behind them, floundering for something—anything—within her realm of control. Without meaning to, she thinks about her promise to Charlie that morning. Her promise to come early if he asked and to be there to pick him up. Tears burn hot in the corners of Heather's eyes. She draws a breath deep into the recesses of her lungs. And when she's certain that Nick's attention is focused elsewhere, Heather slips her phone out and dials the police.

I'm sorry, Heather. I heard you fighting with Nick in the parking lot. You must be terrified. If you think something is happening inside those school walls, you're right. Don't worry, I'm keeping watch on things. I'm here, Heather.

BH

Chapter 14

Heather falls into the chair by a desk at the police station, opposite of Officer Fowler, who she was told to ask for when she came in. The most recent note she's received promised help. Someone to watch over things. Heather has to believe it's the truth, that someone out there is helping her. Because she doesn't know who she can trust. And she's exhausted from carrying so much extra weight from the emotional burden that she could never have imagined for herself. Heather drove Theodora home and once she'd settled in, Nick insisted on staying there with Theodora to avoid her witnessing any more traumatic outbursts from her mother. As if Heather doesn't have the right to every one of them.

Officer Fowler pulls a form out from a folder and clicks his pen open, ready to write. "What can I do for you today, ma'am?"

"I need to report a missing person."

"Name?"

"Charlie Hartford." Heather changed the children's last

names from Lauer to Hartford at Nick's insistence. He said it would benefit them to be recognized as being connected to him, with his prominence in the area and his connections. Heather agreed.

"Age?" The officer drawls on as if the routine bores him.

"He'll be nine in April."

Officer Fowler glances up, a spark of recognition in his eyes. "You're Heather Hartford."

"Yes, I am."

Fowler lowers his eyes back to the form, and Heather scowls at him. "I'm sorry. How do you know who I am?"

The officer clears his throat. "The headmistress over at Bronswood was here just shortly before you arrived. She told us what happened regarding your son. She was extremely concerned for Charlie's welfare." His eyes narrow in Heather's direction, and Heather catches the insinuation that she may be at fault. He continues, "I'm sorry for your loss."

"Excuse me?"

Heather's heart jumps into her throat at the speculation that Charlie is deceased, and Officer Fowler sits up a little straighter and immediately backtracks. "Sorry that you are dealing with the disappearance of your son," he corrects. His face has transformed into a picture of professionalism.

Heather allows herself to relax only slightly. "Well, thank God someone is finally showing some interest in the situation because you know when I was over at the school—," Heather is rambling, grasping for any shred of information that might shed light on this impossible situation. She tells him about the empty classroom, about the teacher she's never heard of before. The more she talks about it, the more certain she is that something is very wrong.

"I've noticed a bunch of families haven't been to school in some time which is highly unusual since, you know, many of the families attend that school specifically because it gets their kids out of their hair for a while and it looks great on boarding school applications but you really need to look into it because—."

Officer Fowler holds a hand up and cuts her off. "Ma'am. Slow down. We understand that you're worried about your son. Can you tell me where you were today after you dropped Charlie off at school this morning?"

Heather's annoyance at having been interrupted rises to the surface, but she answers his question obediently, knowing he might be the only person who will help her. "My daughter and I went to meet a friend for brunch at The Cafe."

"And can your friend confirm she was with you at The Cafe?"

"Well, no. My friend never showed up. I tried to reach her but I still haven't heard from her." Heather fidgets uncomfortably when she realizes she still hasn't heard from Zola. But she can't worry about that now.

Fowler nods, making his notes. "Mm hmm. Go on."

"Then I went back to Bronswood, to the recreation hall, er, gymnasium, to help with the gala layout and decor."

"How long were you there?"

"Maybe an hour or a little more."

He nods again. "And can anyone confirm they saw you there?"

Heather blinks rapidly. "Yes, several people."

"Ok, and where did you go after that?"

"I went home to find more items for the gala."

"And how long were you there?"

Heather is getting increasingly frustrated at the string of questions that don't seem to accomplish anything. "Until it was time to leave to pick up Charlie from school. Around 2:45pm."

Fowler hasn't looked up from his paper. "And was anyone with you in your home? Any employees, nannies, cleaning crew, who can confirm you were there?"

"No, it was just me and Theo. And——." A lightbulb flicks on in Heather's mind, shining a light on what is happening here. "Wait. Am I a suspect here? Do you think I had something to do with Charlie's disappearance?"

Fowler straightens his shoulders and reclines in his chair. "Mrs. Hartford. Can I call you Heather?" Heather rolls her eyes. "Heather, I'm going to be straight with you. Headmistress Rosler told us what happened in her office today. She submitted the security footage that clearly shows you picking up your son from school this afternoon at approximately 1:10pm." His eyes look like two tiny slits as he watches her. Like a shark taunting its prey.

Heather leans closer to the desk. "Officer, something is very wrong here. You don't understand. I think that the footage has been tampered with. It must have been altered to look like I picked up my son. But I didn't." When he doesn't respond, Heather pleads. "You have to believe me."

Fowler's face relaxes, and he sits forward, palms resting on his desk. "I want to believe you, Heather. I do. But surely you can see what this looks like." Fowler shakes his head, staring at her with an expression that looks remarkably similar to pity. "We have to operate on the facts, not hearsay. I can see the video footage. You're telling me you were at home at the time, but there was no one with you who can corroborate your story." Fowler's voice trails off.

Heather's hands feel like blocks of ice. She brings one up to place on her forehead to cool herself down. "Officer Fowler, I'm not stupid. I see how this looks. But doesn't the fact that I am here, at my own insistence, begging you to help me, tell you I'm not lying to you? If I had done something to my own son, my firstborn," Heather's eyes well up with tears, "would I be pleading with you to help me find him?"

Fowler leans forward onto his elbow, resting his weight on the desk. He seems to consider Heather for a moment, and locks eyes with her for several seconds before returning to his report. "How are things at home? Everything alright there?"

Heather swallows against the knot in her throat. "Of course. Everything is fine. Why do you ask?"

"Ms. Rosler suggested things might be… difficult at home." Officer Fowler uses the tip of his pen to gesture at Heather's cheek. "Sometimes kids are a lot more privy to things going on between their parents than we'd like to believe. Any reason to think Charlie might feel unsafe? Perhaps he was frightened and ran?"

Heather's eyes drop to her lap, and she forces herself to bring them up to meet Officer Fowler's in an attempt to smother her shame. "Everything is fine. This isn't what you think." She can't bear to say more, and she turns her face on instinct to make it harder for him to see the healing bruise on her cheek.

Fowler betrays nothing. "Alright then. The investigation is open, and we will get to the bottom of this," He waits for Heather to make eye contact. "For now, I recommend not even considering leaving town. Keep yourself reachable by phone."

Heather knows he's saying that because she's under a microscope, but she's satisfied enough that he's opening an investigation. She has nothing to hide.

She reaches for her purse to pull her cell phone out. "I will. I will do anything to get my son back. Thank y—." She digs in her purse, aggressively shoving things aside. "I—I—can't find my phone. I must have left it at home." She looks up, her eye wide, apologetic. "I'm sorry. I will find my phone and then I won't let it out of my sight again."

Fowler goes back to making some notes on the form in front of him. "We'll be in touch."

Chapter 15

It's past Theodora's bedtime when Heather arrives home from the police station. She had to wait much longer than she expected to file her report. Heather's mind is elsewhere, focused on everything that's happened today. She's distracted walking into the kitchen, replaying her conversation with Officer Fowler in her mind. Trying to generate the answers she needs from the information she wasn't given.

Her head is down as she goes over the things she needs to do. *Canvas the neighborhood. Call the other parents. Send a school-wide email. Ask Tom Stafford to use his investigatory resources to unearth any leads.*

As she lifts her eyes, Heather sees her phone laying on the island, face up, and she sighs in relief. The only thing that's gone right today. Heather notices the screen is lit up, and she frowns when she realizes the phone is showing a recent message. She prays it's Officer Fowler with an update. Instead, she finds a series of new text messages from Paul.

I HAVEN'T HEARD FROM YOU IN DAYS. COME ON HEATHER. TALK TO ME. PLEASE?

DON'T BE LIKE THIS.

I JUST WANT TO SEE THE KIDS. I'M NOT THE SAME MAN I WAS BEFORE.

PLEASE HEATHER. I JUST WANT TO TALK.

Heather's guard is down. She startles when Nick's voice rings out from behind her.

"How long have you been sneaking around with Paul behind my back?" Ice cubes clink against glass, and Heather turns around slowly to see her husband leaning against the wall, swirling his scotch on the rocks before taking a deep drink. "Did you think I wouldn't find out?"

Heather watches him for signs of movement, unsettled by how drunk he seems. He rarely drinks to excess. She feels her survival instincts take over. "I'm not sneaking around with Paul. He wants to talk about the kids. That's all." Heather speaks slowly, giving him time to absorb her words as she turns her head away from him. "I didn't tell you because there's nothing to tell. I haven't even responded to him." She picks up the phone, holding it out for him to see. As if he hasn't already seen that.

Nick walks over to where she stands, and Heather braces herself with each slow footstep. Her hands tremble as he cranes his neck down to meet her eye-line. She can smell the liquor on his breath. "I have eyes and ears everywhere. Your carelessness has already cost us Charlie. God only knows where he is." Nick pauses, the muscles in his jaw firing as he clenches his teeth. Like he's trying to will away the pain. "And if you so much as think about telling Paul about what happened, he'll try to take Theodora, too."

His voice is barely a whisper. "As if that loser could do anything about it, anyway. I'll make sure Judge Reynolds knows that he's trying to take them back to an abusive environment. You remember what Paul was like. Or do you need a reminder?" Nick's eyes narrow, and he chuckles. A sick grin spreads across his face. Heather can't tell if it's for Paul or for her.

Heather has never seen Nick quite like this. She stays where she is, unsure of what he needs to calm down. The alcohol isn't helping, and she wonders how much he's actually had tonight.

"Nick, you're scaring me." Her voice is timid. When Nick turns toward the table where her phone is laying, Heather risks a step towards him, suddenly needing to reassure herself that they're in this together. That they're on the same team.

But Nick doesn't give any indication that he's heard her. Taking another step, Heather slowly moves to wrap her arms around him. "Honey, let's just sit—."

"Don't!" Nick slams his tumbler down, sending glass flying across the room, and he shoves Heather backwards to create space between them.

Heather stumbles and flails to catch her balance, but it's no use. She tumbles onto the floor. Her forearm lands on a shard of glass that pierces her skin and delivers searing pain to every corner of her body. She clenches her teeth to keep herself from crying out.

As Heather struggles to sit up, she cradles her arm against her torso. Warm blood trickles towards her elbow, staining her jumpsuit and dripping onto the hardwood floor.

Nick's eyes clear, and he rushes to the counter, opening a drawer to pull out a dishtowel. He kneels down and wraps the cloth tenderly around Heather's arm, holding it firmly as he kisses her cheek. "I'm sorry. Jesus, I'm so sorry I hurt you. I think…" He starts to sob, his chest heaving. "I just miss Charlie so damn much already. I'm so fucking angry, Heather." Nick drops his head to her shoulder. "I'm sorry."

Heather sits there, tears streaming quietly down her face, and waits for Nick to rip himself away from her. She can't bring herself to say anything.

After several minutes, Nick finally climbs to his feet. He wipes his eyes on his sleeve, and he stumbles toward the living room. On his way out, Nick loses his footing and swings an arm out to catch himself, striking a vase with Heather's latest floral arrangement. Heather shudders as it crashes to the floor. When the shattered glass settles, Nick straightens and continues his exit from the kitchen, crushing the blooms under his shoes.

In the living room, Heather hears the distinct sound of Nick pouring himself another glass of scotch. She waits, afraid to move, for Nick to come back for more. But he doesn't.

Heather holds the air inside her lungs as she listens, terrified that her breathing will mask the subtle sound that will warn her he's coming. Until, finally, Heather hears Nick's footsteps climbing the stairs that lead to their bedroom. Finally, she allows herself to exhale.

Heather gathers herself, trying to make sense of what had just happened. It's never been like this. Of course, it hadn't always been bad with Paul, either. Men like Paul have a way of easing you into it. Making you feel like you earned it.

Heather knows she wants to run, not just for herself, but for her kids. The feeling is too reminiscent of the way things started last time. And she has no idea how much worse this will get. She knows that Nick loves Charlie and Theodora. But so did Paul. Nick is hurting. But so is Heather. She has seen all of this before and she knows how it will end if she doesn't escape.

But Heather can't leave. Not without Charlie.

Heather scrapes herself off the floor and picks up her phone.

She limps to the bathroom and locks the door before she sends a quick text message.

CAN YOU MEET ME AT THE LIBRARY TOMORROW MORNING? PLEASE. IT'S IMPORTANT.

She waits a few minutes and prays for an answer.
The phone buzzes.

I CAN BE THERE AT 10:00AM. DOES THAT WORK?

Heather confirms the time and erases the messages. She runs the tap and washes her hands in case Nick didn't pass out, in case he is listening and waiting at the door. To make amends or to release some more of his pain, it doesn't matter. She presses an ear to the door, and when she feels like it's safe, she goes back to the kitchen to clean up the mess and get ready for bed. Why, she isn't sure. She knows she doesn't stand a chance of getting any rest.

I wish I could explain everything, Heather. It's just too risky. Things are getting messy now. There's something I need to dig deeper into. Or someone, rather. But I promise, I'm still here, Heather.

Chapter 16

Heather is finishing a new floral arrangement in a fresh vase when Nick comes downstairs from his morning shower. She busies herself with the blooms, needing to focus on something that feels normal. Heather already has Nick's morning protein shake waiting on the counter for him. She pulled it from the refrigerator a moment ago and gave it a good stir to blend the separated layers.

"Is that a new flower? I don't think I've seen it before." Nick observes.

There is no reason that Nick would know this flower, or any flower, since he's been too busy to pay any mind to the garden that Heather is cultivating in their backyard. Heather lets her mind wander back to their early days together. When Heather would ask for his opinion on the different plants that she thought about adding, and Nick would tell her that it was her thing. That he'd prefer to play with the kids in the backyard than tend to some plants that would probably die soon anyhow if left to his care. If Nick was in a good mood, Heather would tease him, insisting that, like all living things, plants wouldn't die if they were given proper care and attention. To which Nick would inevitably flash her one of his most charming smiles.

For a moment, Heather lets herself forget that her husband's pearly white teeth are still sharp enough to bite. "They've bloomed only recently. It's called a snowdrop." She pauses, debating how much she wants to share. When Nick doesn't reply, she continues. "It's said to symbolize hope and rebirth."

Nick stares at the bright colors as he approaches Heather slowly. He leans in, and Heather can feel the warmth radiating from his skin onto her cheek. Nick whispers in her ear, "How perfectly appropriate. I'm sorry. About last night." He drops a soft kiss on her cheek and turns to pick up his smoothie.

Heather shrugs a shoulder and deliberately changes the topic. "Will you remember to talk to Tom this morning, please? I'd feel so much better having a private investigator looking for Charlie, too."

Nick hangs his head and lets out a deep sigh. "I've said I'll have a chat with him. And I will."

Heather picks up another stem that she's already trimmed, and she trims the end again. She handpicks its place in the arrangement. "Thank you, honey. I know you're doing all you can. I'm just so worried…" A sob chokes Heather's throat, and she drops her sheers.

Nick gently takes Heather in his arms, and her body betrays her by relaxing. "We are all worried. But I'm sure Charlie will turn up soon. We have to stay hopeful. For Theo."

Heather nods and pulls away. She stiffens her posture and tries to pull herself together. She knows Nick will ask his friend to help. He promised he'd make some calls about Charlie the second he arrives at his office this morning. It was his suggestion during their meeting with Headmistress Rosler. He was the picture of a concerned father, while Heather played the part of a raving lunatic.

The minute she heard the garage door close, Heather throws all the food down the garbage disposal. Nick wants to pretend that they are coping well. For Theo. For himself. For everyone else. But even the sight of food sends Heather reeling. How can she even think about eating while her son is missing?

Nick has made his promises, but Heather is growing concerned because it's been nearly twenty-four hours and he hasn't mentioned it since. What was he doing yesterday while Heather was at the police station?

It's just as well, though, because Heather knows he wouldn't be thrilled if he knew what she was about to do.

Heather drags Theodora into the library entrance, eyes darting around. She is, understandable, on edge today. How could she not be? Her son disappeared yesterday. On top of that, she didn't sleep last night and then skipped breakfast this morning, which hasn't helped matters. Now, she's received another note, and she's no closer to figuring out who's behind them.

As soon as she slips through the second set of automatic double doors, Heather sees a woman sitting on the bench in the lobby, hunched over a book, her face hidden behind a short drape of silver hair.

"Mom."

The slender woman stands up, and Heather strides forward and falls into her arms, sobbing. Heather's mother, Pamela, guides Heather gently to an empty reading room, and they sit down at the table.

"What's going on, Heather? I haven't heard from you in months, and you contact me out of the blue with something vague but important. I didn't even know what to think." Pamela sighs. "I've been so worried."

Heather pulls a tissue out of her purse and dabs at her eyes. She slides a coloring book and a pack of crayons from her bag for

Theo as she explains. "I'm sorry I haven't called. I've been busy at the school and Nick… well, he just thought we needed some time to focus on our family and get more involved at Charlie's school."

Her mother lowers her eyes, and Heather thinks she looks disappointed. "Heather. Do you think I'm blind? I am your mother. And we've been down this road before. I've always known something wasn't right with Nick. No one is that charming." Pamela covers Heather's hand with her own. "Did he hurt you?" Despite her determination to maintain a brave front, Heather's face betrays her, and Pamela sighs. "What did you do, sweetie?"

"It's not Nick!" The words tumble out before Heather can stop herself, and she checks on Theodora to make sure she isn't paying attention. Heather glances again at her daughter and lowers her voice. "And I didn't do anything." She considers mentioning the bruise on her cheek, maybe even the cut on her arm, but she decides against it. She's here for Charlie, not herself.

She sucks in a deep breath. "It's Charlie."

Pamela sits up in her seat, deep lines pinching together between her brows. "What about Charlie?"

"He's missing."

"What do you mean, he's *missing*?"

"Something happened and I don't know what to do. I dropped Charlie off at school yesterday morning and when I went to pick him up, he wasn't there." Pamela gasps, covering her mouth with one hand. "That's not all," Heather continues. "They told me I had already picked him up. They showed me security footage. But… but it's impossible." Heather stares at her mother, praying she'll believe what Heather is saying. "I swear I didn't pick him up. I don't know how they had that footage, but something is very wrong and I'm terrified someone took Charlie and God only knows why, or what they're doing…" Heather barely gets the words out before her voice becomes too wobbly to understand.

Pamela is quiet, and Heather wonders what is running through her mind. Pamela seems to have come to a conclusion. "You've reported this to the police, haven't you?"

"Yes, but I'm not sure how helpful they are going to be. They've been acting like I'm a suspect in all of this." Heather drops her eyes. "The school headmistress submitted the video footage to them before I even made it into the station to file the report. It looks terrible."

"And Nick? What did he say?"

"I can't get a good handle on what he's thinking. He was so upset when we spoke to the headmistress. But then he just seemed angry with me. Like I lost Charlie on purpose. Or like I did something to him. As if I could ever."

Pausing only to take a breath, Heather adds, "Nick is going to talk to a friend of his this morning who's a private investigator. And a very good one at that." Heather shakes her head, not wanting to admit her fear out loud. "I just don't know who I can trust if they are convinced I had something to do with this. I have to do something. I'm not going to just sit around waiting for someone else to find my son."

Her mother frowns as she considers all of this. "What do you need me to do? How are you going to find Charlie?"

Heather's head slumps to one side. "Right now, can you just sit here with Theo for a while? I'll grab some books from the kid's section." Heather checks the door behind her before she lowers her voice and continues. "I need to use the computers and do some digging on the school. Something isn't right and I can't use the computer at home. I can't risk Nick checking the search history and telling the police."

Pamela nods. "Go. I'll be right here if you need me."

After situating Theodora with her grandmother, Heather heads for the check-out counter to rent some time on the computer.

She sits in front of the screen, drumming her fingertips on the desk, not knowing where to start. She types in the search bar: *Bronswood*. The results are overwhelming and the articles are scattered across a vast range of subjects, from building architecture to teacher profiles. She starts at the beginning. *History of Bronswood*. She clicks on the first article, which is a few years old.

> Bronswood is widely regarded as Northern California's most prestigious elementary school. Built in 1870, the bricks and stones of this building are over a century old. Originally built as a response to the demand for medical care during the gold rush, the free hospital served many until funding was no longer sufficient to keep its doors open. The building was modified in 1894 to tend to the mentally ill and eventually abandoned in 1906 until Prudence Addler saw a need in the community that was going unfulfilled.
>
> Bronswood opened its doors in 1910, intending to serve the children of the state's most prominent figures as a way of adding security and advanced education to the future generations of oil and technology tycoons. Affluent families from all over the state flocked to the school, drawn in by its exclusivity, longer school hours, advanced curriculums, matriculate quality, and security measures.
>
> The Bronswood curriculum is funded largely by the exorbitant yearly tuition and bolstered by extraordinarily generous donations of

the parents and its annual gala fundraiser, which holds a silent auction, a Michelin star dinner, and live entertainment.

Tuition has risen each year, weeding out those who can no longer afford its cost. In recent years, the school has come under scrutiny for its lack of diversity and equal opportunity.

In response, the school has begun to offer a limited number of scholarships each year and the competition for these spots is fierce. Applicants must show exceptional IQ scores, well-rounded interests, advanced aptitude in either architecture, music, art, or language. Staff also evaluated social skills through a series of interviews and observations of the children in various social settings. On top of it all, parents of scholarship students must commit to serving the school in a variety of ways for a certain, what some are calling unrealistic, number of hours each year.

"The point of the scholarship is to provide opportunity to children of the working class. We don't have time to volunteer for one hundred hours each year. If we did, we'd probably also be able to afford the tuition," one mother commented when asked if she was familiar with the Bronswood scholarship program.

Bronswood has committed to awarding ten

scholarships each year, increased from the
original three by popular demand. Children
in the scholarship program must maintain a
high level of marks in order to remain at the
school. Bronswood claims it remains committed
to serving the families in their community with
the highest quality of care and education.

"Educated children make educated choices.
Together, we can educate the world."

Heather goes back to the list of search results without finishing the article and scrolls through the other pages. Many articles feature the same basic information. Several praise the school for its humanitarian efforts. Some articles spotlight the headmistress of that year or add exclusive insights about the curriculum design from former headmistresses. Heather's eyes are growing tired. She rubs them with her fingers before returning to the screen. Page after page of glowing reviews, until one old headline buried in the sixth page of search results catches Heather's attention.

BRONSWOOD STUDENT GOES MISSING

She clicks the article and leans in closer to the screen.

Local first grader, Caleb Norton, was reported
missing four days ago by his parents when they
went to pick him up and were told by his teacher
that an uncle listed on Caleb's emergency contact
list had already been to the school to pick him
up. The school claims that Caleb recognized his

uncle and confirmed that his uncle was indeed supposed to pick him up that day. But there was one major problem. According to Caleb's parents, Don and Janet Norton, Caleb's uncle Matthew was across the country in New York for business at that time. Security footage during this time was unavailable. Authorities have been unable to reach Matthew Norton for comment.

Calebs' parents were unavailable for comment, but previously, when police asked why Caleb might corroborate the story that his uncle was supposed to pick him up, his parents could only speculate. "We don't know why Caleb agreed. He's only six years old. He was probably afraid and confused and didn't know what to say."

By all accounts, Caleb Norton was a bright young man selected for a 75% tuition waiver among the inaugural batch of Bronswood scholarship students. Police have no leads, and the investigation into Caleb's disappearance continues.

As the search continues, authorities ask anyone with any information that might lead to Caleb's whereabouts to come forward immediately.

-James Cannon, Journalist, California Chronicle

    A connection at last. The only thing that Heather can latch onto right now that gives her hope. Another boy went missing six years ago and people know about it. A quick look into whether or not Caleb has been found since then proves fruitless, and the bit of optimism deflates.

But this is something.

Heather goes back to the search home page and finds a missing persons database. She types in Windwood, California. A painfully high number of results fills her screen. She filters the results to show only those children ages five through eleven, the age range in which a student at Bronswood could be.

The list remains heartbreakingly long.

Heather opens a new window and searches for some of the names individually, wondering if any others had news articles dedicated to their disappearance the way that Caleb Norton does. She comes up empty-handed and can't understand why each of these children doesn't have a dedicated person searching high and low for them.

Heather thinks about her next move and decides the best source for help is Officer Fowler. She grabs her phone and is about to move into an empty reading room where she won't disturb anyone. Instead, she looks around to find herself alone in the computer area and opts to stay put so that she has her search results in front of her. She'll keep her voice down.

The phone rings four times, and Heather is about to hang up when the line connects.

"Officer Fowler here."

Heather shoots up in her chair, sitting a little straighter. "Officer Fowler, hi. This is Heather Hartford."

"Mrs. Hartford. What can I do for you?"

"You mean besides tell me you found Charlie?" Heather pinches her lips shut between her teeth, regretting snapping. If her grandmother were here, she'd remind Heather that you catch more flies with honey than you do with vinegar.

When Officer Fowler lets out a gruff sigh, Heather quickly continues. "I'm sorry. I'm a bit out of sorts today."

He continues, his tone soft. "Understandable. I wish I had better news for you."

"I actually didn't call you for an update on Charlie." Heather hates how much it feels like a betrayal to her son to admit she isn't asking after him.

Her only reprieve comes from knowing that her call is still entirely for him. "I wanted to see if you could tell me what happened with a couple of other missing children's cases in Windwood. Tell me if they've ever been found?"

"Should I be offended that you are checking our track record?"

Heather doesn't respond, and Officer Fowler continues. "Sorry, small joke. And a poor one. Of course, I can look into some cases for you. Who are you looking for?"

Heather looks at the screen in front of her, trying to decide where to start. Which child, aside from her own, deserves to be thought about first? "Tabitha Keller?"

"Tabitha Keller." Fowler repeats the name. "Age six. Reported missing three years ago. Never found. Investigation ongoing."

"Investigation ongoing? As in, someone is still actively looking for her?" Heather knows what the answer will be, but she prays she's wrong.

Officer Fowler sighs again. "I know what you want me to say. But the truth is, nothing has shaken loose in all this time. Her parents call every few months hoping for good news and every time, I have to hang up the phone because Mrs. Keller forgets to disconnect before she starts to sob." He waits for a moment. "We keep an ear to the ground."

A tear rolls down Heather's cheek. She knows that person could easily be her, and she takes a deep breath as she continues. "What about Nathaniel Barrett?"

Heather can hear the tapping of a keyboard on the other end of the call. "Nathaniel Barrett. Age nine. Reported missing five years ago. Investigation ongoing."

They repeat this song and dance twice more before Officer Fowler starts to sound irritated, like he's running out of patience. "Mrs. Hartford, let me stop you right here. We'll be here all day if you intend to check on every child in the missing persons database, and our resources are best used on cases that we have active leads on at the moment. I can save us both a lot of time when I tell you if you see them in the search results, their case is still open."

Heather isn't ready to hang up yet. She clings to the hope that something he can tell her will shed some light and point her toward Charlie. What he could possibly tell her, she has no idea. But she has to keep going.

"I understand. Just one more, please."

Officer Fowler relents. "Name?"

"Caleb Norton."

Silence. For a moment, Heather thinks the call disconnected. She looks down at her phone and sees that the call is still active. "Hello? Officer Fowler?"

"Sorry, I'm here. Did you say Caleb Norton?"

"Yes." Heather can hear him typing again, but this time, it sounds quick and frantic. "I believe he went missing around six years ago. He would have been about six or seven years old."

Officer Fowler's voice comes out in short, clipped sentences. "Caleb Norton is not in the missing persons database."

"Does that mean he's been found?" The cells in Heather's body begins to vibrate. She tells herself not to get her hopes up, but her body ignores her plea.

"Where did you hear that name?"

Heather nearly informs Officer Fowler about the article she found on the internet, but something in the way his tone has changed makes the hairs on her neck stand up. Suddenly, this lead feels too precious to share. "I don't remember."

"You don't remember? You don't remember how you heard of a missing child who isn't in the database you've been reading to me for the last fifteen minutes?"

Heather wracks her brain for an excuse she can offer. A lie to appease him. Instead, something snaps inside of her from being held taut for so long. "In case you haven't heard, my son went missing last week. And I still have a husband and a daughter who need me. I've had quite a lot going on. Forgive me if I can't remember every little detail of every pointless conversation I've had in the last few days."

Heather waits for him to scold her for withholding information pertinent to a case. Or to tell her she needs to calm down. To remind her she's speaking to an officer of the law.

But when Officer Fowler speaks again, his voice is gentle, as if he remembered that he's speaking to the mother of a missing child. "Of course. You've been under immense pressure, Mrs. Hartford. I'm sorry. I was only concerned that a missing child slipped through the cracks." Heather hears what sounds like his chair squeaking as he shifts his weight around. "I'll look into it, but please let me know if you remember anything else. Perhaps he's not actually a Windwood case."

"Of course. I'll let you know. Thank you for your time, Officer."

"Take care, Mrs. Hartford."

The line disconnects, and Heather slaps her phone down on the tabletop a little too loudly. Her hand is shaking. She isn't sure if it's nerves from the confrontation she just had, or from the feeling that Officer Fowler isn't as trustworthy as she once thought.

Chapter 17

Heather gathers herself and goes back to the article she found, still centered on the computer screen. She scans down to the bottom to find the name of the writer again. James Cannon.

She quickly searches for anything else written by him, but this seems to be the only thing he's ever written. Or at least it's the only article of his that's been published on the internet.

Heather reads the article again, and her mind replays her conversation with Officer Fowler. The way he reacted to Caleb's name compared to the others she listed. The way he snapped at her when she couldn't tell him why she knew Caleb's name.

She makes the split decision to print out the article so that she can have it on hand whenever she may need it, but when she clicks the command to print, an error message appears. She tries again, this time highlighting the section that she wants to print. Same error message. She tries a different menu, but no luck.

Heather finally resigns herself to leave the computer to ask for help. She peeks her head in on her mother and Theo. Her mother looks up and smiles comfortably before returning to the storybook she's reading to Theodora, who appears to be incredibly content in Pamela's lap.

At the desk, two librarians are busy stamping books, clicking the mice by their computers, and filing the books away in one of the three carts behind them. One librarian looks to be significantly older than the other, and without intending to be too judgmental, Heather approaches the younger woman, assuming she'd be more helpful with computer issues.

Heather leans in to read the woman's name tag. "Excuse me, Samantha?"

Samantha looks up from her task with a bright smile. "Hi, there! What can I do for you?"

"I'm at the computers and there is an article that I'd like to print out, but for some reason, it isn't working. User error, I'm sure. Could you help me?"

Samantha stands up. "I'd be happy to take a look!" As Samantha walks around the large desk, Heather glances over at the older librarian, who looks up for only a moment with a knowing smirk and returns to her task.

Samantha appears at Heather's side and Heather leads her over to the computer she's been stationed at.

After several minutes, and several attempts—most of which were things that Heather had already tried herself—Samantha throws her hands in the air. "Darn! I don't know what is wrong with this thing. Maybe Margaret knows some trick that I don't." Heather watches as Samantha goes back to the front desk and says something to the older librarian.

They both return, and Margaret speaks before she's even reached the computer. "Well, my goodness. I'm just not sure what on earth an old dinosaur like me could do for you. What's this thing called again? A computer, is it?" Margaret winks at Heather and Heather struggles not to blush. "I'm only teasing, dear. Truly, I can't stand how fickle these machines are. But, I've learned a thing or two in my *many* years of experience. Let's have a looksie." Margaret leans in towards the screen. "Oh! A news article. Why didn't you say so?" She takes a small notepad out of her pocket and clicks open the pen in her hand. After jotting a few things down on the paper, she turns to leave. She waves them along without looking back. "Follow me, ladies."

MARGARET PULLS OUT A set of keys and unlocks a windowless door on the backside of the library. Stepping through the doorway is like being transported back in time. Before them sits a row of large machines with the yellowish tint that comes with age.

Margaret turns around to face them. "These are microfilm readers. They became popular during wartime and they've never failed me. So long as you have the filmstrips and a working lightbulb, everything you need is at your fingertips. Each of the original newspaper pages gets scanned onto a film strip that gets projected onto the screen." Margaret walks over to one machine and flicks on the power switch. The machine roars to life. "Now, they can be tedious to do research on if you aren't sure what you are looking for yet. But if you already know what you want, it's a breeze."

Margaret walks to a large filing cabinet on her right and unlocks the door. "The filmstrips are sensitive to light, so we keep everything locked up."

Heather watches Margaret pull her notepad out and expertly navigate the filing system. "Margaret, do all libraries have these machines?"

"Oh no, dear. Only the research libraries with... classics like myself who understand which are the superior pieces of technology." Margaret pulls out a tin and brings it over to the machine she turned on. "Besides, I love having these pieces of history on hand. The vintage look makes me feel young again." She chuckles and feeds the filmstrip into the microfilm reader and waves Heather over.

Heather ducks her head under the large hood with Margaret, and Samantha brings over two chairs for them to sit on.

Margaret scrolls through the film at lightning speed as she explains to Heather what she's doing. "This film is all the California Chronicle newspapers from 2004." She presses another button that scrolls at a much slower speed. "We have all the major national newspapers and all the California papers." She stops for a moment as she checks her notepad. "Here we are. We've made it to November. Now we just need to go a little further until we reach the date we're looking for. Would you like to try?"

Heather shakes her head a little. "You clearly have everything under control."

Margaret smiles. "Yes, I do, dear." She scrolls for a few more minutes, slowly checking each page for the article headline Heather was reading on the computer. "Ah! Here it is. Does this look like the article you were reading?"

Heather skims through the first part of the article. "Yes! This is it!" Heather feels tears well up behind her eyes as all the emotions from this week come rushing in at once. She continues to read through the article as Margaret fits the page to the print screen and clicks the button, sending it to the printer. Heather frowns. "Wait, this article…"

"Yes, dear? What about this article? If it's wrong, we'll keep looking."

"No. It's not that." Heather worries her bottom lip. "This has more than the article on the internet. I'm sure of it. I don't remember this bottom portion."

"Really?" Margaret brings over the printed page and hands

it to Heather. "Is it possible there was more and maybe you needed to click on the next page?"

Heather shakes her head again. "No, I'm certain I'd read to the end. I saw the writer's name at the bottom, just like this." She points at the paper.

"Well now, that just proves my point." Margaret rewinds the film back onto its spool and puts it back into its tin. "We need these machines because those fancy computers just can't be relied on." She closes the cabinet door and turns back to Heather. "Is there anything else I can help you with, dear?"

Heather looks up from her paper. "No, thank you so much, ladies. You've been an enormous help." She returns their smiles before walking back to her computer.

When she sits down, she clicks over to the browser tab that has the internet article and compares it to the paper in her hand.

She was correct. The article in her hand has a section that was deleted from the internet version.

As the search continues, authorities ask anyone with any information that might lead to Caleb's whereabouts to come forward immediately.

Before you move on to your next article, my journalistic integrity demands that I confess some digging of my own has shown an unusually high number of boys reported missing in Windwood over the last few years.

Their stories have been buried.

Sources remain concerned as to the location of Timothy Smith, Bradley Jacobson, Miles Donner,

Anthony Brando Jr., Roberto Jimenez, Edward Rutherford, and Winston Andrews. And these are only the names I've been given as of the time this article is being written. Who knows how many others have been buried over the years.

We must not let this stand. We must find and protect the children of Windwood. They can't silence us all. Please contact me with any information. Every lead counts.

-James Cannon, Journalist, California Chronicle

 Heather can't believe what she stumbled upon. This can't be true. If it were, and if people knew about this, who would move to Windwood?
 Heather stares at the screen as if the article may disappear. She exits the article to return to the search bar. She types in the search bar *Missing Windwood Children*. Nothing comes up.
 She tries again. *Missing Windwood Boys*. She finds a result that takes her back to the missing persons database, but nothing specific. She's been staring at the screen for so long that Heather's eyes cross and the words on the screen blur together, but she won't give up. Why is no one talking about this? Is James Cannon a conspiracy theorist?
 Without a better option, Heather searches for every single name mentioned in the article, one by one.
 A search for Bradley Jacobson turns up nothing, not even a missing person report. The same is true for Edward Rutherford and Winston Andrews. By now, Heather is all but certain that she's just been wasting precious time, and she fights a wave of tears when she realizes that this lead might be another dead end.

A single search result with the next name averts a complete breakdown. Meet the Student of the Month: Miles Donner. Exceptional trumpet player and devoted friend.

Heather allows herself a sigh of relief. It's her first glimmer of hope that these names might be real and not fictionalized to sell copies. She knows that chances of finding useful information in a school post are next to nothing, but she clicks on the link anyway, for the sake of completeness if nothing else. And when the article appears on her screen, Heather's heart skips.

The article features a picture of a handsome young man holding an award in front of two ornate wooden doors. *Bronswood's* double doors. Heather would recognize the intricate patterning anywhere.

She scowls as she skims the article once and then again. The article praises Miles' efforts in both academics and extracurriculars, touting him as the probable valedictorian in his graduating class if he stays on course. But Bronswood isn't mentioned anywhere. After a third read, Heather is certain.

There is no mention of a school—any school—anywhere in the article.

Another search result describes Roberto Jimenez as an important contributor to his community and a star humanitarian. No school mentioned. And no picture.

Heather drums her fingers on the tabletop, still clutching the article in her other hand.

After a minute, she searches for each of the seven names in the article paired with *Bronswood*, and she's shocked when this tactic proves successful. Each time, the name pops up under the "student register" headline. However, when Heather goes to click that result, she's taken to a locked page which is restricted to password access only.

She may not be able to access the student registers, but she's now confident that each of these children attended Bronswood.

Heather leans back in her chair, wondering what it all means. She returns her fingers to the keyboard. *James Cannon.*

No additional results found. She adds *California Chronicle* with no luck.

Heather goes back to the reading room where her mother is reading a book with a sleeping Theo in her lap. Heather lowers her voice so as not to wake her daughter. "I'm not sure what I found, but I found something. I don't want to leave a trail on my cellphone. Can I use your phone to make a call?"

Pamela points to her purse, which is out of reach with Theo asleep on top of her. "Of course. It's in there."

Heather pulls out the phone and slips into the next reading room so she doesn't wake Theodora.

Heather dials the number to the California Chronicle to see if she can track down James Cannon.

"Greg Hiller, California Chronicle."

"Yes, hi. My name is Heather Hartford, and I'm hoping to speak to James Cannon."

"Sorry, there's no one here by that name."

"Do you know where I can find him? He was a journalist there in 2004."

"Might be another paper you're thinking of. There's never been a writer here by that name."

Heather presses further with the article in her hand. "That can't be true. I'm looking at an article that he wrote back then."

Greg pauses for a moment. "Well, I've been here longer than that and I've never heard of him. Anyone can post an article claiming they wrote it for the California Chronicle, though we do our best to weed out any false claims."

"This is certainly for the California Chronicle. Is there someone else who might remember James?"

Greg sighs, sounding bored. "Are you sure you're reading this article on the official California Chronicle Website?"

Heather hasn't mentioned that she has a copy of the original paper or that it's different from the online article. Something tells her not to, hoping maybe something Greg tells her will explain why the online article was chopped. Knowing for certain that she has the correct paper, she tells him she's sure.

Greg gets the date and the headline from her and asks her to hold while he checks their website. She waits for several minutes, listening to him mutter some muffled words to someone nearby while he searches. "Sorry, there's no article by James Cannon, and there's nothing about Caleb Norton. Not currently, and not in our archives."

"But I'm looking at it—."

"Look, Heather was it? I'm sorry, I'm a little busy right now. I wish I could be more help, but there's just nothing here."

The statement is followed by a dial tone, and Heather stares at the phone in her hand, wondering if she's ready to handle whatever this is that she's uncovered. She goes back to the computer to repeat the search process that led to the discovery of the article. She clutches the paper tighter in her hands.

She types in exactly what she did before and clicks through each page.

The article is gone.

Heather tries to swallow the lump that forms in her throat. She looks down at the paper crumpled by her hand, and she realizes that it's now the only lead she has.

Chapter 18

Heather returns to the school the next morning. She parks on the far side of the Bronswood parking lot and watches the other parents drop their children off. Theo sits in her car seat singing along to *Beauty and the Beast* on the portable DVD player. When her daughter begins to whine, Heather bends her arm at an awkward angle to pass a granola bar back to Theo without taking her eyes off the car line.

She breaks focus only for a moment to glance down at the article she uncovered at the library. Second only to her own son, Heather is desperate to spot Zola, or the Haplys, or the Landers or the Morrows, who also stopped showing up to school last week. Anyone to prove her growing suspicion wrong, that kids have been disappearing from Bronswood for years. To quiet her imagination, picturing horrible things happening to those missing children. To soothe the ache in her gut screaming at her that whatever is happening to them is happening to Charlie, too.

Heather made several attempts to contact the missing families yesterday, but all of her calls went unanswered, and her messages went unreturned. She even went so far as to drive over to the Landers's home to see if they were there, but it appeared Shay was right about Caleb Landers being transferred for work. The house looked vacant.

She turns her attention back to the school. The last of the children enter the building, and Heather lays her forehead on the steering wheel, tears silently streaming down her face. In the back, Theo bops her head along to Be Our Guest.

Heather pulls herself together, and glances down at the California Chronicle article, reaching into her purse for a pen. In the margin, near the list of names identified by James Colins, she writes the names of the boys who have stopped showing up at school.

Sequoia Landers. Thatcher Morrow. Elliot and Bronson Haply. Adam Engler.

She thinks for a moment and adds Beck Rodgers with three question marks, still unsure of why he's been missing.

Heather takes a deep breath, and she swallows hard as she writes one more name.

Charlie Hartford.

She puts the paper away and decides to make the drive out to the office of the California Chronicle. The PTA triplets will expect her at gala preparations, but she doesn't care. It's the first time in two days that Heather has anything to chase, and she's not about to sit around waiting for others to do what she can do herself.

When she looks up, there's a note stuck to her windshield. She looks around for the person who left it, but there is no one.

I know it hurts. But you can't waste any time. Bronswood won't let you unearth its secrets. You need to be more cautious than ever. There are eyes everywhere. I'll show you what I can as soon as it's safe. I'm with you, Heather. I'm here.

BH

Chapter 19

The commute to the Chronicle office passes quickly. Heather's mind bounces in every direction, reviewing the pitifully little progress she's made. She's spent far too much time dwelling on the shady notes she's receiving which has gotten her no closer to her son. She called the police department again for an update on Charlie's case, but no one offered any news. When she asked who they had spoken to, the officer on the phone informed her that no one had come forward with any new information. Beyond the headmistress, who has been a picture of cooperation, they have no other leads to go on. Heather pressed further about Charlie's teacher only to be told again that there is no Miss Kilgore at Bronswood, and that there never was. Police had, however, spoken to Charlie's actual teacher, Miss Crawford, who confirmed that Heather had arrived at the school shortly after 1:00 pm to pick up her son on Monday. Faced with dead end after dead end, Heather is keenly aware of how badly she needs this lead to work. To actually lead somewhere.

Heather pulls into the parking lot of the Chronicle and unbuckles Theo from her car seat. She grabs her bag and makes her way to the entrance.

A pair of bells attached to the door jingle as Heather and Theodora enter the building. Heather considers recommending a new method for announcing arrivals because not a single person looks up to acknowledge her. Some employees are hunched over their computers, tapping away at the keyboard, their eyes never leaving their screen. Others are talking excitedly over some papers in their hands or darting around the office. All appear too busy to notice Heather at all.

She waits several moments before waving down a man who has just removed his glasses to rub his eyes. "Excuse me."

The man looks at her lazily, as if he's already bored by her. He doesn't look a day over eighteen. Practically a child. He looks like he just rolled out of bed and ran a hand through his wild hair. "Can I help you?"

"Yes, I'm looking for James Cannon. He wrote an article some time ago, and I wanted to talk to him about it." Heather opens her purse to reach for the paper.

"James Cannon? Sorry, there's no one here by that name. Maybe a different paper?" The man's eyes drift back to his screen.

Heather smothers her irritation and interrupts his work again. "Excuse me. Sorry. What about Greg? I spoke to a Greg something or other on the phone yesterday. Is he in?"

The kid leans back in his chair and cranes his head over his shoulder without peeling his eyes away from what he was typing. "Greg! There's a lady here to see you!"

"Thanks," Heather grumbles.

A minute later, a man comes stalking down between the row of desks. He's got a solid twenty years on the kid whom Heather has just annoyed by existing. Greg is wearing baggy khaki cargo pants and a blue plaid flannel shirt that's at least two sizes too large for him. "I'm Greg. What can I do for you?"

"Hi, I'm Heather Hartford. We spoke on the phone yesterday about James Cannon's article on the missing boys."

"Yeah, look I told you, there's never been a James—."

"Just look at this!" Heather interrupts him and thrusts the article into his hands.

Greg takes the papers cautiously, and he stares at her for several moments before dropping his eyes to look at the headline. Heather waits while his eyes flicker over the writing. "What are these names you wrote off to the side?"

"More boys who have stopped showing up at school recently."

Greg scans the paper and when he reaches the last name on the list, his eyes go wide. He looks at Heather, and Heather just nods.

Greg looks at the California Chronicle title at the top of the page. "Well, I'm not sure what to tell you about James Cannon. Like I said, I looked into it and couldn't find any record of his existence at the paper. This sure looks like one of our papers, but all of our papers have been printed physically and digitally for years now. Since I can't find its online edition, I can't be certain." He looks at Heather and holds up the papers. "Can I make a copy of this?"

Heather nods.

"Great. Be right back."

He trots off and returns a few minutes later, handing the original article back to Heather. She checks to verify that the article hasn't been tampered with, and she relaxes a little when she recognizes an ink smudge on the righthand side.

Greg fidgets a bit and stuffs his hands into his pockets. "Tell you what. I'll do some digging and see if anything shakes loose on this. I can't make any promises."

Heather forces a small smile. "Thank you. I really appreciate it. You have my information."

He responds with a curt nod and spins around to hustle back to whatever he was doing. Heather stuffs the article back into her purse and takes Theo's hand to leave.

As they exit the office, Heather hesitates for one fleeting second to consider mentioning the bell above the door. She decides not to bother, and she flings the door open. Her hand whips up to shield her eyes against the sunlight that temporarily blinds her.

Heather is just reaching for the door to her car when she hears a woman calling out behind her. "Ma'am! Ma'am, wait!"

Heather turns around to find a woman jogging towards her. Judging from her appearance, she looks to be about Heather's age. She's wearing no makeup at all, and her hair is pulled up into a frizzy ponytail.

"Hi, sorry. You don't know me, but I heard you were looking for James Cannon." The woman whoops in a breath.

"Yes!" Heather lights up. "Do you know where I can find him?"

The woman shakes her head. "No, I don't know him personally, but I've heard his name around the office."

She takes a step closer to Heather and lowers her voice. "I don't know what happened, but something went down some years ago and no one likes to talk about him anymore. It's all very hush-hush."

"Do you know where he went? Where he might be now?"

"I can't say for sure because he was gone by the time I started working here, but I heard something about Lake Harding. There's a bunch of cottages up there. Might be worth looking around there."

"Thank you so much. I will."

Heather commits Lake Harding to memory, and she gives the woman a grateful nod before turning to buckle Theo into her car seat.

"I hope you find your son." The woman's voice sounds from behind Heather as she walks away.

Heather is about to climb into her car when something clicks into place. She turns on her heel and calls out to the woman. "How did you know my son is missing?"

The woman turns to face Heather and shrugs. "I heard Greg talking about it on the phone just before I ran out here."

Heather nods, unsure if that revelation should put her at ease or unnerve her. "I'm sorry. What did you say your name was?"

The woman looks around, as if checking that they're alone. "It's Kara. Kara Luval."

"Thank you, Kara." Heather wants to press Kara for more, but Kara seems skittish suddenly. Heather doesn't want to scare her off. "If you think of anything else, would you call me? Greg has my number."

Kara nods. "Good luck."

Heather makes a note to follow up with Greg in the next few days before she starts the car. For a split second, she considers a nap. It's been days since she's had any actual sleep and she can feel its effects coming on stronger.

HEATHER PULLS INTO THE garage to find Nick's car waiting there. Her heart drums rapidly in her chest. This week, she's had to step lightly around him. His moods oscillate wildly between needing physical affection to cope with Charlie's disappearance, to the angry destruction of whatever is nearby, to neglect of both Heather and Theo. He's been drinking more since Charlie disappeared, becoming less predictable by the hour, and Heather fears how dangerous that makes him.

Heather climbs out of the car and lifts Theo from her seat.

She enters the house first and looks around. It's quiet and there's no sign of Nick, so she brings Theo inside.

Theo is complaining about being hungry, so Heather plops her in a chair at the kitchen island and slices an apple, putting it on a plate with some cheese cubes. "Be a good girl and stay right here with your snack, alright? Mommy will be right back."

Heather walks quietly from room to room. "Nick? Honey, are you home?"

A low grumbling comes from the sitting room. "Where have you been?"

Heather carefully migrates into the room to find her husband's body thrown carelessly across the leather armchair, head slung back awkwardly so that Nick is looking up at the ceiling. A tumbler with two fingers of scotch sits on the side table next to him and on the bar cart sits an open bottle of Lagavulin 16.

"Hi, honey. I was just out running some errands with Theo and then we went to the park for a while." Heather stands on the opposite side of the room, not daring to come any closer.

Nick appears to take a great deal of effort to lift his head to look at her, his eyes like two small slits. "What did you just say?"

Heather wonders what she might have said to draw his focus this intensely. "I said I was out with Theo. We had some errands to run and then she wanted to go to the playground."

Nick pulls himself upright and stands, turning his body just enough that he can reach his glass. He tosses back what's left of his drink and stumbles over to the cart to pour another. "Do you even care that our son is missing? Really. Charlie has been gone for two whole days and you just walk around like nothing's happened. Embarrassing me with your outbursts, then flitting off to the playground." He downs another finger and fills his glass again.

"Of course I care. I'll do anything to get my son—."

"*Our* son." Nick interrupts.

"Of course. To get *our* son back. But we still have a daughter who needs us. One who is too young to understand what is going on. We can't disappear on her." Heather waits while Nick seems to consider what she's telling him.

Nick takes a few steps towards Heather, his drink sloshing in his glass. "Why is it that mothers don't seem to give a shit about their sons? Huh?" He takes a sip. "You know, my mother didn't give a damn about me. Well," he chuckles, "to be fair, she didn't give a shit about my sister either."

Heather is stunned. And terrified. Nick never talks about his parents. She didn't think he had a sister. He's not making sense anymore.

He takes a few steps closer to Heather, and she stiffens, unsure whether to run or to stand her ground. "And now, here you are. And you clearly don't give a damn about Charlie." He leans in close to Heather and whispers, "You disgust me."

Heather's mind reels with thoughts she wants to scream at him. *I disgust you? Look at everything I'm doing for Charlie! And what are you doing? Nothing. Pretending like everything is fine.* You *disgust* me.

Nick sneers at her and then stumbles up the stairs, spilling his drink on the way. Heather releases the breath she'd been holding and returns to Theo.

She unclenches her fists and looks at the tiny moon shaped cuts in her palms. She has to work faster. Her husband is a human bomb, ready to explode.

Chapter 20

Heather has to drag herself out of bed the following morning. Her head is so foggy that she can't tell if she slept poorly or didn't sleep at all. Her grief over Charlie threatens to keep her in bed, but her obsession with finding her son yanks her out of it. She needs to follow up on some of her leads. Besides, she can't risk Nick thinking she is getting lazy. Heather knows he expects her to put on a strong, united front, but she can't stop dwelling on the way she used to know how to keep him happy. Now she never knows what may set him off.

Heather throws back the covers and slogs down to the kitchen to make the breakfast she knows she won't eat and the shake that she knows Nick won't drink because he's still sleeping off his bender from last night. She can't remember the last time he went out for his usual morning run. Was it last week? Or last month?

When Nick finally comes downstairs almost an hour later, Heather is in place, standing in the kitchen where she always stands, journal open on the counter next to her.

"Morning," Nick mumbles.

"Good morning, honey. Did you sleep alright? I made your protein shake if you want it." Heather moves toward the refrigerator to get it for him.

"No, that's alright." Nick pours himself a large tumbler of coffee and walks over to Heather. He kisses her lightly on the cheek. "I've got to get to work." He leaves without another word.

Heather throws her food away and goes back upstairs to get herself and Theo dressed. Heather grabs the first black athleisure set she sees and throws her unwashed hair up into a messy top knot before she heads to Theo's room.

A part of her needs the comfort of her morning routine with the kids, the steady rhythm they created together, and she hates herself for still craving it, knowing that Charlie isn't here with her and Theo.

On her way to Theo, she stops at the door to Charlie's room and slowly opens it. For a minute, she sees him sitting there on his floor, building some elaborate Lego structure. When she blinks, he's gone again, and the hole in her chest grows larger. She gently shuts the door and pads down the hallway to her daughter.

Heather's imagination runs again at the familiar motions of dressing her daughter for the day. Theodora giggles as Heather pretends she can't find Theo's head under her shirt. "Where's Theo?" Theo's head pops out, and she yells "boo!" Heather's heart fills up as they walk down the stairs to the kitchen where she knows Charlie will be eating a bowl of cereal, waiting for them. Just like he always is.

Except this time, he isn't there. And the devastation is too much today.

She plunks Theo down in a chair and steadies herself on the countertop as sobs roll through her body in waves. She wipes her nose on her sleeve and turns to get the cereal box from the pantry.

Her hands shake as she tips the box over Theo's bowl and she spills some cereal on the counter. She looks over at Charlie's empty seat and imagines the pieces of cereal that toppled over the edge of his bowl as he ate last week. She curses herself for cleaning them up. For having wiped away such tangible proof of his presence.

Heather watches her daughter eat her cereal. Twenty minutes pass before Heather scoops Theo up and heads to the car. She has to finish their morning routine. She has to get to Bronswood on time.

Not to drop her son off at school. But to search for any shred of hope that might tell her where to find him.

HEATHER'S STOMACH SCREAMS AT her for food, and she resents it for needing nourishment with everything going on. She wonders if Charlie is being fed wherever he is. She wonders if he is even alive to need food.

She blinks back a fresh set of tears and sits up straighter in the driver's seat, sipping the black coffee she poured herself this morning in an attempt to erase the fog living in her head for the last two days.

The Bronswood car line is filling up.

All the same families are at drop off. Heather even made certain to arrive early enough to see Harriet, Liv, and Shay walking their children to class.

None of the missing families have returned.

Heather watches the last car pull away, and then she waits long enough to see Harriet, Liv, and Shay exit through the great wooden double doors together. They are talking rapidly with a lot of hand gestures. Shay leans in towards the other women, and they laugh. Heather hates them for laughing. How dare they be happy while she slips further into despair with every minute that Charlie isn't with her.

Heather watches them from behind her oversized sunglasses,

morbidly curious about what they'd say to her if she told them everything that she's uncovered. Harriet looks up and spots her.

 Harriet doesn't say anything to the other two women. She stares right at Heather with sad eyes. Heather throws the car into gear and drives away.

Chapter 21

Heather drops Theo off at her toddler Gymboree class with her mother. Pamela tells Heather to take as long as she needs. Pamela will take Theo for a trip to the park and lunch after class, which gives Heather time to drive back to the library to make some phone calls and investigate the Lake Harding cottage residents.

When Heather arrives at the library, the first thing she does is check out another time block at a computer. She steels herself as she fires up the search engine and starts with her first lead. The cottages surrounding Lake Harding.

Lake Harding is a large body of water with extraordinary depth. While most lakes average ten meters in depth, Lake Harding descends to an incredible three hundred meters at its deepest point. Locals are drawn to the area because of the sheer volume of fresh water the lake holds and also because of its shallows. The shallow areas of the lake are so wide that an unusual amount of photosynthesis occurs, keeping the area lush, green, and thriving.

As a protected nature reserve, Lake Harding is home to a

minuscule one hundred fifty-five permanent residents, making it easy for Heather to look into property records. Over the years, property values have soared at these shoreline cottages. The cottages are all built along a single road that winds around the lake, which should be convenient for Heather to drive along.

Heather navigates to the California state property records database and scans through the list for James Cannon.

No such person is listed on any of the titles.

She does, however, find a Beth Cannon.

Satisfied, Heather clicks the button to print out the address, and decides that she'll drive to the property tomorrow, when her mother has a little more time to stay with Theo.

Record not found.

This new roadblock hits her like a physical punch to her gut. She hangs her head, but for only a moment. She cannot stop.

With the leads on James Cannon exhausted for now, Heather switches gears and turns her attention closer to home. She tucks herself away in an empty reading room and digs through her purse for the article with the list of names in the margin. Setting the paper down on the table in front of her, Heather pulls out her phone and dials the number for each of the four missing Bronswood families.

No one answers. No one returns her calls.

She calls her mom to ask if she can stay with Theo a while longer. Heather already confirmed that the Landers house has been abandoned, but that still leaves her three more homes to check. Pamela assures Heather she and Theo are getting along swimmingly.

Heather packs up her purse and sends a quick text message before she leaves.

I DON'T KNOW WHERE YOU RAN OFF TO, ZOLA. OR WHY. BUT PLEASE CALL ME BACK. PLEASE. I NEED A FRIEND.

A tear splashes onto the phone screen, and Heather wipes it clean before drying her eyes. She tosses the phone into her purse and makes her way to her car. Her body feels like lead, and Heather wills her muscles to move. To move faster, for Charlie's sake. And for hers.

THE MORROW AND ENGLER homes appear to have been recently vacated, just like the Landers. Heather peeks into one window at the Morrow residence through a crack in the shades, and all that remains is the furniture draped in sheets. It's easy for Heather to believe that the Morrows might be gone considering the awful rumors of infidelity floating around. So far as Heather can tell, it's a topic that every Bronswood wife seems to have experience with, yet none are willing to own up to it happening to them. Instead, they chatter about who else's husband was seen with a twenty-something year old, pretending their husbands aren't doing the same thing during all their late work nights and long sessions at the club. Heather would be lying if she said it never occurred to her that Nick may be seeking comfort, or a distraction, elsewhere lately. But walking in on your spouse in the act? Well, now that's something different entirely. Heather imagines Marian Morrow couldn't just stand by and pretend it never happened.

But the Englers, as far as Heather knows, remain a mystery. When she asked around, no one seemed to know anything about where they'd gone or why. Furthermore, not a single Bronswood mom has mentioned the strange coincidence that all these families left the area at nearly the exact same time.

Of the parents of Charlie's classmates who did answer Heather's calls, none provided her with any useful information. A few were polite enough to ask their children who their teacher was—*Miss Crawford*—and their classroom number— *D-3*—the room across the hallway from the vacant room Heather has been seeing Charlie enter each morning since the beginning of the school year. Before Heather could dig any further, the parents must have sense her hysteria because each conveniently had to go somewhere after offering their condolences.

It doesn't make sense to Heather.

Then again, nothing makes sense to Heather anymore.

She climbs back into her car and drives towards the Haply home. It's only a few blocks away. As she drives, Heather pieces through the million unknowns in her mind. Where are these families disappearing to? Why? And why now? Where is Charlie? Does James Cannon have clues about what happened to him? Does anyone?

Heather's train of thought comes to an abrupt halt as she pulls around the corner and comes in view of the Haply residence. There's a huge moving truck in the driveway, and a small herd of workers cart boxes from the house to the storage area of the truck.

Heather parks on the opposite side of the street and makes her way to the front door. She doesn't see anyone she recognizes, and she hesitates for a moment before calling inside. "Cherie? Are you home?" She waits a moment. "Hello?"

A sickly looking woman makes her way down the stairs. "Can I help—oh! Heather. What are you doing here?"

Heather realizes her mouth is gaping, and she must look horribly rude for staring. Cherie Haply's normally bronze skin is pale and nearly see-through. She's lost a good amount of weight that she didn't have to spare. She looks fragile. And her roots are showing. Then again, Heather can't imagine that she looks any better.

Heather quickly screws on a weak smile. "Cherie, I'm so glad you're here. I just came by to check on you and the boys. We haven't seen you around school, and Charlie was asking after them."

Cherie's eyes fill up, but she holds herself together. "You

are so sweet. The boys have been quite ill, but otherwise, we are doing well."

Heather glances back at the moving truck. "You're moving? Now?"

Cherie waves a hand like it's nothing. "Yes, it was all very sudden. Harry got a job offer that we just couldn't refuse. It's across the country, and they expect us there right away."

Heather suspects there is far more that Cherie isn't telling her, and she prods a little further. "I can't believe you were going to leave without saying goodbye. Could I just say goodbye to Elliot and Bronson? Charlie will miss them so much." Heather's insides scream at her each time she says Charlie's name, but she has to get to the truth. For his sake.

Cherie's chin is quivering. She looks like she wants to say something, but changes her mind. "No… No, I'm sorry. That's impossible. They're just too ill. They're asleep."

Heather nods. She's about to ask another question when Lana Haply, the Haply twins' younger sister, bursts into the room. "Mom, can we go now? I want to see Elli and Bron," she whines, tugging on her mother's dress.

Cherie's eyes flash with terror, and she turns back to Heather like a deer caught in a hunter's scope. Cherie keeps her gaze on Heather as she responds. "Yes, sweetheart. We'll go upstairs in just a minute to check on them. Run along, and I'll be right there."

The girl cocks her head to one side. "But Mom——."

"I said run along." Cherie's tone is forceful, leaving no room for further argument. Defeated, Lana throws her head back and slumps her shoulders, dragging her feet out of the room.

Cherie turns back to Heather. "Kids." She shrugs her shoulders with a sad smile. "I'm sorry, I really must be going now. It was so good of you to stop by."

Heather nods. "Of course. I hope the boys feel better soon. Take care of yourself."

Cherie's eyes fill again, but she says nothing as she turns to follow Lana.

Heather knows she's about to miss an opportunity. If she doesn't act now, she might never have a chance, and she hears herself call out before her sense can catch up with her. "Charlie is missing!"

Cherie freezes but doesn't turn around, so Heather continues. "I dropped him off at school on Monday, and then when I went to go get him, they told me I had already come to pick him up. But I hadn't. No one knows where he is or what happened to him."

Cherie's whole body turns slowly to look at Heather. Her tears are falling freely now, creating uneven splatters on the dusty doorstep. "I'm sorry about Charlie."

Heather tries again, unwilling to give up. "Cherie, please. I know they're keeping something from me. And I think you might be able to tell me what it is." Heather pauses, holding Cherie's gaze, pleading with her eyes. "Please, I need help."

Cherie's head drops, and she swipes a finger under her nose, sniffling. She looks up, her face like stone. "I'm sorry, Heather. But I can't help you." She turns and leaves Heather alone on the doorstep. The movers continue to haul boxes out of the house, completely oblivious to the fact that Heather's world is collapsing around her.

You aren't the first to start digging. James Cannon did too. You're right to follow him. I shouldn't give you this but, 1453 Lake Harding Loop. You won't find Charlie. But I can show you something else. I'm still here, Heather.

BH

Chapter 22

Heather stares at the scribbled note in her hand. It was left on her SUV windshield while she was at Cheri Haply's house yesterday, though Heather still can't figure out how someone managed to leave it without her seeing.

An address. Heather has no way to be sure, but she hopes it belongs to James Cannon. Or at least, Beth Cannon.

The signature on the paper is cryptic; nothing more than a symbol that Heather has never seen before.

Heather sets the note down, having gleaned nothing new from her fifty-third read through, and shoves several potato chips into her mouth, hardly tasting a single one. Grease clings to her forearms each time her hand blindly plunges into the family-size bag. She's pulled her chestnut locks up into a messy knot today and parked a few rows closer to the car line this morning hoping to get a better view of the families dropping off their children. She certainly doesn't know every family at the school, but she knows every family with a second-grader. If there are more children disappearing, she's going to figure it out.

Today, Heather brought an old copy of the second-grade class rosters that she was given at her first PTA meeting, and she ticks off each family as she sees them enter the building.

She nearly adds the Kenneth family to her no-show list when Victoria Kenneth comes flying into the parking lot at the last minute. Heather is watching Victoria smooth her unkempt curls when a rapping on the window next to Heather startles her so badly she nearly sends her bag of chips flying across into the passenger seat.

Heather turns to find Harriet waving at her through her window, and she presses the button to roll the window down. "You scared the hell out of me, Harriet."

Harriet smirks. "Sorry, I didn't—," Harriet's eyes fall to the oversized bag of potato chips in Heather's lap, and Heather tries to pretend that nothing is amiss as she cleans the grease from her hand with a baby wipe. "Jesus, Heather. Are you alright?" Harriet curls her top lip, looking at the bag with disgust, like it may as well be filled with acne and three pounds of pure fat.

Heather continues to wipe her hands without looking up at Harriet. "My child is gone. Would you be alright if you were me?"

Harriet's shoulders slump, and she reaches a hand through the window and places it gently on Heather's shoulder. "No, I wouldn't be. We are all so sorry about Charlie. But Heather," Harriet presses gently, "you have to take care of yourself. For Charlie, if no one else. He needs you."

Heather leans forward, hugging her steering wheel. Her cardigan slides down her back, sagging in the middle, exposing the tiny points of the bones in her spine. "Something isn't right, Harriet." Heather's voice comes out just barely more than a whisper.

"I understand why you need to believe that. I can only imagine how you must be feeling—."

"*Why I need to believe that?*" Heather sits up suddenly and turns to glare at Harriet. "What the hell does that mean?"

Harriet looks startled by Heather's reaction, and she pulls her hand out of the car window and folds her arms in front of her, softening her face. "Well, yeah. I mean, kids run away sometimes. And I know we've never really talked about it, but it's no secret that things have been," Harriet looks down at the ground, "hard at home." Heather turns her eyes back to the windshield, looking straight ahead.

Harriet lowers her voice. "Heather, Nick comes off charming, but I know he has a temper."

"How could you possibly know that?"

Harriet looks around her and purses her lips together. "Lance told me a story once, about a time when all of our husbands went golfing together. Nick was in rare form. Lance said he seemed agitated from the minute he arrived." Harriet shifts her weight onto one leg. "He said on the eleventh hole, Nick lied about his strokes so that he could make par. When Philip called him out for it, Nick threw his club at Philip's head and kicked the golf cart." Harriet shakes her head. "He put a dent in the side of it."

Heather chuffs. "That's just men being men. They all pitch fits when they're losing at golf." She waves it away, still covering for her husband. Still covering for herself.

Harriet lowers her face to look at the ground. "Heather, we know what happens when he throws a tantrum at home. It's literally written on your face the next morning."

Heather is silent.

"We saw the makeup, we saw the bruising."

Heather keeps her eyes on the school in front of her. "It was an accident. He's just stressed. He always gets stressed about this ridiculous gala, having to show up for his firm. Now with Charlie gone..." Heather trails off, realizing she's defending Nick, and she doesn't want to.

"Ok, you don't want to talk about what's really going on.

That's fine. You want to pretend you tripped on a toy? Alright then. But you need to do *something*. It's clear you're not sleeping." Harriet points to dark circles beneath Heather's eyes. She reaches in to grab the bag of chips from Heather's lap. "And *this* is not food. You are losing weight and you need real nutrients in your body. Come on, get out of the car."

Heather turns in her seat. "What? Why?"

"We're going to the gymnasium. I want you to see the gala setup so far. You need to get your mind off all this shit for a minute." Harriet waves her hand around in the air like she's swatting at a mosquito.

"You want me to forget about my missing child for a minute?"

Harriet bites her bottom lip. "You make that sound worse than I meant it. I only meant that we all want Charlie to come home. But the police are doing everything they can and everyone here at the school is fully cooperating. Let the police do their job and try to give yourself a few moments of reprieve." Heather shoots Harriet a look, and Harriet puts her hands up in peace. "If only to recharge your battery so that you can properly focus on searching for Charlie again."

Heather considers this for a moment, weighing the pros and cons of taking a momentary break from her investigation. With a sigh, she realizes that the effort would at least show Nick that she is trying to put on a good face like he keeps asking of her. She reaches for the handle to open the car door and Harriet takes a big step backwards.

"There you go! Good girl." Heather narrows her eyes at Harriet. "Look, I'm just trying to help you. One of the moms reported you to the headmistress. She said you were making them uncomfortable. I told the headmistress that I'd talk to you, but she will flip if she finds out you're stalking parents in the parking lot again."

Heather pulls Theo out of the car and gathers her things. She throws her bag over her shoulder and takes Theo's hand. Harriet loops her arm through Heather's free one, and they walk to the gymnasium.

Chapter 23

When Heather steps inside the gymnasium, her mouth drops open. She turns to find Harriet grinning from ear to ear. "I know, right?"

Heather slowly follows Harriet deeper into the room as Harriet shows off everything that's been set up at this point.

Round tables draped in cream linens are centered at the back end of the room. Gold-plated forks, spoons, and butter knives rest on top of black dishes that appear to be specifically made to hold silverware. Gold chargers sit beneath fine china dinner plates, and each plate is topped with a cream linen napkin folded into the shape of a star. An enormous centerpiece with the floral arrangement Heather created sits in the center of each table. Heather marvels at the deep purple Queen of the Night, white snowdrops, red winterberries, and maroon hellebores mixed in with golden orbs, a few branches and a bit of greenery.

Heather soaks in the familiar flowers and lets her eyes close. When she does, she's home, in her garden on a crisp Spring morning, snipping old blooms and breathing in the floral scents. Charlie is there chasing Theo around the yard until it's time to go inside and get a snack where they'll beg Heather to make a pitcher of lemonade.

When her eyes open once more, she's back in the place that took her son away from her. She swallows her anger and tries to focus on what Harriet is saying to her.

Unable to avert her curiosity, Heather asks Harriet about the centerpieces being placed so early. "Oh, don't worry. I'll have fresh centerpieces brought in, but I needed to see the full effect before I signed off on them." Heather is stunned by the budget for this event and wonders exactly how much money it brings in for the school each year.

The cracked gold crystal orbs Heather dug out of her basement hang above each of the tables, and tiny white lights sparkle on the ceiling.

Off to one side, Heather sees a bar set up near the hors d'oeuvres tables. She continues to scan the room when Theo tugs on her arm. "Mommy, I'm bored. I want to watch Cinderella."

Harriet gestures to the row of benches that line the wall opposite the bar. "She can go sit down for a few minutes, if you want."

Heather shakes her head, unwilling to let Theo out of her reach. "No, that's alright." She turns to Theo. "We won't be much longer, sweetheart. I can carry you."

Theo starts to whine. "I want to watch my movie."

"I can put her at a table if that's better for you. You'll be able to see her from wherever we are in the room, Heather." Harriet's voice is careful, and Heather can tell she means well.

"I said *no*. She'll stay with me." Heather's voice comes out harsher than she meant it to, but Harriet acts like she didn't notice.

They are about to walk over to the dance floor and auction area when a pair of double doors bang open. Two blonde heads burst through the doors. They appear to be deep in debate about something, faces close together, hands gesturing to the front of the room. Shay looks up, and her eyes connect with Heather's. Liv turns to see what Shay is staring at. They exchange a glance before pinning a pitying smile to their faces as they walk over to Heather.

Liv's arms are outstretched and she locks Heather in a hug that Heather doesn't return. "Heather! My god, I didn't expect to see you here. How are you holding up, sweetie?"

Heather takes a step backward when Liv releases her. "As well as could be expected, I'm sure."

Shay reaches a hand out for Heather's. "We are all just heartbroken and praying Charlie comes home safe."

When Heather doesn't respond, Harriet explains she is just showing Heather around the space to take her mind off things.

Liv and Shay nod. "Of course," Liv says. "We were just working out all the auction details, so we'll get back to it."

Liv turns to walk back to where she entered the room, and Shay says goodbye to Heather. "You will let us know if you hear anything? Jeanie asks after Charlie constantly."

Heather nods and glances briefly at Liv, who has stopped walking and is giving a pointed look to Harriet that Heather can't interpret. Shay whips around to join Liv, her white blonde curls swinging like curtains that were shut too quickly.

Harriet continues to lead Heather to the dance floor. Heather scoops up Theo, who rests her head sleepily on Heather's shoulder, and follows Harriet.

They stop in the center of the dance floor and Heather spins around, taking in each of the twelve white porcelain busts that surround the vinyl subfloor.

"Harriet, those look amazing." Heather faces Harriet. Harriet is practically glowing. "Truly, the details are incredible."

"Thank you. They turned out well, didn't they?" Harriet smiles.

Heather starts at one end of the half-statue semicircle. There is a small square table in front of each porcelain figure. On top of each sits a display post describing the auction item to be bid on, a clipboard for the bidder to write their bid, several heavy but slender gold pens, and a laminated card with a brief history of the headmistress at that station.

The faces are so detailed that Heather wonders if the sculptor had access to a cast of the women's faces.

Heather makes her way around the tables, craning her neck awkwardly around Theo, who has now fallen asleep in her arms. She tries to shake the feeling that the white porcelain eyes are watching her wherever she goes.

Harriet trails next to her, chattering away about the process of securing each bust.

Heather comes to a halt when she reaches the last table. Headmistress Rosler stares back at her with piercing white eyes, and Heather freezes where she stands.

"I know those eyes. I've seen them before." Heather's voice is breathless, addressing no one in particular.

Harriet is next to her suddenly and leans forward, eyebrows pinched together. "Headmistress Rosler?" Harriet asks from behind her. "Well, of course you know her eyes. We all do." Harriet studies Heather, her eyebrows pinched together.

"No. No, that's not what I mean. It's like I've seen them before, somewhere else."

Harriet scowls at her. "Hmm. Probably just some intense déjà vu. Happens to me too." Harriet laughs uncomfortably.

Heather can't quite interpret what Harriet is thinking, and she looks down at the auction description. It is an all-inclusive ten-day stay at a private villa in Greece. There is a name and a bid already written on the clipboard.

Heather turns her body sideways, so that she doesn't have to crane her neck around Theo as she reads the name. Bruce Bannar.

Heather's heart drums faster. Picking up speed the longer she stares at it. "The Hulk?"

Harriet's mood brightens, and she beams. "Oh, that! An old silent auction trick. We pick a theme each year and we always fill in the starting bid on the paper to get the ball rolling." Harriet leans in a little closer with a sly smile before whispering, "And to make sure we are hitting our fundraising goals." She rights herself once more. "This year we went with superhero names, but we always change one letter so that it's just a silly coincidence." Harriet giggles. "Not that anyone would notice anyhow. In our experience, the wealthiest of the wealthy don't spend their time watching Marvel movies, and they certainly don't look beyond the first name. All they see are numbers."

Heather's eyes haven't left the page in front of her. "The Hulk was Charlie's favorite hero." A lump solidifies in Heather's throat at the realization that she just referred to her son in the past tense.

"Is it? How funny! Maybe it's a sign. You know? The universe telling you that Charlie is ok." Heather feels nauseous.

"Who suggested the Marvel theme?" Heather whispers. She already knows the answer.

"Well, I can't remember for sure. I think maybe it was one of Liv's ideas. But Headmistress also has the final say."

Heather drags her eyes up to meet Harriet's. Her whole body feels numb. "You should be really proud. The gala is going to be perfect."

Harriet is beaming, but her brow creases in the middle as she studies Heather's expression. "You're still coming, aren't you? I've already placed you at our table."

"Oh, I don't think so. It just wouldn't feel right, with Charlie missing."

"Heather, please come. You can't just sit in your car withering away. There is still a life here for you and for Theo. She's going to start school soon. You need to stay plugged in."

"Theo won't be going to school here."

Harriet's jaw falls open. "What are you talking about? Surely Nick already made sure she has a space."

"Harriet. This school stole my son from me. God only knows what happened to him." Heather chokes back a sob. "There isn't a single cell in my body that's willing to risk that with Theo."

Harriet blinks a few times more than she needs to. "Does Nick know that?"

"No. And you are the only person in the world I've ever said that out loud to. So if he finds out—."

"I won't tell him, Heather. I promise." Harriet looks sincere.

"Thank you, Harriet." Heather hugs her with one arm, the other gripped like a vice around her daughter. "I've got to get going. Nick will expect me when he gets home."

AS SHE MAKES HER way out of the gymnasium, Heather turns around to push one of the double doors open with her back, since Theo is still fast asleep in her arms. The door stops abruptly when it slams into something hard.

"Ouch! Shit…"

Heather hears a deep grumble from the victim and she scrambles to apologize.

"I am so sorry! I didn't see you. My back was turned—." Heather turns around at last. "Stephen! I'm sorry, are you alright?"

Stephen grins as he rubs his head where the door must have hit him. "Don't worry about it. I can see you have your hands full."

"Yeah." Heather looks down at Theo and sees her daughter's eyes fluttering open from the commotion.

"Hey, Theo. How are you doing?" Stephen crouches down to say hi, and Theo buries her face in Heather's neck.

"Not a morning person," Heather throws out. "So, what are you doing here?"

Stephen holds up the toolbag in his left hand. "Liv asked if I could come in to hang some things and fix a few rickety chairs. I guess they aren't up to standards."

"I didn't realize you were on Liv's payroll. Should I start calling you *Mr. Fix-It?*" Heather asks dryly.

Stephen leans in, close to Heather, and he lowers his voice. "Are you doing ok?"

Before she can stop herself, everything inside of her comes rushing to the surface, and she unloads on Stephen. Heather tells him about her breakdown at breakfast yesterday morning, and about Harriet trying to take her mind off of everything.

"—And then there's Nick, and he's trying to pretend like everything's fine except it's not fine, and he definitely isn't fine, and I tried to talk to him yesterday and he—." Heather snaps her mouth closed before she says something she'll regret but Stephen presses her on it.

"He what? Heather, what happened? Did he hurt you?" Stephen searches for her eyes, but Heather can't bring herself to look at him.

"No. No, he didn't. He's just under a lot of stress and it's getting to him. To both of us," Heather corrects.

Before she can register the movement, Stephen drops his bag and wraps his arms around her.

Heather isn't sure what to make of the fluttering in her stomach, and she hurries to divert attention away from whatever is happening between them right now. "Well, you should get in there. I'd hate to see what Liv is like when her contractors are a no-show."

Stephen nods. "I'll see you, Heather."

Heather answers with a half-smile and continues her trek to the parking lot.

She hears Stephen call out behind her, "Let me know if you need a handyman!" She turns around just in time to catch Stephen smiling to himself before he disappears into the gymnasium.

Chapter 24

Heather stares at the note left in her palm. *1453 Lake Harding Loop. You won't find Charlie. But I can show you something else. I'm still here, Heather.*

At first, the entire situation frightened her, and she considered taking the note to the police. After she calmed down, she decided against it.

Heather still isn't certain if Officer Fowler is really on her side. The more she thinks about it, the more it feels like the note-writer is trying to help her, and Heather decides there could be any number of reasons they might want to stay anonymous. They may be in trouble too. They may have had a child taken from them.

Heather worries that if she tells anyone about the note, any future notes may stop coming. And she's not ready to lose an ally.

Heather starts her car to let the heater warm her chilled body. She told Harriet she was going home, but Heather isn't ready to face Nick yet. Just a few more minutes of quiet safety.

The radio clicks on and the smooth sound of Elvis' voice rings out as he begs his lover not to destroy them with her suspicions.

Heather doesn't remember leaving the radio on, and she frowns as she tries to read which station she's listening to.

Except it's not the radio playing *Suspicious Minds*. It's a CD. One that Heather didn't own and certainly didn't push into the player on her own.

Heather sits up straight and cranes her neck as she surveys the parking lot. Someone was in her car. Did she leave the car unlocked? Is the intruder still here at the school?

Heather hits the lock button on the door, and she contorts in her seat to lay eyes on every inch of the inside of her car. Theo stirs in her car seat as Heather climbs into the backseat to look in the trunk. When she is certain there is no one hiding inside, she returns to the driver's seat and wonders if she might actually be going insane. But the song is still playing. Someone was inside the car.

As she turns the music down, Heather swivels to make sure that Theo is still asleep, and she scans the note again, begging her heart to slow down to a normal pace. Tracing her fingers across the writing, she whispers aloud, "Who are you?"

There are surveillance cameras all over the parking lot, but she doesn't trust the school to help her. Not after her behavior in Rosler's office and certainly not now that Rosler knows she's been creeping around in the parking lot during drop off and pickup.

Heather thinks of the bust of the headmistress in the gymnasium, and she wonders how similar Headmistress Rosler is to the young woman who lived back then. She imagines a rigid woman with pale eyes and a forced smile. Even in her mind's eye, the expression looks out of place, like a piece forced into the wrong jigsaw puzzle. It's hard for Heather to imagine that the headmistress was ever a teacher, one of the guardians responsible for shepherding young hearts and minds.

She thinks about the photo of Bronswood's first class from Rosler's desk. The children were all smiling, overflowing with the carefree joy that seems innate at such a young age. Despite the intensity of their teacher, all the children looked happy. All the children except for one.

Heather remembers the serious boy from the photo. His arms crossed in front of his chest, isolated from his classmates. The way his chin tipped down just slightly, and he wore an empty, serious expression. Heather wonders what might have caused his angst that day.

Her eyes relax as she thinks about the boy. The edges around his face soften, and he begins to blend into his surroundings. Pale blue eyes against a sandy background. Empty sadness where there should have been wonder and light.

As Heather returns to the present moment, the boy's eyes sharpen. She knows she's seen them before. That same haunting intensity. Those particular angles at the corners. The exact shade of pale blue-grey, now obscured by a layer of white. It's not a little boy's eyes that stare back at her.

They are Headmistress Rosler's.

Chapter 25

Heather is convinced that the brief history of Headmistress Rosler on display at the Gala isn't nearly the complete story about the woman who currently rules Bronswood. Heather races back to the library where an extensive search only bolsters Heather's hunch.

Headmistress Rosler isn't who they all think she is.

In fact, she doesn't seem to have existed at all prior to becoming a teacher at Bronswood. There are no articles mentioning her name prior to her brief interviews and biographies after obtaining the title of Headmistress. There are no mentions of Anastasia Rosler on any social media pages. No public records with her name on them.

Anastasia Rosler doesn't seem to exist.

But, if that's true, then who is the woman who has been at Bronswood for the last thirty years?

THE DRIVE TO LAKE Harding is about an hour north of Heather's house. She calculates that she might have just enough time to drive the loop of cottages and make it home before Nick does. She has to try. This can't wait until tomorrow. Besides, she isn't sure that she wants to give the person sneaking around her car the heads up that she's coming. Heather plugs the location of the nearest cottage into the GPS system that Nick recently installed in her car and heads to her mother's house to drop off Theo for a few hours, since it's twenty minutes in the same direction.

Heather wonders what she might find at Lake Harding, if anything at all. That someone left her a note instructing her to go there leads her to believe there must be *something* there. It can't be a coincidence that someone resides there, in the same area Kara told her to look for James. Can it? The note told her she wouldn't find her son, but she can't stop herself from hoping that's where Charlie is.

Heather drives slowly around the lake loop and searches for the address she was given. It's nearly halfway around the lake, and she slows down as she approaches. It looks empty. The lights are off, and there are no cars in the driveway. Her car rolls to a stop in front of the dark cabin and she climbs out.

Heather looks around and sees a few people mulling about. An older couple sits on their porch a few cabins down the road. A family is walking their dog on the other side of the road. Somewhere close by, the growl of a lawnmower sheering grass is whirring.

Heather approaches the door and prepares herself to knock. She has to believe that whoever lives here will have answers for her. Answers that will lead to her son.

She raises her hand, but before she can pound on the door, it swings open to reveal a young woman holding a bag of garbage in one hand.

The woman's eyes go wide, and she drops the bag on the ground. "Heather? What are you doing here?"

Chapter 26

Heather stands there, speechless, feeling her heart thumping wildly in her chest.

Zola jolts forward and throws her arms around Heather's shoulders before dragging her inside. "My god, get in here." Zola slams the door behind them and locks it. She guides Heather to the sofa and sits beside her. "What are you doing here?"

"What am I doing here? What are *you* doing here? And where the hell have you been? You had me scared to death! And pissed, to be perfectly honest." Heather's words tumble out in rapid succession. "I needed you this past week. Do you have any idea what I've been going through?" Heather leans closer to lock eyes with Zola. "Charlie is gone. And something at the school is seriously wrong. They know what happened and they're covering it up. I know it."

Zola closes her eyes and takes a deep breath while Heather spirals. "Wait. Heather, slow down. What do you mean *Charlie is gone?*"

Heather stands up, her body on fire, needing to move,

needing to run. She walks to the other side of the room and turns to face Zola. "He's gone! They took him from me. They have him and I have to get him back." Heather narrows her gaze at Zola. "And you just left me? How could you do this to me?"

Zola shakes her head. "I didn't know. You have to believe me. I didn't know." Zola blinks hard, her eyes filling with tears. "I'm so sorry, Heather. I didn't want to disappear on you. I had to keep Beck safe. I didn't want to drag you into this mess."

"What do you mean you had to keep Beck safe?" Heather throws her arms out to the sides. She wants to scream. "Drag me into what? Zola, I don't understand."

Zola sighs. "How did you know to come here? How did you know where I was?"

Heather brushes her anger aside for a moment and collapses back down on the couch. "I *didn't* know to come here. I wasn't looking for you." Heather looks down at her lap. "I'd pretty much given up on that." She steels herself and looks up. "I was looking for James Cannon."

"You were looking for James Cannon?"

"Yes. Charlie isn't the only boy who is missing. I went to the library to do some research, and I stumbled on an article he wrote for the California Chronicle years ago." Heather reaches for her purse. "It was a plea for help, really. Turns out there are several former Bronswood students that have vanished over the years, and I think he was investigating it." She pulls the papers out of her bag and hands them to Zola. "I called the Chronicle to ask about it, but they denied the validity of the article. They denied even knowing who James Cannon was." Heather watches Zola's eyes roam over the article. "By the time I got off the phone with them, the article was gone. Like it had been erased from the internet."

Zola is nodding her head, following along. "So, how did you find this cottage?"

Heather can't imagine why that is so important, but she answers anyway. She's been bursting with this information, craving someone she can trust to work through this with her. "I went to the Chronicle office to show them in person. They gave me the same story. But when I left, a woman flagged me down to tell me she's heard the name James Cannon around the office and suggested I try the Lake Harding Cottages." Heather thinks about the note in her purse and decides against showing it to Zola. "Property records didn't show a James Cannon. But there was a record for Beth Cannon." Heather weighs how to explain how she arrived here when Beth Cannon's property record was unable to be found. She decides a clipped version of the truth is best. "I got an address. So I crossed my fingers and came to check it out."

A tear falls from Zola's eyes, splashing onto the paper. Despite her anger, Heather reaches a hand over and wraps it around Zola's. "What is it? What's wrong?"

Her friend pulls her hand back and swipes at the tears trickling down her cheeks. "Beth Cannon is my aunt. James was her husband."

Chapter 27

Heather searches for a moment before finding her next words. "James Cannon is your uncle? How is it possible I didn't know this? We've been best friends since middle school. You've never once mentioned them."

Zola looks at her, eyes brimming with apology. "I know. It's complicated. I hadn't spent any real time with them since I was a little girl. When we were kids, things were bad for you at home with your parents. And then there was Paul. It just never felt right to suddenly unload a complicated family tree on you. It felt so irrelevant."

Heather thinks about this for a moment. "You said *was*. James *was* her husband. Where is he now?"

Zola sniffles. "They were killed in a car crash. Nearly three years ago. They were coming back from a party to celebrate the lead reporter at the Chronicle being the recipient of the John Chancellor Award. It was late and dark. A deer sprinted out onto the road, and they swerved and collided with a tree. My uncle was killed instantly. My aunt died later that night at the hospital."

"Oh my god, Zola. I can't imagine how horrible that must have been."

Zola nods and dabs at her eyes before she continues. "I got the call that they had left a will, and they left the cottage to me along with a small nest egg. There was a letter explaining that it was just in case Beck and I needed it." Zola lets out a little huff of air. "Like even from a distance, they could predict the shit that was going to go down with my ex-husband." Heather watches, seeing the memories forming behind her friend's eyes. Zola straightens as she adds, "But this isn't about me, Heather. Right now, it's about Charlie."

"What does this have to do with Charlie? Do you know where he is?" Heather is certain Zola doesn't know where her son is. Just moments ago, Zola hadn't even known that Charlie was missing. If she did know, then Charlie would be here right now.

Zola's shoulders sag. "Of course not. But Heather—."

The sound of small feet padding down the hallway interrupts them.

"Mom?" Beck's voice calls out to Zola.

The two women turn to face him, and his eyes connect with Heather's. A grin splits open from ear to ear. "Hi, Mrs. Hartford! Is Charlie here? Did you bring him?"

Heather tries to find the words to answer, but nothing comes out as Zola jumps up to wrap her son in her arms. "No, sweetie. I'm sorry, Charlie isn't here."

Beck starts to protest. "When do I get to go back to school? I want to see my friends. Why do we have to stay here?"

Zola crouches lower to look at him. "I know, Beck. I know this is hard for you. It's just for a little while longer. I promise." She squeezes him tight. "Why don't you go play your video game while I talk to Charlie's mom? I'll make you a little snack to eat."

Beck drags his feet as he heads back to his room.

Zola doesn't move until they hear his door latch shut. She

stands up slowly and turns back to Heather. "Come on, I need to show you something."

Heather stands up and follows Zola to the other side of the cottage. Zola catches Heather's gaze before leading the way into a small room, just barely bigger than a walk-in closet. Zola flicks the light on.

THE TINY ROOM LIGHTS up, and Heather is entirely unprepared for what's revealed.

Before her is what looks like a detective's crime wall. One side of the room is covered in photos, articles, newspaper clippings, handwritten notes, maps, and pushpins attaching string from one photo to the next like a spider's web. The other side of the room contains several boxes. A box at the top of one stack is missing its lid, and a row of hanging file folders is exposed.

Heather slowly works her way around the room, and Zola talks from somewhere behind her. "Uncle James and Aunt Beth moved out here when I was young, and James got a job as a junior beat writer at the Chronicle. He worked his way up pretty quickly." Zola nods towards the papers and photos on the wall as she says, "One day, an anonymous tip came in that there was something happening to the boys at Bronswood. My uncle was given a list of three boys' names to look into."

Heather glides her fingertips gently over the pictures on the wall, each labeled with a handwritten name on a sticky note. Every little boy from his article. She can't help but wonder if there's a stranger out there, somewhere, with Charlie's photo pinned up on a wall.

Zola continues. "James went digging, and he found out that far more than just those three had fallen off the Bronswood map without explanation. But no one believed him." She clicks her tongue and lowers her voice. "My mom told me the case ruined him. He became a recluse, obsessed with proving that the disappearances were happening."

Zola walks to where Heather is standing and stops at her side. "There were rumors floating around that he was gunning for a Pulitzer, and that he created the story himself. There were worse rumors that he was the one taking the boys."

Heather moves slowly from face to face, reading the names on the attached sticky notes. She recognizes Miles Donner from his picture posing as student of the month. "Why would the staff at the Chronicle tell me that James Cannon didn't exist?"

"My mom said her sister called her once, sobbing about James getting fired. James told Beth that he found proof that someone at Bronswood was involved in some kind of illegal side business. He said there was a paper trail, but no one ever saw it so far as my mom knows because nothing ever came of it."

Zola starts to rummage through some folders. "James went to his boss to show him he finally had proof to support his story, and that he was going to expose Bronswood and everyone involved. His boss shut him down and fired James for unethical behavior and insubordination. There was a huge altercation in the office, and James's boss threatened to destroy James if he ever showed his face there again. Supposedly the rest of the staff was ordered never to speak a word of it, at the risk of staining the Chronicle's reputation for journalistic excellence."

Heather shifts uncomfortably, trying to process everything Zola has told her. "So you have been here? All this time. With all of this." Heather stretches her arms out. "And you never said a word. You just… left me."

Zola spins Heather around to face her. "I didn't want to. I didn't know anything about this until my uncle died, and I came up here to clean out the cottage and I found this." Zola takes a step back and gestures wildly at the walls. "But Heather, something is very wrong at Bronswood. This is the reason I followed you to that horrible place and applied for their damn scholarship. It's the reason I told you to pretend like you didn't know me when I got there."

Heather scowls at her, feeling the fury rising inside her chest. "Why did you let me come at all?"

"You were trying to find your place there with Nick." Zola looks sad, and her eyes are begging for Heather to believe her. "I swear, I didn't know what you were getting into. And I had to be sure, and I didn't want you getting hurt in the process. I watched you endure years of Paul's abuse and I've watched you all this time with Nick—"

This time, her husband's name shocks Heather back to reality. "Nick! Shit, what time is it?"

Zola glances up at a clock on the wall. "Just after three o'clock."

"I have to go." Heather runs to the living room to get her purse. "I have to pick up Theo from my mom's and get home. Nick is going to kill me."

Zola races after her, following Heather to her car. "Heather, wait! Let me know that you're alright when you get home. And come back tomorrow." Heather shakes her head, looking down at the ground. "Please, Heather. I will tell you everything I know."

Heather sighs. She has to know what Zola has discovered. "Alright. Tomorrow."

"Bring Theo. I know Beck would love to see her."

Heather nods and climbs into her car and drives off.

Chapter 28

Heather has to force herself to focus on the road in front of her. The area is unfamiliar, and the sun is beginning to descend onto the horizon sending a ray of light piercing her eyes at exactly the right angle to compromise her vision.

Heather drives along, trying to process everything that's happened today. She's trying desperately to cling to this new thread of hope. She found Zola, and she can find Charlie, too.

But why didn't Zola tell her where she'd gone to? Her best friend in the world let her drown in her own grief, alone. Zola said that she was trying to protect Heather from whatever this was that she's getting involved in. But why couldn't she have just said as much before she left?

Heather's brain is a tangled mess of moving parts, none of which seem to fit together.

Where is Charlie? How many boys have gone missing over the years? And why? What does Zola know? How much had James figured out? Who can Heather trust?

Heather jolts when an unwelcome thought intrudes. *Paul!*

Have the police contacted Paul to tell him about Charlie? Why hasn't he reached out again since his last text?

Heather needs help. And she isn't sure who she can turn to.

Heather glances down at the dashboard of her car and realizes she's driving a solid fifteen miles per hour over the limit. She hadn't noticed herself picking up speed while her mind was racing, and she gently taps the brakes to slow the vehicle down. The last thing she needs is to explain to Nick why she got a speeding ticket near Lake Harding.

Something slides into place inside Heather's head, and she pulls the car over to the side of the road.

Heather pulls her phone out, finds the phone number she needs, and dials before she can think better of it.

The line connects after a single ring. "Sacramento Police Department."

"Hi, I'm looking for Officer Pierce."

"Hold please."

Heather drums nervously on the steering wheel.

"This is Officer Pierce."

"Josh?"

"Who's this?"

Heather swallows a gulp of air. "My name is Heather. Heather Hartford. I don't know if you remember me, but I knew Meg's father, Mark. I was at the wake last September."

"Heather! Of course. Wow! Uh, what can I do for you?"

"I was wondering if you could look into a couple of things for me?"

There is a pause on the other end of the line that Heather can't interpret.

"I can certainly try. Is everything alright?"

Heather's eyes fill up. The phone rattles in her hand from nerves. "To tell the truth, no. It's not. But that's not why I called. I was hoping you could look in on my ex-husband, Paul? He was Mark's cousin. I wouldn't ask except that he still lives in Sacramento."

"I can do that. Any particular reason I'd need to?"

Heather wonders how much he knows about her history with Paul. "I'm sure Megan has told you about... what happened between us?"

"I know enough." Josh doesn't ask Heather to expand, and Heather relaxes for a moment.

"Ok." Heather takes a deep breath. "The short story is that lately, over the last month or so, he's been calling and texting me."

Some shuffling sounds come from the other end of the line, and Heather thinks she hears a desk drawer slam closed. "What kinds of things has he been saying?"

"Nothing too horrible. Mostly, he's been demanding to see the kids more. To change their visitation schedule." Heather scrambles to add, "Which I don't have to do, right? Legally? I have full custody."

"No, you don't have to do that."

"Good." Heather takes another breath. "It's just that his messages were becoming more and more aggressive. Not threatening, exactly. Angry."

"Ok." Josh waits for Heather to continue.

"Then, out of nowhere, they just stopped." Heather starts to shake again. "And I'm just scared that I don't know why. It's not like him to just let anything go."

"Don't worry." Josh clears his throat. "I'll look in on him. Make sure he is where he's supposed to be."

"Thank you. I really appreciate it."

Realizing that she's still racing against the clock, Heather restarts the car, and she pulls back onto the road, feeling calmer than she had before. She drives for a moment when Josh speaks again. "Is there anything else I can help you with?"

Heather thinks for a moment. She nearly let him disconnect when she remembers something else. "Actually, yes! If I sent you a photo of a note that I received, could you tell me who wrote it?"

"A note?"

"Yes. Someone left a note on my car the other day, but they didn't sign their name to it." Heather considers telling him it was just a good citizen who dinged her car and wanted to exchange insurance information, not wanting to sound paranoid. But then she realizes that if he wants to see the note, the first thing he'll see is that she lied to him.

"Well, I can have a handwriting analysis done on it. But the information will be very limited without any samples to compare it to. We can determine, with reasonable certainty, whether one person wrote it or more than one. Whether the person is right or left-handed. Male or female, most likely. But we can't look at a piece of writing and tell you who wrote it." Heather doesn't respond right away, and Josh adds, "But I'd be happy to send it along for analysis if it will help you narrow down your search."

Heather considers this and decides it's better than nothing. "That would be great. Thanks."

"No problem. Send me a photo or scan of the note when you can, and I'll see what I can find out."

"I will. Thanks, Jo… sorry, Officer Pierce."

"Take care of yourself, Heather. I'll be in touch."

Heather hangs up the phone and tosses it into the passenger seat. She should feel marginally better now that she has someone she can talk to who is outside of this Bronswood world she's trapped inside. But, for reasons she can only guess at, she feels more on edge than ever.

Heather hopes it means she's getting closer.

Chapter 29

By the time Heather reaches her mother's house to pick up Theo, she can feel the full effects of sleep deprivation setting in. Her thoughts are punchy, and her head feels foggy from the emotional fatigue. She knows she needs to be focused on the dark roads in front of her, but she can't get herself to obey. She rolls her window down just enough to let in the bite of the frigid air to keep her alert. Paranoia creeps in as she weighs how she feels about Zola right now.

Zola has been Heather's closest friend for most of her life. She's the one who tried to get Heather to leave Paul. She's the one who took Heather, Charlie, and Theodora in when Heather finally mustered the courage to escape. Zola's the one who helped Heather find an apartment of her own. Zola even encouraged Heather to go talk to Nick at the business mixer when she noticed Nick staring at her. She should be the one standing beside Heather through all of this.

But Zola is also the one who vanished without a word. She's the one who knew something was happening inside the walls of

Bronswood, but she didn't tell Heather. She's the one who didn't come back for Heather when Heather told her that she needed her. In truth, Heather is furious. But she also has questions that only Zola can answer, and if she wants answers, she has to put her anger aside.

Right now, she needs to get home before Nick gets really suspicious about where she's been. She'd texted him when she got to her mother's apologizing for getting caught up with her mom and losing track of time. Heather hoped maybe he'd be working late or out for drinks with one of the other husbands. Or hell, out with another woman for all she cared right now.

After her text, Nick sent back a sweet reply to tell her it wasn't a problem and that he would have dinner waiting for her and Theo. Heather can't help but wonder if it was for her mother's sake, in case Pamela saw the message.

She's nearly home when her phone ringing jolts her from her thoughts. She grabs the phone and sees an unknown number on the caller ID. Ignored.

As she nears her street, the phone lights up again. Unknown number. Heather tosses the phone on the passenger seat as she pulls onto her street. She slows to a roll as she approaches their house.

There is screaming.

It's dark, and Nick is standing in the yard yelling at the front door.

Heather's heart seizes. Has the home invader returned and Nick caught him in the act?

She wonders if she should stay back, but as she rolls closer, the combination of the porch and street lights slowly reveals that it isn't Nick that she's looking at.

It's Paul.

Heather pulls into the driveway watching Nick shout from the porch, and Paul yells back with his hands up.

Heather turns to Theo. "Mommy will be right back, baby. Ok? I'll be right back." She gets out of the car. "Paul! What the hell are you doing here?"

Everyone is shouting at once.

Nick turns on her. "I knew you were messing around with him, Heather! You stupid bitch!"

Paul returns fire at Nick. As much as he can, given his physical state. Paul was once a large man, towering over most. But, an infection post weight loss surgery left him frail and fragile-looking. "Don't talk to her that way, asshole. It's not like that."

Heather injects all the strength she has into her voice. "Both of you, calm down right now!"

Nick runs his hand through his hair, and a wild laugh bubbles from his throat. "I don't fucking believe this."

Heather takes a step towards Paul, but she freezes when he walks towards her. He seems to notice, and he stops moving. "Heather, you won't talk to me. You haven't answered any of my messages." Paul's eyes narrow pointedly, as if he's asking her a different question all together.

"There's nothing to talk about, Paul. I'm not giving you the kids. Not now. Not ever. You can't have them."

Paul drops his hands to his sides. "I'm not the same man I was back then."

Nick scoffs. "Yeah fucking right."

Paul shoots a look at Nick. "Shut up! This isn't about you. Except that you're about as big an asshole as you seem." Paul turns back to Heather. "I'm not here to talk about custody. I know Charlie is missing. The police called me in for questioning. What the fuck, Heather?"

Heather looks down at the ground. "Why did they call you in? You don't even live here."

"Because he's my son!" Paul roars.

Nick steps onto the grass. "He's not your son anymore!"

Paul steps backwards with his hands in surrender, looking frightened. And weak. "Heather, our son is missing. I'm trying to *help* you, but you won't talk to me."

"Paul, you need to leave now." Heather pleads with him. Heather has been trying to lie low. To manage Nick's mood swings. But the longer Paul stays here, the worse it's going to be for Heather when he leaves.

Nick sneers at Paul. "Yeah. You need to get the fuck out of here right now. Before I call the cops and have your sickly little ass thrown in jail."

Paul seems to snap at that, and he rushes to Nick. The two men size each other up and Paul jams a finger into Nick's chest. "Fuck off, Nick! I know exactly who you are. I know exactly how men like you operate."

"Is that right?" Nick laughs, cocking his head to the side. "And how would you know that?"

Paul lowers his voice. Heather doesn't recognize the sound that comes out of his mouth. "This is about Charlie. And it's between me and Heather. If you get in my way, I'll kill you. And if I rot in a cell for it, who cares, right?"

Heather picks her head up and sees Nick staring down at Paul. A sinister smirk painted across his face. Heather looks at Paul. "Paul, please. You have to leave. Don't come back here."

Paul seems to consider this for a moment. He takes a couple of steps backwards and yells over to the car, where Theo is crying. "Theo, baby! Daddy loves you! See you soon!" He walks towards the street where his car is parked, stopping just next to Heather, and lowers his voice. "I'm not going anywhere, Heather. I'm going to be right here. And I'm going to help get our boy back."

Paul gets into his car and drives away. And Heather turns to get Theo out of the car. She carries Theo into the house.

"What did he say to you?" Nick asks, his voice like ice.

"He said goodbye." Heather answers. They enter the house, and Nick locks the door behind them.

Chapter 30

Heather lies in bed. Sleep continues to evade her. She replays the evening over and over in her mind, desperate to change the outcome.

As soon as Paul left, Nick sent Theo to her room, telling her dinner would be ready soon. Once Heather knew for certain Theo was safely tucked away, she ran to the kitchen to busy herself preparing food, deliberately keeping her body between Nick and the block of knives. She noticed the way Nick was careful not to come too close to her, as if he knew not to test the limits of his fury. Or perhaps he was just acutely aware that the gala was coming up in just two days. He still expects Heather to attend with him, and they both know that she won't be able to if she's covered in bruises.

Nick knew that he didn't need his hands to hurt Heather last night. His words alone sufficed. But a part of her wished for a wild hand to connect with her face. It might have ended quicker. No amount of venom Nick spit seemed to sate him.

Nick hurled every insult he could at her.

Stupid. Whore. Ungrateful. Fat. Ugly. Useless. Bitch. Worthless.

None of that meant much to Heather. But his final cut sliced deep into her gut.

Horrible mother.

Heather wanted to fight back. She wanted to defend herself; to scream at him that she was a good mother. That she loved her children. But she couldn't. He'd given voice to the dark thoughts that had been consuming her, bit by bit, since her children were born.

What kind of mother stays with a man who abuses her in front of her children?

What kind of mother has a second child with that man?

What kind of mother finally leaves, only to find another man who might be more cunning than the first?

What kind of mother loses her child and can't find him?

When the tears finally fell, Nick lost his composure. His hand flew out and connected with the vase of fresh flowers Heather cut from the garden that morning, sending a burst of yellow winter jasmine, purple aconite, creamy witch hazel, and bright pink English primroses soaring across the island to shatter against the wall.

Theo appeared in the kitchen doorway, crying because the loud noise frightened her. In an instant, Nick knelt down and swooped her up into his arms to soothe her. Heather watched as Nick's entire being shifted in a single blink, and he became the father she fell in love with. The transformation was more frightening than anything else that happened that night.

Heather listened as Nick explained how clumsy he was. He said he'd knocked over the vase. He passively instructed Heather on what he expected from her as he told Theo they could go back to her room and play together until dinner was ready while mommy helped clean up the glass so Theo's tiny feet wouldn't get a boo-boo.

Heather didn't move until they were out of sight. Then she swiftly swept up the glass and finished the macaroni she had been making for Theo.

When she went to tell them Theo's dinner was ready, it was as if nothing had happened. Theo ran to the kitchen and, as Nick passed by Heather in the doorway, he dropped a sweet kiss on her cheek and thanked her for cleaning up.

HEATHER STARES UP AT the dark ceiling as she runs through a list of acceptable reasons she might be gone with Theo for most of the following day. Nick doesn't go into the office on Saturdays. He'll expect to keep Theo with him if Heather needs to run errands. He always keeps the children around whenever possible. Whatever debate Heather tries to get into with him, she always loses.

She will tell Nick that she is taking Theo to visit her mother. It's the safest choice since Nick despises Pamela. He argues constantly that Pamela is always inserting herself into their relationship, and righteously insists that Pamela is too judgmental.

In the beginning, Heather bought into Nick's rhetoric about her mom, and she was all too happy to have an excuse to avoid Pamela's overbearing concern. Looking back now, Heather wonders how early in their relationship her mother saw through Nick's charming facade and guessed the truth about the monster underneath. Heather has never told her mom the full truth, but then again, Pamela has watched her daughter go through this before.

HEATHER MUST HAVE DOZED off eventually because when she wakes up, it's light outside, and Nick isn't lying in bed next to her. He normally gets out of bed before her, but Heather is already awake, waiting for him to move first. That Heather didn't see him get out of bed this morning immediately puts her on edge. She has no idea what kind of mood he woke up in.

Over the last few years, Heather has learned to read the way

Nick stretches in the morning. Is it jerky and stiff? Or relaxed with a deep exhale?

She listens to the way he walks to the bathroom. Does he stomp his feet, making it a point that Heather wakes up to hear him? Or does he tread lightly, so softly that the only tip off that he's moving is the occasional pop of a knee or crack of an ankle joint?

She watches the way he leaves the room to go for his morning run. Does he swing the door wide open, uncaring if it hits the door stop a little too hard? Or does he sneak out and quietly latch the door shut behind him?

With none of Nick's usual clues to tip her off, Heather doesn't know what to expect as she climbs out of bed. As she treads softly towards the bathroom, Heather goes to Nick's side of the closet to see if his running shoes are missing. They are. She turns to the bedroom door and when she finds it closed, she finally releases her breath.

HEATHER PADS DOWN THE kitchen where Nick is standing behind the island, sweating from his run. Theo sits in a chair across from him, eating chocolate chip pancakes. Nick sips his shake and leans across the counter with a fork. He playfully sneaks a bite from Theo's plate. Theo giggles wildly as he makes a dramatic monster sound. Nick looks up. "Morning, honey. Did you sleep well?"

Heather walks over to where Theo sits and plants a kiss on her cheek. "Well enough. How was your run?"

Nick takes a drink from his cup. "Great! I made progress on my mile time. Six minutes and fifty seconds."

Heather smiles. "That's very impressive. Theo, isn't it amazing how fast daddy is?" Heather rubs her daughter's back in tiny circles.

Theo's mouth is overflowing with pancake. "Mm hmm."

Nick laughs. "Can I make you something for breakfast?" Nick slides a cup of coffee across the island to Heather and pulls her food journal out of the drawer. He jots down eight ounces of coffee, half a teaspoon of stevia, and one tablespoon of cream.

Heather takes a tentative sip from her mug, not noticing at all the way it tastes. "Thank you. But no, that's alright. I'm not quite ready to eat."

"You need to eat something. Let me at least make you a protein shake." Heather knows better than to argue as Nick plunks an aggressive amount of vegetables into the blender along with a bit of fruit, protein powder, and coconut water.

He logs her breakfast in her journal, and he swipes another bite from Theo's plate.

Heather thanks him again for his thoughtfulness, and then carefully brings up her plans for the day. "I was thinking of taking Theo to my mom's house for the day. My mom has a few new things for Theo to play with, and she mentioned a free children's event at her church that she thinks Theo would enjoy."

Nick shakes his head, smiling at Theo. "No way. We are having a daddy-daughter day! Aren't we, Princess Theodora?"

Theo giggles, nodding her head as she digs a chocolate chip out of the pancake and feeds it to Nick.

Heather tries again. "I know you aren't a huge fan of my mother. But it's just this once. These days don't come around often. Plus, it would give you a chance to catch up on some of the things you wanted to do around the house."

Nick tilts his head to the side, staring into Heather's eyes. She prays he can't see her plans. "I said *no*." He looks back at Theo as he talks to Heather. "You go see your mom. Theo and I will be just fine."

Heather bites her lips closed to keep them from quivering, and she gambles by placing a kiss on Nick's cheek. She needs a minute to calm herself and think. There is only one place at home that will help her do that. "Thank you, honey. I think I'll go out to the garden for a minute to gather some flowers before I leave. I'll take a bouquet to my mother."

Nick nods. "Just let me get cleaned up first."

He leaves to shower. Heather dumps the rest of her breakfast down the garbage disposal without another word, and she draws a deep breath as she tells Theo to be good for daddy. Heather prays Theo won't tell Nick all the places she's been going to the last few days, but she also knows better than to tell Theo to keep a secret. Asking Theo *not* to tell Nick is all but a guarantee that she will. Heather needs to make today count.

Chapter 31

Heather spends longer than she ought to select just the right flowers, retreating into their colors and smells. Feeding them and watering them, helping them gather their strength during these cold winter months.

A chill in the air bites at her cheeks as she sinks deeper into the solace her garden provides. The only sounds to keep her company are the chirps of some Scrub-jays and mockingbirds. Heather looks over her shoulder to the empty patch of grass where Charlie should be, lying next to Theodora, pointing out each blue bird to her as they swooped down to take perch inside their primrose tree.

Heather turns back to the flowers in front of her and snips a few more stems, pulling the vibrant yellow and deep purple blooms close to her nose. She inhales their scents, letting the rich green notes of the daffodils and the sweet notes of the pansies wash over her.

The garden does its magic, and Heather relaxes, if only for a few minutes.

She swallows her disappointment at needing to leave so soon.

Then she swallows her disappointment in herself for wishing she could stay here instead of continuing the search. She doesn't have any time to waste.

After saying goodbye to Theo and Nick, Heather makes her way back to Lake Harding.

You aren't the first to start digging. James Cannon did too. You're right to follow him. I shouldn't give you this but, 1453 Lake Harding Loop. You won't find Charlie. But I can show you something else. I'm still here, Heather.

The note instructed her to come to Lake Harding. Which leaves Heather wondering if someone is following her. If someone is watching her now. If someone will try to intercept her.

Her anxiety is nearly maxed out by the time the front door of Zola's cottage swings open. "Hey!" Zola frowns. "Where's Theo?"

Heather steps inside. "I couldn't get Nick to let her go. I didn't want him to get suspicious, so I let her stay with him."

Zola shakes her head and closes the door behind Heather. "I'm glad you're here. I was worried when I didn't hear from you last night."

Heather sighs and lowers herself onto the couch, thrusting the bouquet of bright yellow daffodils, snowdrops, and purple pansies out for Zola to take. "You'll never believe what happened. I got home last night, and Paul was there, and he and Nick were fighting in the front yard." After Heather confirms Beck is still reading in his room, Heather tells Zola the entire story.

Zola delicately sets the bouquet down on the coffee table and leans back against the sofa. "Are you okay?"

"Yeah." Heather's eyes flicker up to Zola's. "I'm fine."

Zola narrows her gaze at Heather. "You know you can't do that with me. You can't hide the fact that Nick has hit you before."

Heather rolls her eyes at the prodding. With years of experience, she's adept at minimizing all marital problems. "He didn't touch me last night, I promise. He smashed a vase, is all."

Heather pauses, deciding how much she wants to say. "I think he's being careful because the Bronswood Gala is in two days."

"You're not seriously going to that, are you?"

"Nick says it's important that we go and continue to show support. A united front. He thinks it will help Theodora next year."

"But, Heather—."

Heather holds a hand up to stop Zola. "Theo isn't going to Bronswood. But Nick doesn't know that yet. As soon as I find Charlie, I'm leaving."

Zola just nods. They sit quietly for a few minutes, and Heather considers the question she came here to ask. She just got her best friend back. The thought of losing her again terrifies her. But she has to know. "Where have you been, Zola? Why did you just leave when I needed you?"

"I didn't want to, Heather. I swear." Zola takes a deep breath. "When my aunt and uncle died, I didn't come up here right away. I only came up a couple of years ago to clean the place out. I found a closet with this…" Zola hangs her head, shaking it slightly, "…crazy wall. Of course, I didn't think much of it then. I looked through it briefly because I was curious to see what this case was that he was so obsessed with."

Zola stands to move to the kitchen to pour two mugs of coffee, and Heather follows, joining her at the bar top counter. Zola slides a cup across the counter to Heather. "Anyway, there was something about it that was bothering me. Maybe just that I had Beck with me and there were all these missing boys. I couldn't even imagine what that must feel like. So I let the room sit there." Zola sips the coffee from her mug. "A few months later, when you told me Charlie was going to Bronswood, I recognized the name of the school that kept popping up in my uncle's articles. I didn't want to alarm you unnecessarily." Zola looks at Heather sympathetically. "You're already prone to anxiety."

Heather nods, knowing it's true, and Zola continues. "I started going through my uncle's things again, but there is so much stuff in there. I haven't been able to make sense of it all. He was pretty disorganized and his notes were all over the place. So when you suggested I apply for a scholarship for Beck, I agreed because I wanted us to be close again, and I wanted our boys to be together. Plus, I thought getting into the school would help me understand the case my uncle was putting together. I thought maybe getting close to the women there would give me some insight." Zola huffs. "We've seen how far that's gotten me."

Heather takes a large drink, relishing its warmth. "But why did you disappear without telling me? I still don't understand."

Zola wraps her hands around the hot mug. "My uncle found a connection between the boys in his article."

"That they are all students of Bronswood. Right. I already figured that out."

Zola shakes her head. "Not only that. They are all scholarship recipients. Their parents wouldn't be able to afford a single semester at Bronswood. Let alone an entire elementary school career."

Heather sets her cup down a little harder than she intended, and it bangs against the countertop. "Scholarship students are missing? But Charlie isn't a scholarship student." Heather chews on the new information, rolling it around in her mouth. "What did James think happened to the boys?"

"I'm not sure. But I started asking questions a while ago, and I even tried to butter up Harriet once, which was no easy thing since Shay and Liv are always around." Zola rolls her eyes. "I complimented her ring. I asked how she managed to do so much all the time. But when I asked if she'd heard the old rumors about scholarship boys disappearing, Liv turned on me."

"How do you mean?"

"She basically tried to muscle me back against a wall, and she told me that there's no proof of anything like that and that those rumors were started by some nobody whack job trying to make a name for himself at the paper."

"James Cannon." Heather sighs.

"James Cannon," Zola agrees. "She told me they already squashed him for libel, and if I wasn't careful, they'd take care of me, too, for spreading slander and trying to smear the school's reputation."

Heather is stunned, unsure of whether she can believe Zola. Normally, she'd be the first to argue that her best friend would never lie to her. But then Zola vanished without a word, and now Heather's history with Zola is at war with the sting of fresh betrayal. "I can't believe it… Liv has always been so kind to me. A little over the top, but sweet."

"That's because Nick is one of them." Heather bristles at the implication that the Triplets don't actually like her without Nick. "One of the elite. The wealthy. The powerful." Zola shakes her head.

"But—"

"Liv kept pushing towards me, shoving me further against the wall." Zola interrupts her, continuing her story. "Shay and Harriet just watched." Zola stares down into her cup and swirls the liquid inside, as if it was strengthening her to continue. "Liv told me she knew there was something wrong with me from the day I set foot in the school. She told me to be careful. Then she asked me to remind her if Beck was a scholarship student." Zola stares at Heather.

"She said that to you?" Heather believes her. She can't deny the conversation she overheard in the bathroom. She knows they can be cruel when they want to be.

Zola nods, her eyes full of hurt. "I couldn't take the chance that anything might happen to Beck. And I didn't want them to find out how long we've known each other. I was just trying to protect you." She sniffles. "But now Charlie is gone, and I hate myself for leaving you last week."

A tear slips out and rolls down Heather's cheek. She steps around the countertop and hugs Zola tightly. "How could you have known? I'm just glad I got you back."

After a few moments, they separate. Heather lowers herself onto a nearby barstool, drained with nothing to latch onto. "What are we going to do? Is there any hope? What can we do to find Charlie?"

"Yes." Zola's voice is certain, and Heather feels a small flicker of optimism spark inside her chest. Nodding towards the investigation room, Zola says, "I think we have to dive deeper into my uncle's madness."

Heather nods, considering this. "Let's get to work. I don't know how much time we have."

Chapter 32

Heather and Zola step back into James's home office. Heather takes another look at the young boys' faces on the corkboard. Steeling herself, she writes the names of the boys that disappeared after James's time on their own note cards, and she attaches them to the board.

Sequoia Landers.
Thatcher Morrow.
Elliot and Bronson Haply.
Adam Engler.

She hesitates, then adds *Charlie Hartford*.

As she digs through an open box, Heather discovers a photo of Rosler with her students. She recognizes it as the same picture that lives on Rosler's desk. "Zola, did you ever find any notes on this photo?"

"No, I didn't. Why do you ask?"

For a moment, Heather considers whether she still trusts Zola enough to tell her what she's thinking, but she realizes she doesn't have much of a choice. Zola is now the only hope she has of finding Charlie. "Look at this little boy. Does he look familiar to you?"

Zola takes a moment to think. "He does have a quality I feel like I've seen before." She chuckles under her breath and returns to the folder she's sifting through. "Honestly, he's so serious that he reminds me a bit of Headmistress Rosler."

It was a throwaway comment, so Heather startles Zola when she yells, "Yes! Exactly!"

Zola stares at Heather as if she might have lost her mind. "What do you mean by *exactly*?"

"He looks just like her. They have the same intense blue eyes. Same unflinching expression. He looks like he could be her son." Heather stares at his picture while she talks.

Seeing the photo again, she's more certain than she's ever been.

Zola peers closer. "Yeah, I guess they look pretty similar. But Rosler doesn't have any children."

Heather's eyes connect with Zola's. "Not that we know of…" Heather tacks the photo to the wall, beneath the missing children.

Zola shakes her head. "No. No, I'm almost certain it's true. I read it in a profile, I think. Let me see if I can find it."

Zola drags a box off one stack and pulls the top off. She flips through a folder filled with newspaper clippings. "Here! Yes, this is the profile I found last week."

She hands it to Heather.

Heather scans the words on the page.

Sure enough, it describes Rosler's motivation for teaching young children. She and her deceased husband had tried to conceive for many years with no success. Rosler found peace in teaching other children when her heart was broken. Becoming a small but integral piece of their development, and helping them grow into thriving members of the community, fulfilled her.

Heather sets the article down. "Then who is this boy? Do we have a list of names? Any way to look them up?"

Zola gestures to the boxes in the room. There must be at least twenty. "Grab a box and pray one has a yearbook in it? If not, we can request one from the school library."

They spend the next hour digging through boxes of notebooks, pictures, articles, tapes, files, and a rather old blueprint for the school. They sort quietly in tandem until Zola finally speaks. "Have you found anything about Rosler from before she came to work at Bronswood? All of this is from her teaching days and her tenure as Headmistress."

Heather doesn't look up from the pile of papers in her lap. "No. She doesn't seem to exist before then. She clearly kept a very private life. Even when I was at the library, I couldn't find anything about her."

"I suppose if even my uncle couldn't find anything, there's probably nothing to be found." Zola sighs.

Heather drags another heavy box over to her pile. "It's like she appeared out of thin air." She lifts the lid. "Oh, my god!"

Zola looks up, and Heather tips the box so Zola can see the row of thin yearbook spines lined up neatly inside. Heather smiles with relief and nods, feeling hopeful. "What year did Rosler start teaching at Bronswood?"

Zola pulls an article out and reads aloud. "Mrs. Rosler began teaching a group of twelve second graders in 1980."

Heather looks for the corresponding yearbook and frees it from the box. She flips through the pages and finds a printed version of the photo pinned to the wall. The same photo that sits on top of Rosler's desk. After a little more digging, she finds the page containing the individual photos of the children, grouped together by class.

The little boy is simple enough to identify. He wears the same unsmiling expression in his individual photo, though his shirt is a different color.

Heather reads the name underneath his photo. "Colin Hughes. Any notes on a Colin Hughes?"

Zola shakes her head. "Not yet, but I'll keep an eye out for it."

Heather sets the book aside, keeping it open to the page with the boy's picture. She wonders how likely it is that she'd be able to find information about him at the library.

They dig through boxes for another hour, working quickly. After a while, Heather's stomach demands her attention, and she realizes she hasn't eaten since yesterday morning. "Let's take a break and eat something. I'm sure Beck is getting hungry, too."

Zola looks relieved. "Good idea." She moves to stand up, but something seems to catch her eye. A stack of papers with photocopies of checks is bowing inside an open hanging file folder. Zola grabs the folder and brings it out of the closet to the kitchen, where she calls for Beck.

Beck appears a few seconds later. "Is it time for lunch? I'm starving."

When Zola doesn't answer right away, Heather nods and asks what he'd like to eat, just as she has for years, playing second mother when she and Zola are together. Beck asks for a classic peanut butter and jelly sandwich but with crunchy peanut butter and blackberry jam, and a cup of orange juice. Heather moves to grab the items from the pantry, noticing how normal it feels to be making lunch for her second son. Her comfort fades into guilt when she remembers that she's making only one sandwich for Beck. Charlie isn't next to him.

Heather glances at Zola while she smears crunchy peanut butter onto one side of the sandwich, trying not to press so hard that the peanuts tear a hole in the slice of bread. "What did you find there?" Heather swipes some jam across the other piece of bread.

Zola flips through the pages. "I think these are the payments my uncle dug up." Zola glances up, noticing Beck sitting in front of her. She dumps a small bag of chips and an apple onto his plate. "Sweetie, for today, you can go watch TV while you eat."

Beck lights up and grabs his plate too quickly, spilling some of his chips on the counter. He doesn't notice as he races to turn on the TV. Zola scoops the chips into one hand and turns to place them in the trash as she continues. "Photocopies of checks from Bronswood to various organizations. Each with a memo that says *charitable donation* on it."

Heather furrows her brow. "Payments to the police?"

Zola nods. "But not just them. Payments to WebTech, the governor, several payments to *CASH.*" Zola slaps the pages down on the counter. "And payments to Ned Marsh, the owner of the California Chronicle. No wonder they shut my uncle down and made him go away. He must have found out they were getting paid by the school too, to cover up whatever they are doing there."

"But what *are* they doing? Where are the kids, and why can't we find any of their families?"

Zola picks the papers back up. "I don't know. That's what we need to find out. And we need to find out what these cash payments are. They're enormous. $200,000. $325,000. Half a million dollars!"

Heather forgot to hand the cup of juice to Beck, who slips back into the kitchen and reaches across the counter to take it. "Sorry, sweetie."

When Beck returns to his lunch, Heather turns to Zola. "If only we could track down one family of a missing boy. It'd help if they could explain what happened and why they left."

But Zola is no longer paying attention to what Heather is saying. Instead, she's staring at the page in front of her, her expression inscrutable. "Zola, what is it?"

Zola flips the last page in the stack and turns it around to show Heather a large, handwritten note on the back. The lettering is scribbled in all caps.

THE GALA AUCTION!!!

Chapter 33

After lunch, Beck goes to play video games, while Heather and Zola return to the mess in James's tiny office. They turn it upside down. Most of the papers read like nonsense, illegible scribbles alongside highlighted texts with seemingly random circles and arrows. Rosler appears in several more photos and articles featuring Bronswood, but Colin Hughes does not. Colin's name had been mentioned once in the 1981 yearbook, but not a single photo of him was found on any of its pages. The many copies of checks include dates spanning years with no obvious pattern or consistency in either amount or recipient.

The trail goes cold each time Heather feels like they might have the answer.

From the little they can decipher, it's obvious that James believed something was happening at the annual Bronswood gala auction and that the payments were hush money.

It still doesn't explain why Rosler doesn't seem to exist prior to being hired on at Bronswood. Or what exactly is going on at the gala. Or the extent of who is privy to the secrets buried beneath the piles of money.

Heather is about to give up and switch to another task when her phone buzzes. It's a text from Nick asking when she'll be home. She hadn't realized how late it was.

She hammers out a quick reply and tells Zola that she has to get home. "I'm going to call Harriet on the way and ask if I can come help finalize the Gala setup. Since James provided us with this old floor plan that he dug up, maybe I can sneak into the back rooms and look around. Or maybe I can talk to Harriet. I have to try something. The Gala is in two days, and we have to stop whatever is going to happen."

Zola nods and tells Heather to keep in touch. "I'll keep looking and see what else I can find." Despite her lingering anger, Heather feels a wave of gratitude for Zola's help. It means the world to her that she is no longer searching for Charlie alone.

HEATHER RACES HOME, CALLING Harriet on the way. She steadies herself, and when Harriet picks up the phone, Heather does her best to sound cheerful. "Hey, Harriet! Yes, I'm hanging in there. Listen, it really was helpful to stay involved in the Gala setup. Can I come by tomorrow and take a last look? I found a few more things that I think would just really showcase the details. Yes? Great. See you tomorrow."

Heather hangs up the phone and checks in with her mother to see if Nick tried to contact her, covering all her bases before she returns to the house that is rapidly feeling more like a prison.

WHEN HEATHER ARRIVES HOME, she quickly realizes just how badly she needs to get some sleep. Theo's laughter rings throughout the house and draws Heather into the living room. She finds Theo on her knees, crouched over as she paints Nick's toenails a deep shade of red. At first glance, it looks like his toes are bleeding.

Nick looks up. "Hi, honey! Princess Theodora felt I needed a makeover. And I quite agreed." He turns his face from side to side to give Heather a panoramic view of the makeup that appears to have been haphazardly splashed across his face, far more like paint, and a lot less like makeup.

Nick is wearing a plastic tiara on top of his head and a purple costume feather boa wrapped around his neck. A tutu is stretched out to maximum capacity, threatening to snap any second, over the top of Nick's athletic shorts, and he's showing off a pair of gag dress socks with little pink butterflies on them that he received as a white elephant gift during a Christmas party. He grins at her. "What do you think of the new me?"

Something in his tone breaks Heather's heart. Could Nick turn a corner and become the type of husband and father that pulls the broken family back together, rather than push them further apart?

Heather smiles as she performs a mock inspection of Nick's new look. She can't help but laugh at the sight. It's the most absurd thing she's seen in a very long time, and she forgets for a moment about the monster lurking under the paint. "Oh, well, I think you look quite dashing, sir." She laughs again with an adoring smile on her face, and she catches sight of Nick's empty mug on the floor. "Can I get you a refill?"

Nick beams. "Why yes, milady. I'd just adore another spot of tea. Lavender honey, if you please."

Heather nods approvingly and walks over to retrieve his mug. She takes it to the kitchen, where she sniffs the inside of the cup. No trace of alcohol, which is a welcome surprise. She quickly puts another kettle on the stove.

She walks to where she set her purse down and makes sure that the blueprint of the school is still inside. Heather peeks her head around the corner to ensure that Nick and Theo are still busy playing before she goes to the pantry with the blueprint to stuff it inside one of Theo's cereal boxes, knowing Nick would never touch the cereal himself or be so lazy as to feed it to Theo.

Heather grabs the tin of loose-leaf lavender honey tea and exits the pantry to fill the steel tea ball infuser. When the water is ready, she pours it into Nick's freshly rinsed mug and plops the ball into the boiling water. She waits for a minute and then washes the infuser before setting her shoulders in place.

Heather picks up the handle of the piping hot mug, and steels herself against the sting of playing with what's left of her family.

Chapter 34

Heather wakes up the next morning conflicted. Nick waited up for her in bed last night, and when Heather slipped under the covers, he rolled over and softly brushed the hair from her face and gently kissed her lips. For the first time in a while, he didn't taste like whiskey. She laid perfectly still, afraid the moment would turn against her. He whispered to her that she felt tense, and he ran his fingertips over her body. Nick traced her lines and curves and then slowly kissed her everywhere. He dropped a soft kiss on every part of her body, like a hundred tiny apologies. Heather's head swirled with confusion.

Before she realized it, she was relishing the physical affection, forgetting everything else that had happened in the past week. Just for a minute. Reveling in the way Nick's touch brought back their early days as husband and wife. Before every dark day that came later.

Heather didn't want Nick to touch her, and she hated him for thinking about sex right now. She didn't want her husband to make love to her. Heather wanted her son back. She didn't want to enjoy this. But she craved love, starved from its absence.

She was ashamed of the way her body responded against her will, and she let her mind float away to someplace else. Someplace with her children. Someplace without Nick or Paul or Bronswood.

When they were finished, Nick held her gaze and whispered, "I love you, Heather."

She told him she loved him too and her heart splintered a little beneath the weight of such an ugly truth. As her mind crashed back into her body, she rolled over and silently cried herself to sleep.

AT BREAKFAST, HEATHER SMILES and tells Nick that she's going to pop by the school to help Harriet with a few final touches. She tries to sound chipper, but her pulse is racing and it's throwing her off.

Nick cocks his head to one side with an approving grin. "I think that's a great idea. I'm glad you're still getting involved and keeping your mind occupied with positive things."

Heather forces a smile across her lips. How dare he tell her to focus on other things. Her child is still missing and no one else seems to care. Except for Zola. "I'll meet her in a couple of hours. Are you ok with watching Theo?"

Nick cracks a huge smile on his face and looks at Theo mischievously. "Oh, I think we can find something to occupy our time with. Right, Princess?"

Theo rubs her tiny hands together and giggles. "Right."

Heather tries to pretend like she doesn't hate the fact that Theo is too young to understand, let alone care, about what's happened to her big brother. It's not her fault. She tries not to hold it against her daughter, but as she watches Theo delight in having the full, undivided attention of her parents, the anger Heather carries threatens to boil over. Rather than scream, revealing herself to her family, she turns to go back to her room to get dressed.

Before leaving the kitchen, she looks over at Nick. "Do you want me to get Theo dressed before I go down to the basement? There are a few things down there I think Harriet would like."

Nick scoffs. "Heather, I'm perfectly capable of helping my daughter get dressed," he says, as if he's ever done anything more than lay clothing on a bed. He's never helped a near three-year-old get dressed, and Heather doubts he has the patience to do so, which sets her on edge. Before Heather can argue, Nick prompts her, "Better get going. You wouldn't want to keep Harriet waiting. You know how she can be."

Heather does know how Harriet can be. She didn't, however, know that Nick knew how Harriet can be.

She returns to her room to put on some comfortable athleisure wear and prepares to descend into the basement. Standing in front of the door at the top of the stairs, Heather takes a deep breath, releasing it slowly before pulling the door open.

She flicks on the light switch just inside of the door, despising the way it reminds her that the light switch at the bottom of the stairs is on the opposite side of the enormous room. She takes the steps slower than any average human, repeatedly chanting the list of items she's come to retrieve.

Fairy light strings, gold silk table runner, small square crystal vases, black chair covers.

Heather reaches the bottom of the stairs and races to the light switch on the other side of the room. The light flutters on, and Heather's body goes rigid.

The tiny door to the miniature storage room hangs open. Heather stares at it, unblinking. She can see the space inside, too small to be practical. It looks like a coffin. Heather's feet remain glued in place. She stares even though every instinct screams at her to look away. There are scratches all over the walls. There's blood on the floor, running like a stream. Heather can't see where it's coming from.

She snaps her eyes closed, hoping to shut out the image scorched into her brain. When she pries them back open, the tiny square door is closed, padlock securely in place.

Her heart races, and she counts her breath to steady herself. *Four counts inhale, four counts hold, four counts exhale, four counts pause.*

The second her body releases her, Heather scrambles to find an empty box and begins loading the gala items into it, promising herself that she will try to get some more sleep. One decent night just isn't enough to erase the damage from a week of insomnia.

Just one item left, and Heather exhales in relief as she closes the box lid. As soon as it shuts, the lights go out, plunging her into darkness.

"Theo? Is that you?" Heather calls out, but no one answers. "Theodora! Turn the light on! Mommy is down here!" The door at the top of the stairs slams shut, stealing the last bit of Heather's light. "Theo!" Heather screams.

Panic comes for Heather, reaching out for her throat and strangling her in the darkness. She shuffles her feet, arms stretched out in front of her as she feels her way to the nearest wall. She gasps for breath as she finds the staircase and carefully makes her way up. At the top, she grabs for the door handle, but the door is locked.

Heather pounds on the door, every second heightening her fear. "Theo! Nick! The door's locked!" She pounds again, wildly, desperately. "Please! Help me! Nick!" Claustrophobia swallows Heather, and the pitch-black masks the way the walls are closing in around her. She can feel them boxing her in. "Someone, please! Open the door!" Her entire body convulses with sobs. "Help!"

Heather falls forward as the door swings open, sending her tumbling into Nick. He catches her and holds her upright. "Jesus, Heather. Settle down." He pets her hair. "Are you alright?"

Heather sputters a response between sobs. "Someone locked me in the basement. The little door was open, and the lights went out…"

Nick rubs her back, and she can smell whiskey mixed into the earthy scent of coffee on his breath as he shushes her. "Sorry, honey. I locked the door." Heather looks at him, horrified. "Not on purpose, of course. Theo must have turned the lights off. I walked by when I left the kitchen and saw them off. I figured you were finished down there and left the door open." He strokes her hair again. "I'm so sorry."

Heather peels herself away from him. Away from his lies. The door shut at nearly the same time that the lights turned off. "I left the box of decor down there."

"I'll get that for you. Why don't you go make yourself some chamomile tea?"

Heather nods, her body still trembling. "Ok. Ok, yes. Thank you." Her words are shaky.

"No problem, babe." Nick is too relaxed. Heather turns to walk away when Nick calls out to her. "Jesus, what would you do without me?"

She thinks Nick meant for it to sound lighthearted, the way he did in the beginning when Heather couldn't reach the flour sitting on the highest shelf in the pantry. But Heather hears the statement for what it really was. A reminder that she can't leave. That she's no one without him.

Chapter 35

Heather parks her car further away from the school than she normally would to allow herself a minute to gather herself and go over the school blueprint.

The recreation hall has several additional hallways and rooms that are marked as supply closets, janitorial storage, and other various offices. Heather knows this because she's seen these labels on doors at the back end of the recreation hall.

But the blueprint in Heather's hands paints a different picture. It's an old blueprint showing passageways, long hallways, a large basement with a door that pulls out of the floor and a staircase leading down to it. Heather has no idea what she'll find, if anything at all. The last time she was back here was long ago and what the blueprint describes as hallways, she remembers seeing labeled as storage and custodial closets. It's not unusual for a school to modernize itself as old layouts become impractical and undesirable. With the sheer volume of funding from its donors, Bronswood could certainly afford any upgrades desired by its current headmistress.

Without meaning to, Heather thinks about Charlie's now-deserted classroom and its stark transformation in a matter of days. A school that can pull off that kind of feat could mask all manner of sins within its walls, and it's a lead that Heather knows she has to chase. She can't afford to leave any stones unturned. Charlie is counting on her.

She folds up the map and tucks it deep into her bag. She forces herself out of her car and grabs the box of supplies before making her way into the building.

LIV SPIES HER FIRST. "Heather! Oh my goodness, what a pleasant surprise." Liv grabs Heather by the shoulders and plants an air kiss on each cheek, being careful not to actually touch her cheek to Heather's. "What are you doing here? Tell me you are still coming tomorrow. I know Nick already RSVP'd for the both of you."

Heather swallows the lump in her throat and sets down the box she's holding. She knew Nick expected them to attend, but she didn't know that Nick had submitted the RSVP. "Oh, gosh, I'm just not sure. There's just been so much going on with Charlie still missing and the investigation. Honestly, I haven't even thought about it."

Liv rests a hand on Heather's bicep. "Of course. I can't imagine how hard it's been on you."

Shay joins them at the tail end of their conversation, just as Heather dabs the corner of her eye with the end of her sleeve. "Oh, Heather. Don't cry." Her words are soft and kind. "I know the police are doing everything in their power to—."

"The police aren't doing shit!" Heather erupts, startling Liv and Shay. "No one is!" She watches the shock on the women's faces, their jaws going slack. They share a look with each other before zipping themselves back up, becoming a picture of composure.

Heather looks around. A few handfuls of people milling about have stopped to stare at her. Her shoulders sag. "I'm sorry. I didn't mean to snap. I've just been under a lot of stress, and I haven't been sleeping."

Liv stops her with a hand held up. "Say no more. Apology entirely unnecessary."

Shay steps to Heather's side to rub a hand between Heather's shoulder blades. She lowers her voice. "We all want Charlie to be found and returned safely to home."

Heather looks down at the floor. "Thank you, ladies. I appreciate that." She looks up to find the women nodding at her. "Have you seen Harriet? I have some things for her. I should go set them up."

Shay looks to Liv. "Yes, I think I last saw her over by the hours d'oeuvres tables mapping out where each tiny bite will be placed." Liv giggles at her own jab before Heather walks off with her box.

HARRIET IS AT THE table, clipboard in hand, checking something off of her list. Heather calls her name, and Harriet jumps. "Oh! You startled me." Harriet laughs as she steadies her voice again.

"Sorry," Heather says, setting the box down on the floor next to her. "Didn't mean to. Here's what I brought." Heather opens the box and pulls a sample of each type of item out for Harriet's inspection.

"These are perfect. I love it! You're an angel. Thank you."

"Of course. Anything to help." Heather smiles sweetly, thinking that of all the women at this school, Harriet is her favorite. A sharp reminder that she can't trust anyone snaps her back to what she came here to do. "Would you like me to set the fairy lights around the centerpieces? Then I can move on to the chair covers and runner at the head table."

Harriet presses her lips into a tight, thin smile. "That would be wonderful. Thanks, Heather."

Heather nods. "I'll just go set my bag down and get to work. Let's show these donors who we really are."

Harriet doesn't seem to notice the pointed way Heather declares her intentions. "Yes, ma'am!" She holds a hand up for a high-five, which Heather returns awkwardly.

"I don't think we're the high-fiving kind of girls."

Harriet laughs. "No. We definitely are not."

Heather walks over to one of the side benches and sets her bag down. She makes sure the snap on the bag is closed. The top of the bag is still relatively exposed as the sides spring open around the snap, but someone would have to snoop around pretty intentionally to find the blueprint stashed inside.

She takes an assessment of the room, noting how many people are here right now, who they are, where the PTA Triplets are and what they're occupied with. Heather moves to the nearest table and swirls a strand of fairy lights loosely around the base of the centerpiece. She flicks the switch on the strand to ensure they light up, casting a beautiful glow up through the stems of the arrangement sitting inside. She frowns. With the lights dim tomorrow, the glow will look far more haunting than beautiful.

Heather swiftly moves from table to table, ensuring each strand of lights is arranged artfully around a centerpiece. Then she goes back to her box and carries it to the head table at the front of the room, nearest the dance floor and auction pieces. And nearest to the doors that she needs to get to reach the unseen spaces in James Cannon's blueprint.

Heather notes that there is a large black backdrop behind the auction busts, separating them from the wall behind them and creating the illusion that donors are not, in fact, dining in a school recreation room. She's grateful for the effort since no one will see her slip through the far door once she's behind the curtain. Everyone is focused on their respective task. It shouldn't be too difficult to slip away.

Heather drapes the black covers over some of the chairs, setting them apart from the rest of the seats in the room. She ties a gold sash around the back of each chair, adding some dimension and aesthetic appeal to the otherwise solid black furniture. Then she moves everything on the table to the edge, taking stock of how the place settings were arranged, and she rolls out the gold runner across the table. She expertly replaces each item that she moved exactly where she found it. The table really shines with a few added details.

With her head down, Heather pretends to busy herself, and she peers up through her eyelashes and scans the room. Everyone seems to be occupied. Inhaling deeply, she moseys over to the auction area and pretends to read about the items before she takes a last look around to ensure no one is watching her. She's ready to move, but she comes to a halt at Rosler's table.

Bruce Bannar.

The name sends her spiraling, and she grips the edge of the table as memories flood her vision. Flashes of Charlie building with Legos in his room. Pictures of Charlie helping her in the kitchen. Memories of Charlie helping Theo on the slide at the playground.

Heather knows that finding the name on an auction listing doesn't mean anything. Harriet explained their strategy, and sure enough, Harriet's story checked out when Heather had looked at the other clipboards. She found each table had its own alias on it. She recognized some names, but others were quite obscure, only decipherable after a few pointed questions or an internet search.

Heather shakes off the voice in her head telling her not to go searching for answers she may not want to hear, and steadies herself as she plunges forward with her plan.

Taking one more look around the room, Heather slips behind the black curtain and runs for the door at the back of the room.

It's unlocked. She slips inside, holding the handle while the door swings shut, closing it without a sound.

Chapter 36

Heather takes a deep breath and scans the deserted hallway in front of her. There are several doors on each side, and she reviews the blueprint in her mind, trying to fuse the old pathways with the newly renovated area before her. If the old blueprint is to be believed, some of these doors will lead to hallways instead of rooms, but without an updated layout, Heather has no way of knowing where to start and no idea which route will get her to the basement.

No one talks about the basement. In fact, some of the notes in James Cannon's files suggested that the type of soil surrounding Bronswood would make a basement unsafe, and Heather wonders if the space was cannibalized at some point in Bronswood's illustrious history. Then again, a space that's not supposed to exist would also make an excellent hiding place.

Without a place to start, Heather decides to check the doors one by one. There are four doors that she can see on the left side of the hall, and two on the right before the main hallway takes a ninety-degree turn to the right.

The first two doors on the left are marked *Storage* and *Custodial*. Both doors are locked.

The doors all appear to be locked. And why shouldn't they be? Children have an innate propensity for finding their way into restricted areas, and Heather can imagine the lawsuit that would ensue if a child got into something dangerous, but she will check them all to be certain. She has too.

Heather approaches the first door on the right marked *K-1* like the kindergarten classrooms in the main building. Perhaps this was an old classroom no longer in use. The door is locked.

For a moment, Heather considers retreating to the gala area and calling this pursuit a dead end. She doesn't have a key to these doors, and she doesn't know who might. Instead, she takes a few more steps. Her heart starts to hammer inside of her chest when she sees that the final door on the left, labeled *Supplies*, is just barely open inside its frame. It looks as if someone came out of the door and wasn't paying attention to whether the door latched shut completely behind them.

Heather's pulse is racing and she feels a little dizzy.

She slowly approaches the door and pushes it open to peer inside.

A dark hallway lies in front of her, leading to another closed door at the far end. Heather knows she can't leave the door open behind her, and fear fills her stomach at the thought of traversing the hallway in the pitch-black. Every cell in her body wants to turn around and go back. The other door is probably locked anyway and Harriet may already be looking for her in the gymnasium. But images of Charlie fill Heather's mind, giving her the courage she needs to move forward and plunge herself into darkness.

She lets the door rest on its latch behind her so that she doesn't get locked inside and counts her breath as she walks down to the other end of the hall.

The silence is broken only by the sound of her breathing, which echoes off the walls, becoming louder and more labored with each step forward.

At last, Heather feels the door in front of her, and she flails to find the handle. She yanks it harder than she needed to. It's unlocked, and the door swings open with ease.

She extends her head inside to see what lies in front of her.

It's a second hallway nearly twice as wide as the one she just emerged from. Two dusty bulbs hang down from the ceiling and provide a little light. Just enough for Heather to see the hallway's unfinished brick walls and dusty carpeted floor. The temperature drops as she enters the passageway, and goose bumps poke along the surface of her arms and neck. She takes a beat to search her brain and orient herself according to the old blueprint tucked inside her purse. She won't have much longer before someone comes looking for her.

Heather does a rough calculation of how many feet she's traveled down the hallway and tries to imagine the same path on the map. If her estimations are correct, up ahead should be the door in the floor that leads to the basement. But she can't see anything. She pushes on the carpet, but there is no door beneath her, unless it sits under the flooring, which she has no way of knowing. There is, however, a door to her right just a few feet further. It's a large, windowless, metal door, reminiscent of the doors on the isolation cells of psychiatric wards. There is a large pad by the handle where an old lock would be, but the mechanism appears to be missing because the door pulls open with an easy tug.

A flight of stone steps leads her deeper beneath the school. Though she's treading lightly, the silence is palpable, and her heals click loudly on each step.

Dim light illuminates the bottom of the stairway, though Heather has yet to see a light switch. She crouches lower as she nears the last few steps so she can check for anyone walking around before she enters the room. She doesn't know what she would say if she were to get caught down here. Knowing what she does about Bronswood's past, Heather shudders at the thought.

The large room at the bottom of the stairs is devoid of any people, but what it houses sends chills radiating through Heather's bones. Rusty cages line the perimeter of the walls. There is a thick metal lining where the bars meet the floor and the ceiling.

The air smells of urine and feces, and Heather pulls the collar of her shirt up over her mouth and nose to keep from gagging.

Gates with padlocks look as if they once held wild animals inside their iron walls, like dogs in a rundown kennel. But these are not dog kennels. Large shackles extend from the stone walls that make up the backsides of the tiny prisons, each with round prongs meant to contain an appendage from reaching further than the chain allows. A plastic basin with old dirty water sits on the floor of each cell, along with puddles that might be spilled water or urine.

Heather walks down the center of the room towards the old door directly ahead of her, wondering how far she will allow herself to go as she processes the horrifying details on either side of her.

One, two, three, four… ten, eleven, twelve.

Twelve cages. Six on each side of the room.

The sound of water dripping breaks her focus, and she looks up to find an old metal basin at the far end of the room, tucked away behind the last cage. A slow leak sends droplets crashing loudly against the basin's metal bottom.

She peers inside each cell as she passes. Some have filthy toys and stuffed animals in them. Like a favorite dog toy that's been well-loved for far too long. One cage has a plate with some gruel still smeared on it, as if mealtime had been interrupted.

Heather is nearly to the other side of the room when she hears a man and a woman arguing loudly from the other side of the door in front of her. Though she can hear that the man is frustrated, she can't make out the words through the wall.

Heather stands frozen in place, listening carefully. There is nowhere to hide in this room if someone comes bursting in through the door. She knows she should leave, but she can't make her feet cooperate.

Suddenly, a loud crack snaps her out of her trance. Heather doesn't need visual confirmation to know what happened. She is all too familiar with the sound of a palm connecting cleanly with a cheek.

She whips around and moves swiftly towards the staircase she came down. She's almost there when something catches her eye in the cell nearest the bottom of the stairs.

She stares at a tiny sliver of neon green hugging the inside of the cell wall. It hadn't been visible from the other direction, but she can see it clearly now.

She creeps into the cage, willing it to be anything but the thing she knows it to be.

She bends down to pick it up and gently cradles the tiny Hulk Lego figurine in her hands. A tear rolls silently down each cheek.

A loud clattering rings out from behind the far door, like the sound of metal serving trays tumbling to the floor, and the noise sends Heather racing up the flight of stairs. She doesn't stop to see if the doors close behind her. She doesn't stop at all until she makes it back to the first hallway, shutting the door behind her. Sweat beads on her forehead as she stuffs the tiny green figurine into her pocket and makes her way back to the recreation room.

Heather is nearly there when the door flies open in front of her, and she's sent crashing to the ground as Harriet barrels through the door straight into her.

"Heather! God, I'm so sorry!" Harriet helps Heather get up.

"There you are! I've been looking all over for you. What are you doing back here?"

Heather straightens her top and checks that the Lego figure is still in her pocket. "Nothing."

Harriet looks over Heather's shoulder. "Maria told me she thought she saw you heading this way."

Heather scrambles for an answer that might appease Harriet. "I was looking for a bathroom. Someone told me there was one back here, but I couldn't find one."

Harriet looks Heather right in her eyes for a few beats longer than normal, as if trying to decide whether Heather is lying. She screws on a sweet expression. "Oh yeah, nothing but storage closets and supply overflow back here. Come on." Harriet pulls Heather back into the gala area. "I want to go over the seating chart with you."

Heather pulls her arm away from Harriet. "That really won't be necessary. I won't be here tomorrow."

"But Heather—."

"I really have to go, Harriet." Heather races for the exit before her tears burst through the dam she's built to show everyone how strong she is. But it's all a façade. She's weak. Far more so than they could ever imagine.

She's nearly halfway across the room when she spots Tom rushing into the space. After a few moments, he spies his wife and makes a beeline to join Shay at the periphery of the room. Heather watches as Shay intercepts him, reaching a hand out gingerly for the side of his face. Tom's cheek is bright red. Heather has to pass by near them to get to the exit, and she can overhear them talking.

"Jesus, Tom. What happened to your cheek?" Shay frets.

Tom pushes her hand away like he hates the fuss. "Nothing. A box fell and I caught it with my face. I'm fine."

"Let me get you some ice for it."

Heather waits until Shay is out of sight before she walks over to where Tom is standing, waiting for his wife to return. "Tom! I'm glad you're here. I wanted to ask you about Charlie."

Tom's brows pinch together. "What about him?"

"I wanted to see if you had found out anything about his case. Nick asked you to look into it last week."

Tom runs a hand across his chin, looking confused.

"He asked you to look into it, didn't he?"

"Oh, right. Yeah, he did. Of course. I just haven't been able to find anything out yet. I'm sorry."

Shay is walking towards them, and Heather hears Shay call out, "Oh, Heather, wait up!"

Heather doesn't wait. She pretends not to hear Shay and leaves the room without looking back.

HEATHER COLLAPSES INTO HER car, barely managing to close the door before violent sobs wrack her body. She buries her face in her hands, scraping herself together when she hears someone yelling her name.

Harriet is jogging towards her car and Heather scrambles to put her huge sunglasses on. Harriet is carrying Heather's bag and Heather's heart stops at the realization that she left it sitting on the bench in her rush to get out of the school.

Harriet is winded as Heather rolls down her window. Harriet hands the bag to her. "You forgot your purse."

Heather sniffles as delicately as she can. "Yeah, I just realized that. Thanks for bringing it out to me."

Harriet nods and juts a finger out to point at the bag. "You might want to check inside and make sure you have everything."

"I'm sure it's fine," Heather says as she tosses the bag onto the passenger seat.

Harriet rests one hand on the door. "Heather, are you alright?"

Heather swipes beneath her nose with the back of her hand. "I'm fine. Really. I just had a moment. Sometimes, I forget that Charlie isn't at home waiting for me to return. And then the reminders come crashing down on me and I just… it just feels unbearable sometimes. You know?"

Harriet looks down at her feet. "As a mother, I can imagine how painful that must be." She looks up at Heather. "I'm sorry, Heather. I really am."

"Thanks." Heather starts the car. "And thanks for returning my purse."

Harriet steps back and Heather pulls out of the parking lot.

She glances in her rearview mirror. Harriet is standing exactly where Heather left her, watching Heather drive away.

Chapter 37

Every second that it takes to drive home, Heather's imagination spirals deeper and deeper into a dark hole. She thinks of Charlie—her sweet, curious little boy—being held in one of those cages. Is he being fed properly? Is he being fed at all? Is he allowed access to a bathroom? Who put him in there? And for how long? Was he shackled to the wall? He must be terrified. Why Charlie? Why?

And where is he now?

Tears pour without end as Heather suddenly finds herself pulling into the garage.

She mindlessly reaches for her bag and walks into the house without closing the car door.

Heather can hear Nick and Theo saying something to her, but she can't make out their words. She can't bring herself to care. She walks past them in silence, tears still streaming down her face.

In a trance, she drags herself up the stairs and into her bedroom. She doesn't change her clothes or remove her shoes. Her whole body goes numb as she drops her bag somewhere on the floor and falls into bed, the new note clutched in her fist. She keeps falling, further and further into darkness until there is no light left.

Heather can't erase the things she's seen. Charlie is gone and the life she knew ceases to exist.

THE NEXT TIME HEATHER opens her eyes, she's tucked away neatly under the covers and wearing pajamas. She doesn't remember changing her clothes or even moving from where she collapsed, and she wonders for a moment if Nick helped her dress and then put her back in bed.

Heather tries to orient herself. It's getting dark outside, so Heather rolls over to flip the light on, and the clock on the nightstand tells her it's nearly six o'clock in the evening. She pushes herself upright and reaches down for her bag, looking for her phone. It takes a minute of shuffling things around, but she finally finds it. There's a text from Nick and a text from Zola.

> **ZOLA: JUST CHECKING IN. HAVEN'T HEARD FROM YOU IN A WHILE. YOU OK?**

Heather cringes. Her best friend must be worried if she risked sending a text. Ever since she learned about Nick reading Heather's text messages, Zola always opted to call instead of text. Glancing down, Heather confirms that she has several missed calls flagged at the bottom of her screen, and she swallows hard as she proceeds to Nick's message.

> **NICK: I'M DROPPING THEO OFF WITH YOUR MOTHER BEFORE THE GALA SO YOU CAN REST. I'LL TELL EVERYONE THAT YOU'RE ILL. BE HOME LATER.**

Heather fumbles her phone in a hurry to flip to her phone's calendar. Nick's message doesn't make any sense. It's Sunday. The fundraiser isn't until tomorrow night.

Her pulse quickens when her phone confirms it is indeed 6:04 on Monday evening, which means the gala begins in less than an hour. She has slept through Sunday and Nick has gone marching off to rub elbows with the people who stole her son and treated him like an animal. Worse than an animal.

Heather calls her mom quickly to confirm that she has Theo.

Heather wastes no time when her mother greets her on the other end of the call. "Mom, Theo is with you? You have her?"

"Yes, of course I do. Did Nick not tell you?" Pamela huffs. "He told me you knew."

"He left me a note. I just wanted to be sure. Look, I can't talk right now but—."

"Heather, sweetie, how are you feeling? Nick said you were really sick—."

Heather cuts her off. "Mom, I have to go. But listen. Don't let Theo out of your sight. Not for anyone. Even if Nick comes. Do you understand?"

"Honey, you're scaring me. What's going on? I—."

Heather hangs up the phone and breathes a sigh of relief that at least Theodora is safe.

She takes a moment and scans her bedroom, unsure of what she's looking for. The sun is setting outside. She moves closer to the window and looks out, scanning the sky. Tracing the way the colors change from midnight blue, to rich crimson, to a vibrant blood orange. Her garden sits on the horizon, soaking in the last of the light before dusk.

Heather pulls herself away and finds her bag lying on its side next to the bed. The edge of the old school blueprint spills out from its opening, and she can't help but wonder how much Nick saw when he was helping her settle in bed. She's shocked to find that she doesn't care. Images of her son's filthy prison flood her mind. Charlie is gone, and she is no closer to finding him now than she was a week ago. Overwhelmed by the impulse to destroy something, Heather yanks the blueprint from her purse. She rips along its seam when two pieces of paper tumble out from between the folds.

The first item is a copy of an old article dated nearly thirty years ago, published in a Blackpool newspaper in the United Kingdom.

Child's Death Rocks Blackpool Community

On the night of October 22nd, Margaret Hughes burst into the emergency ward at Blackpool Victoria General. Her toddler was unable to breathe, and his cough had turned violent. Margaret was desperate for help for her two-year-old son, Declan, who was born with a congenital defect that left him with underdeveloped lungs and an irregular heartbeat.

Margaret claims that Declan's doctor misdiagnosed him after completing what she described as an "incomplete medical examination." He gave her a pack of cough medicine and sent her home, where her son later succumbed to his breathing difficulties.

The Blackpool community is outraged at the mismanagement of Declan Hughes and is calling for justice. The Blackpool community is frequently cast aside with income levels well below the poverty line, and the inability to afford proper medical treatment continues to plague the residents of the community. Hospitals consistently turn patients away without proper care, reserving space and resources for the more affluent patients who can afford the care they desperately need.

Margaret has taken her case to court, suing the hospital for malpractice, and the residents of Blackpool are rallying to support her. Margaret is quoted saying she will not go down without a fight. She will have justice for her son, and she will make it her life's mission to ensure that vulnerable children will receive the care they need. She says she will do whatever it takes.

Declan Hughes is survived by his mother Margaret Hughes, and his older siblings, Colin and Etta Hughes.

There is a small photo printed at the bottom of the feature, but it's so grainy and old that Heather can't make out the details. Operating off a hunch, Heather fumbles to find a second item hidden inside the blueprint: a small, folded square that tumbled onto the bed. She lifts the paper with trembling hands, and she takes a long breath before pulling the edges apart. Sure enough, the page includes a large, enhanced copy of the photo printed with the feature article.

A woman sits with her three young children, their names detailed across the bottom of the photo.

Margaret Hughes, Declan Hughes, Etta Hughes, and Colin Hughes.

Although Colin is smiling in this photo, Heather would recognize those eyes anywhere. Who she isn't prepared to see is Margaret.

She knows her well, too. But not as Margaret Hughes.

Heather knows her as Anastasia Rosler.

How did this article get into her bag? It couldn't have happened while she was asleep since the only person who had access to her bag was Nick. She had left her bag unattended while she was at Bronswood on Saturday. It must have been someone at the school.

Harriet brought her bag out to her…

Heather grabs her phone to call Harriet, praying she'll pick up this close to the gala.

The phone rings until the voicemail picks up and Heather hangs up and tries again. Just when the voicemail message is about to pick up for the second time, Harriet's voice answers. "Hello?" She sounds chipper.

Heather isn't sure how long Harriet will be able to talk. "Harriet, it's Heather. Why did you put this article in my bag?"

"Oh my god, Heather? Honey, are you alright?" she asks, sounding genuinely concerned. "I was so worried when you tore out of the parking lot yesterday."

"Harriet, the article. I know it was you. Tell me what it means. Why are you helping me?" Harriet doesn't reply, and Heather tries again. "Please, Harriet."

Harriet sighs on the other end of the phone. "Hold on a second. Not here." Heather can make out the clicking of Harriet's heels across the floor, and she hears one of the doors to the school gymnasium squeak as it's closed. "Heather, if I'm caught helping you she'll—." Harriet doesn't finish the sentence.

"She'll what? What will she do to you?" Heather demands.

"You don't know her like I do. She's not who you think she is."

"I know she isn't Anastasia Rosler. That woman doesn't seem to exist."

"It's not just that, Heather. It's not that simple."

Heather doesn't have time for vague ideas. "Harriet, she took my son! Where is Charlie?"

"I can't tell you." Harriet's voice sounds like it's quaking.

Heather tries to relax her tone. "Harriet. Please. I won't tell anyone you told me. I just want my son back."

"I can't!" Harriet is getting worked up now. "Don't you see everything I do for her? I make nice with women that I can't stand. I single-handedly run the events that keep her in business. It's not my job to know where the missing children go, Heather!"

"Ok, Harriet. Calm down. I didn't mean to upset you. What business do you mean? Do you mean Bronswood?"

Harriet takes a few deep breaths. "Heather, I'm sorry. I've told you all I can. I have to go now."

"Harriet, wait! If you can't tell me anything, then why did you bother to help me at all?"

"Because… because you don't deserve what happened to you. It's wrong. It's all wrong. And I'm tired of all of this."

Heather can't help but think how exhausted Harriet does actually sound. "Tired of what? What is happening?"

Harriet sighs again. "I've got to go now. I shouldn't be talking to you." Heather is afraid Harriet is about to hang up on her, but Harriet isn't finished yet. "If you only see Rosler in that photo, then you haven't seen everything."

"What the hell does that mean, Harriet?"

"I have to go. I can't miss the auction."

"Wait—!" Heather yells, but the line goes dead.

Heather grabs the picture again, desperate to understand. Her eyes race around, taking in nothing new.

She sits back and shuts her eyes, pulling a deep breath into her lungs. Her mind slows down for just a moment.

Harriet said seeing Rosler isn't seeing everything.

Heather opens her eyes and scans the photo again.

Declan, Etta, Colin.

Declan, Etta, Colin.

Declan.

Etta.

A spark of recognition goes off. Heather stares at Etta. Her face is familiar. She looks like her brother, Colin. Colin looks like his mother, Margaret. But there is something more here. Something Heather can't quite place.

The faces from the photo flash in Heather's mind. Like she's seen them somewhere before. Not Declan, of course. But Etta and Colin are familiar. Something tugs at the back of Heather's brain, but it lays just out of reach.

As Heather stands up, something inside her head shakes loose. The auction.

She has to get to the gala before the auction. The answer is there. James Cannon knew it, and Harriet all but confirmed it on the phone.

Heather makes an impulsive decision to put her gala dress on and race to the school. Hair and makeup be damned. There's no time for that.

There may not be any time left at all.

Chapter 38

Heather waits, her hand resting on the handle of the door that will lead her straight to Hell. A glance at the clock on the wall tells her it's 7:14. The gala started fourteen minutes ago. A loud drumbeat vibrates the floor under her feet, though it takes a few beats for Heather to realize it's actually the throb of her pulse.

She quietly pulls the door open and steps inside, holding the door so that it closes behind her without a sound. No one notices her enter. Heather waits at the back of the room and takes in the scene.

She looks around and finds the table where she was supposed to sit with Nick, the PTA royalty, and their husbands. Nick is there, quietly sipping on a tumbler with a generous pour of amber liquid. Scotch, if Heather knows him as well as she thinks. He's focused on Headmistress Rosler, who is addressing the room, making a toast. There's an empty chair next to Nick, which Harriet suddenly slips in to fill. Harriet leans over, talking in Nick's ear, and Heather watches as his face turns to stone. He gives an almost imperceptible shake of his head, and Harriet quickly rights herself in her chair.

Heather turns her attention to the front of the room where Rosler is speaking.

Rosler stands in front of a microphone on a podium, a glass of champagne folded demurely in her hands. "On behalf of Bronswood, I wish to thank you all for attending tonight." Her face is a fraction warmer than it usually is, and it looks as though the effort is painful. "As you well know, tonight's gala is particularly special. It's the Bronswood centennial gala. I'd like to thank the always effervescent Mrs. Harriet Porter for putting together this stunning event for us to enjoy."

The crowd breaks into applause, and the sound reverberates in Heather's head.

Rosler continues. "The Bronswood Gala is the grand occasion each year where our generous families, donors, and supporters provide the funding that propels our mission here at Bronswood. The funding that helps us continue our purpose to better the lives of future generations, ensuring the gaps left by traditional education are filled. The funding that allows us to enrich the lives of the students here, providing them every possible avenue of advanced study, opening every possible door for them to leave their mark on the world." Rosler pauses and looks around the room, and Heather retreats into the shadows. She wonders if she's imagining Rosler's gaze hovering near Heather's hiding place.

After a moment, Rosler presses on. "Funding to provide the education necessary for children to thrive in all the ways their home environment may not otherwise allow." She adjusts her posture, standing taller. "Tonight's funding not only supports our school's curriculum and enrichment program, it also provides scholarships awarded to gifted children who cannot otherwise afford to attend the state's most prestigious elementary school." Rosler raises her glass. "So, dig deep into your pocketbook and give generously tonight, with full confidence in the community you so graciously continue to support. You know what you're bidding for." She tilts her head. "Let the auction begin."

Heather watches as the families give headmistress Rosler a standing ovation before dispersing to the auction tables. Heather plunges her hand into the pocket of the black peacoat that she tossed on over her dress. She squeezes her son's Lego figure in her hand, afraid it will disappear.

A few patrons slip behind the black curtain, which appears to go unnoticed.

Heather can't stand by and let this happen. She's out of time and she needs to move.

She creeps forward, her eyes following Rosler back to her chair at the head table, where she lowers herself delicately and sips her drink. Rosler's eyes scan the auction area, and she waves someone over to where she's seated.

Heather's focus turns away from Rosler, only for a moment, when Nick suddenly enters her field of vision, leaning down so that Rosler can whisper into his ear. Nick gives a crisp nod, and when he stands, Heather's eyes lock with his.

She curses beneath her breath. He wasn't supposed to notice her yet.

Nick tosses back what's left of the amber liquid in his tumbler and slams his glass down on the table. Rosler doesn't even flinch. Heather is frozen. Prey caught in a snare while the hunter silently watches her shake. Heather takes a step backward, and Nick picks up speed.

He's coming for her.

Heather looks around to see her husband's outburst has only garnered her more attention.

Harriet walks towards Heather, picking up her pace when Nick starts moving. The two are closing in on her, a race to see who can contain the lunatic first.

But Heather didn't come here to be contained. She came for her son.

Heather pulls Charlie's toy out of her pocket, clutching it tightly in her fist before she screams out, "I want my son back! I know you have him. He's here somewhere." She takes a step forward as Harriet closes in on her. "Give him back! Give me back my son!"

Harriet spins her around so that Heather is facing the double doors and tries to move Heather. "Heather, I thought you were sick. Nick said you were home in bed."

Heather can hear the warning in Harriet's words, and without meaning to, she remembers Harriet's cryptic message over the phone.

If you only see Rosler in that photo, then you haven't seen everything.

But there's no time for riddles. The clock is ticking. She only has one chance to find her son. "Let go of me, Harriet! I know she took Charlie. I'm not leaving without him!" Heather spins around, twisting her arm out of Harriet's grasp, and she collides right into Stephen's chest.

"Heather, are you ok?" Stephen reaches out to place his hand on Heather's arm.

Before Heather can react, Nick appears at her side. "I've got her, Stephen."

Stephen looks reluctant to hand her over, but he lets go.

Nick glares down at her, a tight faux smile glued onto his face. His eyes bore a hole into Heather as he talks to her like a child through closed teeth. "Heather, sweetheart. What are you doing here? You're supposed to be home resting." He reaches for her arm, but Heather backs away.

"No! I'm not going home. Nick, they have Charlie. They took my son. She took my son!" Heather points at Rosler, who hasn't moved from her seat. Even from a distance, Heather can see that Rosler's eyes are ice.

Nick chuckles awkwardly, as if she's being silly. "Honey, you're delirious. You've been asleep for twenty-four hours." His eyes narrow. "You're ill."

"I'm not! I'm not sick, and I'm not crazy! Look!" Heather opens her hand and lifts the tiny green Hulk high in the air, showing the entire room.

Nick moves to grab the toy, but Heather whips her hand away and starts moving towards the head table, shouting at everyone as she passes. "This is my son's favorite toy. I found it in a cage underneath this building!" Some people whisper to each other, but Heather keeps moving towards Headmistress Rosler. "I know about the secret hallways and rooms. I know you have been keeping Charlie locked up like an animal." Heather looks around the room, screaming at the patrons. "They are stealing our boys and selling them. This auction is a cover!" Heather notices that Shay and Tom are casually strolling to the back door of the gymnasium, but all eyes are on her. She turns back to Rosler, and she stares straight at the headmistress as she says, "If you've hurt him, I swear I'll kill you!"

Nick grabs her from behind and turns her into his chest, squeezing her tightly. From the outside, it probably looks as though he's soothing her, bringing her down from her frenzy. But Heather's bones rattle as he breathes into her ear. "We're leaving now. Don't make this any worse than you already have."

The strength of Nick's grip around her tells Heather that she won't be able to escape, and she wracks her brain as he guides her out into the foyer. She may already be out of time. But she isn't ready to give up yet.

As the double doors close behind them, Heather turns to meet Nick's eyes. She remembers the blue-eyed man she fell in love with, and she prays he'll be that man today. "Please, Nick. Please, listen to me. Charlie is here. I know he is."

Nick shakes his head. "Charlie is gone! Heather——."

"I know what it sounds like. It sounds insane, but I can show you."

Heather watches the muscles in Nick's face tense as he clenches his jaw.

Against her instinct to keep her distance from him right now, Heather leans in and takes his hand in hers. "Nick, please. We have to find him. Come with me. Please. Let me show you."

Nick hangs his head. "I shouldn't be indulging this nonsense." He sighs and looks up at Heather. "Fine. Show me what you saw."

Heather nods quickly and takes off, leading Nick to the far side of the foyer where they can go around the gymnasium to access the back rooms.

She carefully checks around each corner as she makes her way through the labyrinth once more, praying that each door will open for her.

They finally make it to the basement, and Heather listens for any movement before flicking the lights on to reveal the rusty cages. She turns to Nick, whose face looks pale. "This is where I found Charlie's Hulk Lego figurine." Heather walks over to the cage where she found the toy, and she pulls it out of her pocket once more. "He was here. I know he was. Don't you see? She stole him. And now she's going to sell him."

For the first time that Heather can recall, Nick is speechless. With no other option, Heather continues to tell him what she's discovered. She tells him about James Cannon's article, about the missing boys, and Officer Fowler's strange reaction to the name Caleb Norton.

Nick looks around the room before stuffing his hands into his pants pockets. His head falls back, and he looks at the ceiling. It's a gesture Heather recognizes, something he does to hide when he is close to tears.

Heather keeps pressing. She steps closer to him as she tells him about the payments that Bronswood has been making to prominent figures and companies in the community.

A tear slips from Nick's eyes and rolls down the side of his face. Heather is sure she's getting through to him. She can feel it: that Nick believes her and now he can help her.

Heather steps right up to him and tells him about the Blackpool article. She tells him about Rosler's class photo, and Nick squeezes his eyes shut.

After several moments of silence, Nick straightens and turns to face Heather. He opens his eyes and peers into Heather's.

At once, Heather realizes her mistake.

If you only see Rosler, then you haven't seen everything.

The little boy. Colin Hughes. Heather recognized his eyes when she first saw his picture on Rosler's desk. The flicker of recognition was there again when Heather read the Blackpool article. And now she knows why.

An arm whips out to strike her, and before Heather can call him by his name—his real name—her vision goes black.

Chapter 39

Heather's eyes flutter open, but she still can't see because wherever she is, it's dark. She reaches her arms out, feeling the surrounding space, searching for any clue to tell her where she is.

Her hands hit a flat surface to her left and she scrapes them along the wall, feeling for more. Her eyes begin to compensate for the darkness, and she can make out a few large shapes close by. She continues to feel her way along the perimeter of the room. She touches what she believes to be a cardboard box, then a plastic storage tub that feels familiar. She crouches and runs her hands upwards, slamming almost immediately into a shelf. Her eyes have adapted to the lack of light just enough. She knows where she is.

Heather is in her basement.

Her mind spins with panic. Heather tries to suck in a breath, but she's gasping. She talks to herself, reminding her body that she knows this space and that somewhere on the other side of the room, there is a light switch.

She stands up, but the movement is too quick, and the room starts to wobble. Her legs are frozen in place, but she manages to drag them to the far side of the room, feeling for the light switch that she knows is near.

At last, the plastic panel is beneath her hand, and she wastes no time flicking the switch.

Nothing.

Heather yanks the switch up and down several more times, needing the light to turn on.

Still only darkness.

The walls begin to close in on Heather, and the room feels like a tomb. Dizzy with fear, she falls to the floor.

This can't be it. Heather searches herself for a shred of hope, but there's nothing left inside her. She's empty.

After everything she's been through, after everything she's done, it's all led her to this point. Alone in the basement, trapped, and defenseless in the dark. Heather's thoughts float away to her son, and the ways she's failed to save him. She wonders if this is the way Charlie felt when he was tossed into that filthy prison cell.

Charlie. He still needs her.

This cannot be how it ends. She isn't done yet.

Heather picks herself up off the floor. She has to find a way out of here. She could crawl up the stairs to the basement door, but she knows there's little point. She's certain that it's locked.

She closes her eyes so that she can't see the room shrinking around her and turns back to the light switch to orient herself.

She knows that she's on the back wall. She thinks about the things that are stored down here.

The emergency kit. There is a bag down here somewhere with vital items in case a storm comes rolling through and knocks out the power. Heather searches her mind and tries to remember where she saw it last.

On the bottom shelf, wedged between two boxes. She's sure of it.

She squats down and runs her hand along the items on the bottom shelf, keeping the opposite arm in front of her to feel for any obstacles obstructing her path.

Halfway down the length of the wall, she feels the rough vinyl of the bag. She drags it from the shelf and it drops on the floor. She finds the zipper and opens the bag.

It's impossible to make out the contents by sight, so she plunges her hand inside and focuses on the feel of each item. There's the hard case of a first aid kit, a box of waterproof matches, a portable radio, and, at last, what Heather is searching for.

A flashlight.

Heather clicks the button to turn it on and nearly cries as a beam of light cuts through the darkness.

She stands up and shines the light around the room to cast the shadows away. Just as her pulse begins to slow, the flashlight catches on something Heather wasn't expecting to see. Her purse.

She shuffles things around, searching for something that can help her get out of the basement, still not exactly sure what that might be. She knows better than to expect her phone to be there, but she has to find something.

Her hand grazes a stack of papers, and she pulls out the article about Declan Hughes's tragic death. She stares at the names on the page.

She knows now that her husband is not Nick Hartford. He's Colin Hughes. But what she doesn't know is the extent of his involvement in Charlie's disappearance. Or why.

She needs to know. And she needs help. She needs Zola. Zola will help her, but Heather has to find a way out of the basement first.

Heather aims the flashlight up the stairs towards the basement door. Her head pounds where she assumes she was hit, and she brings a hand to the back of her head to relieve the throbbing. She pushes her fingers through her hair and winces when she snags on a bobby pin.

The pinch shakes loose an idea, and Heather rips the pin out of her hair, taking a few strands with it.

She slings her purse over her shoulder and races for the basement door.

Heather stretches the bobby pin open and aims the flashlight at the tiny hole in the center of the doorknob. If she can insert the pin just right, and push just so, she can spring the lock on the door.

She slides the pin into the hole and pushes rapidly at any gear the pin touches. Her hand is shaking, and she realizes she's going too fast. Heather forces herself to slow down. To feel for the correct placement.

After three more failed attempts, Heather is ready to kick the door in. Charlie is waiting for her, and he's running out of time.

She blows out a breath and carefully pushes the pin into the knob once more. The pin slides slowly along until it comes to a stop between two tiny plates. Heather pushes firmly, and finally, she hears the *pop*.

She removes the pin and rests her fingers on the handle. She takes a moment to steel herself before she turns the knob.

Chapter 40

Heather stands at the front door to Zola's cottage at Lake Harding. She knocks, but no one answers. Heather leaves the porch and walks over to the picture window in the living room. The curtains are open, and Heather peers inside.

Her heart sinks when she spies the corner lamp left on, and a small blanket thrown casually over the arm of the lounger. A book is turned upside-down on the side table next to a mug, giving the appearance that someone is home but away from their reading spot. It's something Zola has always done when she leaves the house. *Just in case*, Zola always said.

Heather stifles a curse beneath her breath.

A moment later, worry creeps into Heather's gut at the realization that she hasn't seen or heard from Zola since before the Bronswood Gala.

Heather walks around to the side of the house and checks the back sliding door. It slides open, and Heather slips inside before making her way to James Cannon's former office.

As Heather's eyes adjust to the dim light inside, she realizes the crime wall looks even more chaotic than it did last week. It appears as though Zola has been hard at work since then.

There are photos, articles, and notes everywhere, all connected by different strings. The yearbook photo of Colin Hughes is tacked to the wall with a question mark next to the following year, when Colin vanished from the yearbook pages. Heather thinks about asking Nick what happened, but quickly dismisses the idea.

The next photo laid out is a group shot of the Bronswood auction winners in the same year in which the first scholarships were awarded. Beneath that, arranged in a vertical column, are photos of the auction winners each subsequent year. Heather scans through the photos.

Several of the persons pictured never appear in more than one photo, which makes sense to Heather knowing what she knows now. Her stomach churns at the idea of winning a child at auction.

Heather makes a mental note to find out more about the auction winners' identities. Maybe the children can be tracked down. Maybe they can be reunited with their families. She quickly pushes the thought down her priority list. Charlie is at the top, and he's the only thing that matters right now. She moves to the next row of documents.

The last row of documents is a staggered series of close-up photos from inside Bronswood, and Heather recognizes photos that were taken for the school newsletter. She wonders briefly how Zola got them before remembering that her friend volunteered to help with the school website.

It's no surprise that most photos feature the PTA triplets. Liv is pictured inside the gymnasium, smiling and carefree as if she has no idea that she's being photographed but is always prepared. Shay sits beside Liv, her eyes focused elsewhere, her full lips pressed into a tight smile.

Heather frowns as she turns her attention to Harriet. Harriet is clearly unhappy about being photographed, and her eyes bore a hole into the camera lens. Harriet is always careful about how much of her serious side she shows, but Heather has seen this look before, as recently as at the gala. Since that night, Heather has wondered why on earth Harriet would ever help her. But in this moment, she realizes she's been asking the wrong question.

It's not about why Harriet would help her. It's about why Harriet knew the truth in the first place.

If you only see Rosler, then you haven't seen everything.

Reaching into her purse, Heather yanks out the Blackpool article. By now, she can't look at Colin Hughes without seeing Nick, and Heather forces herself to focus on the young girl in the photo. Etta Hughes. Heather presses her fingertips to her temple. When Nick was drunk, he mentioned a sister. A sister closer than Heather ever imagined.

The loud clang of a wall clock makes Heather jump, and she reminds herself that she's running out of time. She needs help. She needs Zola. Shaking her head to clear the cobwebs, Heather focuses on the wall again, trying to follow Zola's train of thought.

She scans the row of faces and finds Charlie at the end, grouped with the other missing children. A red string connects Charlie's picture to a headshot of Nick. Another string is connected to a photo of Heather. A question mark lays between Nick and Heather's pictures.

Betrayal stings Heather's eyes at the idea that Zola is questioning her role in all of this. She bites back the tears.

Heather knows so much more now, and she needs Zola to understand. To help her. Stepping closer to the wall, Heather begins to rearrange the information.

Chapter 41

The house is silent. Nick isn't home, and Heather isn't sure where he's disappeared to since his car is in the garage. Heather paces in her bedroom, contemplating her next move. She needs to go back to Bronswood. To find proof. To find her son.

She creeps carefully down the stairs that lead to the kitchen. Nick believes she's still locked in the basement. She needs him to continue to believe it.

As Heather approaches the bottom of the staircase, the front door bursts open. She slams herself against the wall and steals a peek around the corner just in time to see Nick barrel through the entryway. He's not alone. Stephen trails in behind him and gently closes the front door.

Though she can't see him, Heather can tell that Nick is headed straight for the bar cart. She hears the heavy glass decanter clink against the bar top and she squeezes a little tighter to the wall as Nick passes through her line of sight.

Heather looks around the corner again to see Nick sitting in one of the armchairs nearest the front door. He hasn't bothered measuring out a finger or two. His glass is filled to the brim, and he takes a deep gulp.

Stephen takes a few steps closer, his back to Heather. "Take it easy, man. You've been through a lot lately. But getting trashed isn't going to help anything."

Heather waits for Nick's response. But he simply takes another swallow.

Stephen looks anxious, and he rocks back and forth on his heels. "Do you want to talk about it?" Stephen fidgets with his hands. "I mean, you got called in for questioning. What did the police want—?"

"Nothing!" Nick snaps. He looks down at the drink in his hand. "Sorry. I appreciate you giving me a ride to the station and bringing me home. It's just not a big deal. One of the parents at the gala expressed concern over Heather's accusations, so they just needed to ask some routine questions." Nick lets his head fall back onto the cushion behind him. "Due diligence and all that."

Stephen stuffs his hands into his pockets, looking around. For what, Heather isn't sure. "So, where's Theo?" His tone is too casual.

"Grandma's," is all Nick offers in response.

Stephen nods. "And Heather? How is she doing? You said she was really sick this past week?" Stephen takes a few steps to the left and leans against the wall.

Nick takes another drink, nearly emptying his glass. "Yeah, she's been in pretty bad shape."

Stephen glances towards the staircase that leads up to the second floor, and Heather watches his chin tilt upwards as if to get a good look at the top.

A minute passes before Stephen speaks again. He swings himself upright and relaxes his body. "Hey, you look exhausted. Want me to go check on her for you? See if she needs anything?"

Nick narrows his eyes at Stephen. "You'd like that, wouldn't you? To *check on Heather?*"

"What? Nick, I never—."

"I see the way you look at her. The way you two flirt." Nick chuckles cruelly, and he tosses back the last of the scotch in his tumbler.

Stephen pulls his hands from his pockets and holds them up, attempting to look nonthreatening. "Heather's never done anything—."

Nick laughs again. "I'm messing with you, man. Relax."

Stephen lets out a breath and laughs with Nick, albeit uncomfortably.

Nick looks back at Stephen. "You won't find her upstairs, anyway." Nick's eyes close, and his head falls onto the back of the chair. "Theo isn't here. Heather isn't here. Charlie isn't here..." Nick's voice fades away as he shuts his eyes again.

Heather watches Stephen make his way towards the front door. He pauses briefly, and he looks back at the staircase, as if considering whether to sneak up there. Instead, Stephen quietly opens the front door and slips out.

When the door latches closed behind him, Heather glances back at Nick, who appears to be sound asleep in his chair. Heather gathers herself, and she quietly makes her way out of the house. Back to Bronswood.

Chapter 42

It's dark outside when Heather sees the campus security guard exit the Bronswood main building. She always thought it a lovely perk that Bronswood had on campus security. A rare thing for an elementary school. Now, though, it's clear why Rosler may feel the need to employ an added layer of protection.

The exterior building lights flick on, and Heather checks her surroundings before slipping inside the building.

The hallways are deserted; the silence interrupted only by the thready hum of the central air from overhead. Nonetheless, Heather treads softly, wanting to be cautious in case any staff members have decided to linger into the evening.

She passes by the empty classroom that she watched Charlie enter day after day, and she stops to peer through the small glass portal in the door. The room is still vacant, and she wonders when it could have possibly been cleaned out. Or why Charlie never told her he'd changed classrooms.

Heather shakes the thoughts from her head and forces herself to focus. She needs two and only two things right now.

Proof of what's been happening and Charlie's location.

The rest can wait.

Heather continues down the great hallway and around the corner. All at once, she hears footsteps from somewhere down the hall. Swallowing a yelp in panic, Heather darts into Rosler's office and hurries to shut the door behind her, cringing when the latch closes with a solid click. She listens as the footsteps approach, hoping it's just the security guard. It sounds like the person is right outside the door. Heather waits silently, and she counts the pulse in her ears as she holds her breath.

Finally, the clomping of the shoes continues past the door and down the hall.

Heather moves to the desk and flicks on the small desk light. The room glows just enough for her to get a sense of her surroundings.

As Heather orients herself, her hip bumps the desk, and the computer screen comes to life. The date reads Thursday, February 18th. It's been three days since the gala. Without her phone, Heather hadn't realized how much time she'd lost.

Unsure of where to begin, Heather returns to the computer screen. It's locked. Heather takes a few attempts at the password.

Declan. Anastasia. Blackpool.

Nothing works, and she decides to stop before some advanced tracking system comes online to warn Rosler that there's an intruder in her office. Moving on to her next best option, Heather starts digging through the binders on the shelves behind her.

The binders contain everything one might expect a headmistress to keep on hand for quick reference. Course curriculums, attendance reports, and student clubs. One shelf holds copies of the school yearbooks, beginning with 1980. Heather slides the first yearbook from the shelf and flips to the page she knows to contain Colin Hughes. She frowns when she sees he isn't listed.

Flipping to the front of the book, Heather discovers that this is a reprint issued in 2004.

Heather puts the book back and continues to search the shelves for anything that might confirm what has been going on at the Bronswood Gala.

There are binders containing scholarship applications. Binders containing the school handbook and procedures. Binders containing records of the children put on academic probation.

Nothing about the gala.

Heather turns back to Rosler's desk. The polished wooden desk contains several drawers in various sizes, each with a lock at the top of it. Heather begins to tug on the drawers. Each time, the drawer snags on the lock.

Frustrated, Heather grabs the handle of the bottom drawer, and yanks hard. The lock snaps, and the drawer flies open. She prays that the night guard outside is too far away to hear the noise.

Inside, Heather finds several hanging file folders, each labeled with a different year. She opens the most recent one and finds a small stack of typed letters.

She skims the page on top and sees that it's from a prospective parent, thanking Rosler for selecting her child for the scholarship program. Describing how excited she and her child are to attend in the Fall of the upcoming school year.

Heather slides the letter back in the folder and moves to the next one.

A similar letter brimming with effusive gratitude for the woman who took her son from her. She puts the folder back in the drawer and pulls out the prior year's folder.

Heather thumbs through the stack of letters but stops when she comes across one that is not like the others.

It's from a mother, but unlike the other letters, this one is an update about a child the woman adopted four years ago.

Headmistress Rosler,

I felt compelled to share an update with you. Robbie has adjusted so beautifully to our family. He is an incredible young man. It is a blessing and an honor to be able to provide him with the safe and stable home he deserves. He is thriving in middle school, at the top of his class. This is, in large part, thanks to the foundation he received in your care, I am sure. You can't possibly know how much you've changed our lives. You saved our marriage when we discovered we would never be able to have children. You've made our greatest dream come true. Our family is whole. Thank you.

Regards,
Karen

Heather's hand trembles as she reads the letter again. One of these boys is better now, safe, stable, and happy. And a family so desperate for a child now has one.

For a moment, Heather wonders if she should let Charlie go. Maybe Charlie will have a family better than the one Heather has given him. There isn't a child more worthy, and she would give anything to ensure his happiness and safety.

No.

Heather rejects the voice inside her head that's telling her to let go. She won't let him go. No one will ever love him the way that she does. She'll fight. And she vows right there, in the dim light of Rosler's office, that when she finds her son, things will be different.

She flips the letter over and sees a photo paper-clipped behind it. The back of the picture is labeled.

Robbie's 12th birthday. May 5, 2009.

Robbie was taken from his family four years ago, which means he was eight years old. The same age Charlie is now. The realization burns behind Heather's eyes.

She turns the photo over to look at Robbie. She wasn't sure what she thought she'd feel when she saw Robbie's face, but it certainly wasn't a shock of recognition.

She's seen him before. Robbie is actually Roberto Jimenez. Heather saw his picture at the library when she was searching for other missing children.

There is some peace in knowing that Roberto is alive. If he is alive, it means there is hope for finding him. Hope of finding all of them.

This photo confirms everything: James Cannon's theory, the conspiracies within the police department, Rosler's deception. Everything. Heather wonders if it will be enough.

Heather sets the letter on the desktop and continues looking through the folders. The lighting is so poor that she nearly misses a binder lying on its side beneath the hanging file folders.

She draws the binder out carefully so as not to make a mess of the folders above it. When she lays it on the desk, a cautious smile stretches across her face.

The binder is full of pages recording past gala auction items. Each year is separated by a tab divider. Each year's section includes pages of items that are neatly organized by item number, bid sheet, and winner.

This is it. This is exactly what Heather needed.

Now, she only needs to prove that these items somehow correspond to missing children. Taking a deep breath, Heather looks through the most recent year and scans the winners from just days ago.

The auction item numbers are made up of five, six, and sometimes eight digits. They don't appear to be in any particular sequence. Heather runs through a list of possible ways they might be arranged. Alphabetically by the winner's last name, or perhaps by the listed item value.

She flips through the pages as quickly as she can, looking for anything that might connect the auction to the missing children.

She comes to a halt on one item. A ten-day all-inclusive stay at a villa in Greece. Item number 011702.

Charlie's birthday.

The winner listed is Lana Oxford with a bid of $117,800. Item delivery date is in two days.

Heather's heart sinks. Is this Charlie? Is this what his entire life is worth?

It's too much of a coincidence to be anything else. She needs more proof. And she needs it now if Charlie is to be turned over to a new family in two short days.

Heather looks over at the letter she left on the desk. Roberto was adopted four years ago, and she knows his birthday from the photo. She flips through the folder and finds the 2005 auction items. There, on the fourth page, is auction item 50597. May 5th, 1997. Winner: Karen McConnell with a high bid of $76,000.

Going back to the current year, Heather checks the delivery dates of all the auction items. Each of them is dated two days from now. She clenches her fists at her sides.

The boys are still here somewhere.

Heather scribbles a few notes as quickly as her hand will let her, making the connection between Roberto's auction page and the adoption letter, making it clear that police need to look up Roberto Jimenez's missing person's report. She arranges the information on Rosler's desk, taking time to note the page that she knows to be Charlie.

She picks up the phone and dials 9-1-1 before setting the phone down. She leaves it off the hook as she backs away.

Chapter 43

Heather races to the gymnasium, sprinting through the open space to the back door that will lead her down to the cages. She snakes her way through the hallways, bursting through each door, sending up small prayers of gratitude for each that is mercifully unlocked.

Only one door remains.

She grabs the handle and pulls.

The bottom floor is pitch black. It's silent.

Heather makes her way to the bottom of the staircase. A ray of light drifts down from the trail of doors she left open in her wake. It isn't much, but it's just enough that Heather can make out the shapes of the bars on the cages in front of her.

She creeps quietly through the room. The cages are empty once more.

She was certain the boys would be here. Her mind swirls. She has to find them before the police arrive.

Heather makes her way towards the back of the room.

Towards the door she never got to open. She's nearly there when she hears a thump and her head whips to the side.

To her left, she spots another door, set back about a foot, tucked away behind the last cage. She hadn't seen it before.

Another thump.

Something, or someone, is on the other side of that door.

It may be the night guard making his rounds. It may be someone else.

Despite knowing the odds, it may be the children, and Heather has to check.

She carefully pushes the door open and is met with more darkness. She steps inside the room. From what little she can tell, this room is nearly identical to the one she was just in. Only this room smells like it's been cleaned recently.

There, in the quiet, she hears rustling.

Heather ducks down and leans in towards the nearest cage as her eyes adjust to the bit of light she brought with her. The bars feel smooth.

Huddled at the back of the gate in front of her is a boy. He's fidgeting, and his back scrapes against the wall behind him as if he's trying to disappear into it.

Heather's heart leaps. They're here. Her son is here.

She checks the cages, one at a time. A few are empty. Heather counts the children as she makes her way down the rows. One. Two. Three…

Squinting against the darkness, while the light grows and expands inside the room, Heather is able to make out the five missing boys from Charlie's grade, and two other boys that she doesn't recognize. Seven in total. None of them are Charlie.

Heather wants to scream out. But as she nears the edge of the room, she catches sight of another shadow buried in the darkness.

She fights back tears at the unmistakable shape of her son, huddled against the bars. His legs are pulled in tight, and his head rests on his knees. Heather counts the fingers on the hands wrapped around his shins. She follows the line of his shirt up his back to his neck.

"Charlie?" she whispers.

He shifts to tuck himself in tighter.

Heather reaches into her pocket, and she pulls out his beloved Hulk Lego figurine. She tosses it into the cage where Charlie sits.

Charlie's head shoots up, and his arms fall to his sides. Heather hears a chain rattle and sees then that Charlie's ankle is shackled to the wall. Heather follows his movements as he tentatively reaches for the Hulk. She can't make out his expression, but she watches as he lifts the tiny green hero gently into his grasp.

He looks toward the gate where Heather kneels. "Mommy?"

Heather wants to rush to him. To pull him away from this and run. She *needs* to hold him.

Just as she's about to try prying the gate open, the faint sound of sirens in the distance floats into the room.

The police have arrived.

Heather should be relieved. However, by now she's realized that she and the children are deep within the bowels of the school. She's left the doors open behind her, but there is no guarantee that anyone will find them fast enough.

Heather looks around the room. Her eyes fall on a door at the back of the room, and she remembers. "I'll be right back, Charlie. I promise. I won't leave you here."

She runs to the door and pushes it open. It leads to a long hallway. Along the wall, she sees them. Three enormous wheeled carts with rows of metal serving trays on them. The source of the crash she heard when she first discovered the dungeon.

Heather pushes the cart, trying to tip it over, but it's far too heavy. She glances down the hallway, wondering where this corridor leads. Even if she could topple the carts, there's no guarantee that anyone would know how to reach them. Realizing that she's running out of time, Heather runs down the hallway and flings the door open.

She discovers the hallway is connected to the kitchen area of the cafeteria. A noisy area with bustling cooks and cleaners—a perfect cover to mask children's screams during school hours. She leaves the hallway and races for the main entrance to the cafeteria, knowing that it connects to the end of the hallway near Rosler's office.

Heather opens the double doors to the cafeteria and props them open just as she sees a swarm of flashlights entering the building. Charlie. She has to get back to Charlie. She rushes back and props the back door to the kitchen open and flies down to the metal carts.

She reaches for the first cart and tries again to topple it, but it doesn't budge. Heather wedges herself against the wall and she feels the sting of angry tears fill her eyes. She remembers every time she's felt the burn of defeat. Every time she was dismissed as nothing. Every time someone laid a hand on her. Clenching her fists, Heather remembers the day they took her son from her.

Everything boils over at once, and in a swirl of rage, she sends the carts crashing to the floor, toppling one by one like dominoes.

Out of breath, Heather leans against the doorway to the stairs that will lead police to the children. To her son.

Moments later, police appear and come running down the hallway. Heather steps out of the way to let them through.

Chapter 44

Heather is standing in her garden when Nick gets the call from the police. She sees him accept the call on their cordless home phone and walk toward the picture window in the living room.

"This is Nick…" He paces the length of the room. "You found him? He's safe?" Nick falls into the chair behind him. "Oh thank god." His head falls into his free hand, and for a moment, Heather believes he might truly be relieved. "How long until the doctors have finished examining him?"

A few moments later, Nick's head snaps back up. "More? What do you mean, *there's more*?" Nick rises to his feet. "Yes. Yes, of course I'll come down to answer your questions. I can be there in a couple of hours. Is that alright?" He nods. "Ok, thank you, Officer Fowler."

Heather feels her stomach tighten. After everything she's been through, her child is returning to the danger of Nick's purview. Rosler's purview. She has no idea if her efforts will be enough to keep him safe.

Nick disconnects the call, and even from her place outside, Heather knows he's headed towards the bar cart. She hears the clunk of a tumbler against the table and the rattle of ice cubes against the glass.

Desperate to settle herself, Heather grabs a pair of gloves and kneels at the planter beneath the kitchen window.

The windows are open today, and Heather frowns when she hears Nick talking to someone. The thud of glass onto the marble countertop tells Heather that Nick has returned to the kitchen. Heather frowns when she hears a woman's voice, and it takes her a second to realize that Nick has put the caller on speaker phone. She needs another moment to place the voice.

Harriet.

"Are you hearing what I've said? Jesus, Nick. The police have raided the school. Mom is in custody." Harriet pauses and exhales audibly over the phone. "Nick, what are we going to do?"

When he responds, Nick's voice is eerily calm. "Nothing."

"What in the hell do you mean, *noth*—?"

"Do you ever think about that night?" Nick interrupts her.

Heather is having trouble following Nick's train of thought, and she's grateful when Harriet clarifies. "What night?"

"The night that Declan died. Do you remember?"

"Of course I remember. What—?"

"Do you, Etta?" Nick interrupts harshly. "Do you remember him coughing, struggling to take each breath?" He doesn't wait for Harriet to respond as he says, "Do you remember Mom giving me the cough medicine and telling me to make sure he got it? Do you remember that?"

By now, Heather is sure that Nick is drunk and rattling off irrelevant information. Nonetheless, when Harriet answers, her voice is barely audible. "Yes, I remember."

Heather risks a peek inside, and she sees Nick bracing himself on the kitchen table. "Do you remember, Etta? Do you remember the part when she left me with the bottle? When she didn't say anything about how much to give him?"

The silence after Nick's question hangs heavy in the afternoon air. A minute passes without Nick saying anything, and finally, Harriet ventures a response. "I remember, Nick."

"I was only ten!" Nick bellows. "But somehow, it was still my fault! My fault when he stopped coughing." Nick chokes out a sob. "My fault when he stopped breathing."

"Nick, it wasn't your faul—."

"It was!" Nick screams. "It was all my fault, and she never let me forget it." His voice shakes as he adds, "That's why she took Charlie, and you know it. This all started as a way to give kids a better future, but it isn't about that anymore. Not for her." Harriet doesn't argue with him, and after a long beat of silence, Nick says, "You asked me what we're going to do. What we're going to say when they ask us what part we played in all of this." Heather hears him click his tongue. "And my answer is still the same. Nothing. We're not going to say anything."

"What about Heather?" Harriet presses him. "She knows about us."

"And whose fault is that?" Nick's voice is suddenly ice cold, and it sends a shiver down Heather's spine.

"What do you mean?"

"Heather never would have found those cages without help, and you know it."

Heather imagines the corner of Nick's lip pulling up into a sneer, like it does when he's angry.

"Nick, I don't know what you're talking about."

Heather shakes her head because it's just like Nick to underestimate her. Harriet helped her with the Blackpool article, but that was it. Nick's gulp of scotch is loud enough for Heather to hear from her place just outside the window. "Alright, fine. I'm sorry. I'm just anxious about the police investigation." Nick clears his throat, his voice suddenly even and calm. Too calm. "Will you please come over and talk it through before I go in for questioning?"

"Come over now? I...I don't know."

"Please, Etta." Nick's voice is close to tears, and Heather can almost feel Harriet's resolve break.

After a moment, Harriet says, "Okay. I'll be there soon."

Chapter 45

Nick disconnects the call and slams the phone down on the table. Heather hears him mumbling to himself, and she stands to see him head back towards the bar cart. Heather listens carefully as the sound of his footsteps fade, and she waits for the sound of the door latch.

When she's sure it's safe, she slips into the kitchen. The table is a mess. Splatters of amber liquid have pooled on the wooden surface after escaping from Nick's tumbler, and Heather frowns at a haphazard stack of papers pinned in place by the saltshaker. Papers that weren't here just minutes ago when Nick began talking to Harriet.

Glancing up to make sure Nick hasn't returned, Heather nudges the saltshaker aside and lifts the small stack of pages into her hands. The papers are stained with food and liquid, and a moment passes before Heather recognizes them. The notes from her purse.

After everything she's been through, Heather had almost forgotten about the letters. About the stranger who seemed determined to help her, the faceless person who convinced her to keep going even when she had nothing. When she had no hope at all. Even now, she still doesn't know who left them for her.

The most recent note is on top.

I can't touch him, but Charlie is alive. I can't speak to how well he is. You'll see. You have what you need now. I'm still here. Go, Heather. Hurry!

Heather studies the peculiar signature, the sign off on each note that she received.

On the page in front of her, the symbol is circled three times in red pen. A knot settles heavily in Heather's stomach when she realizes Nick knows. He's worked out the identity of the person who helped Heather through the darkest moments of her life, and Heather doesn't have to think to know that this person is in danger now. Knowing that Nick is confined to the house, at least for the time being, provides a minute of reprieve. She prays that Harriet's visit will…

Heather stops, breathing hard as she grips the edge of the table. She stares at the handwritten note. The signature. She can't believe she didn't see it before.

Harriet's ring. The one she never takes off.

Heather has seen the signature before, inside the band of the ring. So much time has passed since Heather first saw it. She had forgotten entirely.

Harriet said that all the grandchildren were represented.

OH CH EH

Declan Hughes.
Colin Hughes.
Etta Hughes.

By now, Heather is struggling to breathe. Of course, Nick knew, and Harriet will be here any minute. Nick's prey is coming willingly into his trap. Heather knows she can't miscalculate this time. Too much is at stake.

Glancing up to check the kitchen door one more time, Heather steals back out into the garden where the balm of fresh air, sunshine, and color has always helped aid in her resolve. She draws a deep breath as she kneels beside a petite plant with vibrant purple flowers.

Chapter 46

Heather has just come into the kitchen when the doorbell rings, and she keeps herself out of view as Nick thunders across the entryway to reach the door. She frowns when she glances at the clock above the sink. It's only been a few minutes since the phone call. Seconds later, Heather sees: the new visitor is not Harriet.

"What the fuck are you doing here?" Nick sighs.

"We need to talk."

Heather knows that voice well, and she dashes to the other side of the kitchen to disappear behind a wall. She doesn't even think about it. Hiding for years, making herself smaller, have become intuitive. The instinct is seeped deep into her fiber.

"I don't have time for this bullshit. I need to go get my son."

Heather peeks around the wall, just enough to see Paul step inside the door. "That's exactly why it has to be now. He's not your son. He's mine. Mine and Heather's. I'm here for my kids. And for Heather."

Nick chuckles. "Well, you can't have her. And the courts will never give you Charlie and Theo." As he speaks, Nick leads the way into the living room, showing no concern whatsoever about Paul's assertion. Heather looks around the corner again. Nick collapses into a chair, but Paul remains standing.

"I'm not the same man I was before. I'm better now."

Nick laughs outright. "Bullshit. You're a drunk, and everyone knows it."

"I'm 754 days sober today," Paul argues, startling Heather with his quiet confidence. "I'm going to give you one more shot at this. I'm here for Heather and my children."

"*One more shot?*" Nick scoffs. "What makes you think I care about—?"

"Because the cops are on their way here as we speak," Paul interrupts him. "You get one last chance to pretend like you're a decent human being."

From her place behind the kitchen wall, Heather watches Nick sit up in his chair. "What in the fuck are you talking about?"

"We know you were part of the kidnapping ring with your mother," Paul says softly. When Nick doesn't produce any sort of response, "Zola has everything. She's talking to Officer Fowler as we speak."

"Zola?" Nick echoes in confusion. "Heather's mousy little friend?"

Paul nods. "The mousy friend who tried to reach Heather after the gala and couldn't get through. The same mousy friend who has copies of hush money checks shuttled through the parent company of your marketing firm. In your handwriting. She called me, trying to find Heather."

Nick stares at Paul, as if evaluating him. Or toying with him. "So, what do you want? If you gave everything to the police, why are you here?"

"I told you. I want to see Heather. And I want my kids back."

Paul fidgets as if debating his next words, and after a moment, he says, "I want to know if the child in custody is really Charlie."

"What in the hell are you talking about?"

Nick laughs outright, but Paul continues, never breaking his quiet confidence. "Zola told me about the videotape. How it looked like Heather picked up Charlie that day." He looks Nick straight in the eye as he says, "I want to know if that was really my son. If it's really my son they called me about today."

This bit of information seems to get Nick's attention. "They called you? You're a fucking drunk."

Paul straightens his shoulders, and he towers above Nick's wilted form in the chair. "I told you. I'm sober. I don't drink anymore."

Nick's head sags to the side. "You're serious, aren't you?"

"Dead serious."

Paul's word choice seems to catch Nick's attention, and the leather groans as Nick sits forward in his chair. "You know, if it's true that police are headed this way, then one more missing person won't mean all that much to me…" Nick lets the threat dangle there, and Heather hears the floor creak as he stands. Paul doesn't move, watching Nick as he makes his way to the bar cart.

Heather hears the decanter top being set down. "Right. Ok then." Nick takes a small sip as he returns to his chair. "My apologies. You were saying?"

Heather can't keep up with him. First a death threat, then civil discourse. She wonders briefly if her husband is losing his mind.

Paul wastes no more time trying to get the answers he needs. "Was it Charlie in the video? Was that my son?"

Nick's brows pinch together as if deciding whether to reveal another secret. He takes another gulp, drinking like his life depends on it. "Of course it was my son," Nick slurs.

Paul leans forward. "How did you do it, Nick? How did you

get Heather on video, picking Charlie up earlier that day? Did you drug her so she'd forget?"

"I picked out her clothes every day." He wipes a bead of perspiration from his brow. "I loved that outfit…"

Heather realizes the truth at the same time Paul does, and she recoils as she realizes what her husband did. What she let him do.

"It was a repeat outfit. The footage was old," Paul says.

Nick nods, and he blinks several times before focusing on Paul. "You love them, don't you?" Nick whispers.

"I do," Paul answers without hesitation.

Nick straightens, and he jerks his head toward a table to his left. "I keep a pistol in the drawer. Get the hell out of my house before I decide to use it."

Nick turns away, and Paul doesn't wait for another word. He glances at Nick one last time before making a beeline for the door.

Chapter 47

Nick blinks heavily, his eyes roving between the front door and the side table. Heather knows Harriet will arrive any second.

Harriet's voice rings out from the other side of the door as she knocks. "Nick? Hello?" The door opens and Heather watches Harriet let herself in. Harriet trots over to where Nick is slumped in his chair. She shakes his shoulders. "Nick!"

Nick's eyes flutter open and it looks like he's straining to lift the heavy lids.

Harriet picks up the glass still clutched in Nick's grasp. "Jesus, Nick! How much have you had to drink?"

"Etta?" Nick drags his head upright. "What are you doing here?"

Harriet takes a step back. "You asked me to come over. We need to talk about what you're going to tell the police."

"Doesn't matter anymore." Nick's words blend into a jumbled mess, barely decipherable.

Harriet sighs. "How can you say that? Of course it matters.

We still have time to get this straightened out." Harriet's lip curls. "But now you've gone and drunk yourself stupid again."

Nick's eyes close and he pushes the heels of his palm deep into the sockets. "I love Charlie. I never thought she'd go this far. Besides all that, Heather wanted to fit in so badly. Mom knew it'd be too easy."

Heather winces at the comment, her entire body hot with shame.

"Nick, I need you to snap out of this—."

"My name isn't Nick! She turned me into something else."

Harriet pauses at the outburst before continuing. Her voice softens. "Colin, please. This doesn't have to be it. No one knows exactly what's happening, yet."

Nick shakes his head. "Heather figured it all out. You helped her, but still. She told Zola. Paul knows…"

Harriet cocks her head to the side. "Where is Heather?"

Nick throws his head back and stares at the ceiling. "In the basement."

"In the basement?" Harriet steals a look at the door that leads to the lower level. "Nick, you're not making any sense."

Nick continues, bouncing from thought to thought with no discernable connection between them. "Charlie knows. He knows everything." His head snaps to attention. "I can fix that, though. You're right, there's time to clean up this mess. I'm good at cleaning up the mess."

A chill pierces Heather's bones, and she doesn't hesitate as she paces across the kitchen. She knows what she needs to do now. Anything to protect her son.

Harriet seems rattled at the implied threat, too. "Colin, whatever you're thinking about doing right now, you need to forget it. He's just a child."

Nick's eyes glaze over. "So was Declan."

Harriet takes a few steps back. "I'm going to get you some water. Don't move."

Nick says nothing and Harriet moves into the kitchen.

Sitting atop the marble island top is a bag of loose-leaf tea, propped up beside the mug that Heather knows is Nick's favorite. It's a warm, blue ceramic mug emblazoned with the kids' fingerprints next to their respective photos. Letters spelling *World's Best Dad* wrap around the bottom of the mug. Lying next to the mug is the single stalk of belladonna that Heather trimmed from the garden.

Heather watches from the back stairway as Harriet glances around the room, only to find it empty.

Harriet boils some water and pours it into the mug along with the prepared metal tea strainer. She fingers the belladonna stem, seeming to contemplate its merit. Harriet is smart, and Heather knows she remembers what Heather taught her about its fruit.

Harriet seems to come to a conclusion, the same one that Heather was guiding her towards. Heather looks on as Harriet plucks each purple berry from the plant. Heather estimates that the stem she trimmed must have contained nearly thirty nightshade berries. A handful would be sufficient for Harriet's purpose. But Harriet squeezes every last one into the mug.

When Harriet is finished, she tosses the stem into the sink, out of sight. She calls Nick to come sit at the island, and she slides the mug across to the chair Nick stumbles into.

Nick places his hands to each side of the mug, flinching a little from the heat. His brow furrows as he lifts the mug to smell the liquid, and he nods as the corners of his mouth curl into a sad smile. Heather wonders if he recognizes the smell of the tea she used to make for him when he had a tough day at work. After several more moments of hesitation, Nick takes a sip to check the temperature. Then he takes a deep gulp.

For a few minutes, Nick sits in silence as he sips on the tea, staring into the mug with an expression of abject sorrow. He rocks from side to side, looking drunker than Heather's ever seen him.

Harriet watches for a moment before she informs him she needs to retrieve something from her car. She pushes a lock of ash blonde hair from her face as she stands. "I'll be right back."

Heather looks on as Harriet moves toward the door. She pauses as she looks back at the basement, as if debating the truth of Nick's admission that Heather was down there. Harriet shakes her head, seeming to disregard the thought and leaves.

Heather hears the car door slam, the engine start, and the screech of the tires as Harriet pulls out of the driveway too quickly.

Heather knows why Harriet left. She doesn't want to be anywhere close when the police arrive, and Heather suspects Harriet wouldn't want to witness what happens next.

But Heather watches. She has to be sure.

Nick takes another drink, and Heather watches him stare down into his cup a bit longer than normal, as if lost in thought.

After a while, he whispers, "I'm sorry, Heather." He wipes the beads of sweat that drip from his brow and stretches his neck out to try to swallow.

"I'm not."

Nick's eyes snap open in terror, and he stumbles backwards as Heather steps into view. She watches as his face twists in confusion. Seconds later, Nick's body goes slack, and he pitches forward, slamming into the counter before crumpling into a heap on the kitchen tile. The mug shatters beneath the weight of his body, and Heather watches until his body stops twitching.

Heather walks over to where Nick lays. She crouches down and picks up a large chunk of the mug with Charlie's smiling face on it. She sets it gently back down where she found it before checking Nick's pulse. His body spasms to life, and his eyes open wide, looking right at her with fright. His mouth falls open, his eyes roll back into his head, and he's gone.

Heather expected to feel happy. Relieved maybe. But instead, she feels nothing at all.

Chapter 48

The garden is calm. Heather looks around, soaking in the peace that's always found her in this space. She takes in the blooms, vibrant and hearty in the harsh winter air. The trees that continue to bear fruit when there is little warmth or sunlight. The strength of the garden fills her as she thinks about everything she's done to get to this point. She is so much stronger than she ever believed.

She will not forget the promise she made in Rosler's office. To herself and to her son. Things will be different now.

Heather isn't certain how long she's been standing in the garden when she hears the sirens again. But it's time to move. She isn't finished yet.

She walks inside, over to where Nick still lies. She bends down, clutching a single belladonna berry in her fingers. Heather squeezes the fruit just enough to burst the skin, and she rubs it on Nick's fingers. She pauses for a moment before gently swiping the berry across his lips.

Heather stands and walks over to the basement. She pulls the door open, and she waits.

Police bang on the door, demanding someone open it up. When they finally break through the heavy wood, four officers come pouring in, and Heather moves to the side. The first officer spots Nick immediately and rushes into the kitchen. The next two officers split off. One heads upstairs towards the bedrooms, the other to the living room.

The last officer enters and makes his way through the open door to the basement. Heather slips in and follows him down.

"Jesus!"

The officer's yell in surprise startles Heather, and she cranes her neck as she follows the path of his flashlight to the tiny storage room at the back of the basement. She stares as he does at the pool of blood that's seeped over the floor, at the tendrils of red snaking across the concrete.

HEATHER IS OUTSIDE FOR what feels like days, waiting for the forensics team to leave. It's approaching the early hours of the morning when she finally sees the gurneys. Nick's body is first. The police wheel it out with the bag partially open. Just enough to see his face.

The second gurney follows. Heather notices immediately that the bag is zipped shut.

She can't help but be grateful that Theo isn't home to see this. Grateful Charlie isn't here to see this.

It's been a long evening of forensic investigators, swabs, searches, and interviews.

The forensics team has finally completed their investigation. At least for the time being. They've cleared out, and the house is empty save for the various markers and tags left behind.

The house is silent. Death swirls around her, hanging thick in the air. The fortress that she once called home is now a graveyard.

Heather wanders around, with no particular purpose in mind, feeling like she's trapped inside of a mausoleum. With nothing to do besides wait to finally see her son.

She steps into the kitchen, kneeling beside the spot where Nick collapsed. A faint grey area remains on the tile. Heather has heard that dead bodies leave a death stain where they fall. Some say it's the separation of the soul.

Heather wonders if scrubbing the tile will remove the stain, or if it's a permanent fixture now.

Chapter 49

After a minute, or maybe an hour, Heather walks back outside. There's frost on the grass, but she isn't cold. She isn't anything at all.

Heather approaches the door and finds the morning paper sitting on the doormat. She hadn't noticed when it arrived. She crouches down and takes the paper in her hand. As she unfolds the issue, her eyes take in the morning headline, and the weight of it drags her down. She falls to her knees. The paper smacks the porch in front of her.

BREAKING NEWS: MISSING WOMAN'S BODY FOUND IN BASEMENT

```
The following report contains graphic details.

Heather Hartford, wife of prominent marketing
VP, Nick Hartford, has been missing since
Monday evening. A friend, who wishes to remain
```

anonymous, reportedly had been unable to contact Heather after the annual Bronswood Gala where Heather was reported to have been out of sorts. Onlookers confirmed that Heather had been unwell. However, our source says she grew increasingly concerned when Heather's husband refused to allow anyone to check in on Heather's wellbeing.

When shocking news of the Bronswood Student Scandal rocked the community just days ago, police called Mr. Hartford in for questioning. Reports say police were alarmed at their inability to track Mrs. Hartford down for questioning given that her son was one of the eight missing boys found beneath the Bronswood school.

A box of evidence reportedly arrived on the police station doorstep one day ago, addressed to Officer Jenkins, who'd been out to the residence recently following a reported break-in.

Based on the evidence provided, Officer Jenkins confirmed the involvement of not only Nick Hartford, AKA Colin Hughes, in his mother's criminal organization, but the involvement of several others, including members high up in the California Chronicle, the Windwood Police department, and numerous multimillion dollar corporations all over the world. Kara Luval, a junior copy editor at the California Chronicle, aided police in discovering a set of meticulous records stored in the archives room at the

Chronicle. Her brother, Anthony, disappeared from Bronswood nearly a decade ago, and Ms. Luval indicated that she'd been pressured to keep the records hidden on the threat of losing her job.

When police arrived at the Hartford residence that evening to arrest Mr. Hartford, they found him dead on his kitchen floor. Preliminary reports show an exorbitant amount of a plant-based toxin in his system. The final autopsy report has not yet been released.

A search of the premises led police to discover the body of Heather Hartford in a tiny closet in the basement of the home.

Preliminary autopsy results showed she had been severely beaten prior to being shoved into the tiny room. Cause of death was determined to be a blow to the head, causing an acute subdural hemorrhage. Investigators suspect that upon discovering he had killed his wife, Nick disposed of her in the basement. Several of her joints and bones were damaged in the process.

Upon removal of the body, several scratches were visible on the walls inside the basement room. Forensics believe that an analysis of the blood and nails found will prove they belonged to Mrs. Hartford, suggesting she may have been alive at the time of the incident.

The investigation continues and authorities continue to look into the possible murder-suicide of Mr. and Mrs. Hartford.

Heather lets out a long sigh, and despite the thirty-degree temperature, she cannot see her breath. She closes her eyes, and when she opens them again, she's standing in front of the tiny closet in the basement.

The space doesn't bother her as it once had, and she drops to her knees on the cool concrete floor. She reminds herself that her children are safe. Her best friend is safe. Because of her. She closes her eyes as grief pierces her bones.

It isn't enough.

Heather screams, causing the lights above her to surge and burst, plunging her into darkness once more.

Chapter 50

ONE WEEK LATER...

Heather watches them from a distance, longing to reach out and touch them just one more time. She'd give anything. She'd endure every ounce of pain again for just one more chance. She would take them far away from Windwood.

It's snowing. Tiny white flakes float slowly down to the ground, coating the grass in ice. Heather imagines it isn't snow falling from the sky, but ash coming from the school she dreams of burning to the ground until there's nothing left but a few smoldering embers for the sheets of snow to extinguish. She'd burn it for everything they did to her. To Charlie. And every other child.

Heather takes a few steps closer and leans against a huge ponderosa pine tree. She knows where they're headed. She's memorized the engraving on her headstone by heart.

HEATHER HARTFORD
1974 - 2010
"TAKEN TOO SOON. WE SEE YOU. WE REMEMBER."

Heather had watched as her mother debated with Zola over which last name to use for her gravestone. Pamela ultimately kept Hartford because she wanted people to recognize her daughter and know the truth of what she endured when her story is brought up. She wanted people to know that her daughter was real, and that she was murdered. She didn't want her daughter's story forgotten.

Pamela is wearing all black again, as she did the day they laid Heather to rest. Her peacoat is dusted with white flakes. Heather follows the path of her mother's arm down to the hand that clutches Theodora's.

Heather watches as her daughter stretches as far as her arms will allow to draw shapes with her free hand in the snow beneath her. Theo turns her head just enough that Heather can see the tip of her cherry red nose.

A tear rolls down Heather's cheek, leaving a frozen trail in its wake.

Zola moves to stand between the two boys. Beck on one side. Charlie on the other.

They are too young to understand exactly how strong the gravity of what happened will be. How it will pull their lives in a new direction. A direction they should never have had to go in.

They stand there for a minute before Beck begins to whine that he's cold.

Pamala turns to Zola. "I'll take the children back to the car. You take as much time as you need."

Zola nods her thanks as Pamela takes Theo's hand in hers and guides Beck towards the car with her free arm. Heather can tell her mother's thin smile is for their benefit.

Charlie stays where he is. Heather hasn't seen his face yet, but she knows it probably betrays nothing. He was always so good at disappearing, even when he stood right next to you. Heather wipes away more tears as she thinks about her son's resilience and his strength.

Heather moves a little closer and watches as Zola bends down, laying a bouquet of crisp pink camellias on Heather's headstone. "I'm sorry, Heather." Heather hears her voice shake. "I'm sorry I failed you."

Zola swipes under her eyes with the back of her hand. "But Nick will never hurt anyone ever again. And the rest of them will pay for what they've done. I'll make sure of it."

Zola sniffles and leans in closer to the stone. She lowers her voice, but Heather can still hear her as if she's standing right beside her. "I'm going to take care of Charlie and Theo. I'm going to take them far away from here. I promise you that."

Zola sits up a little straighter and places one palm to the engraving of Heather's name. "I'm still here, Heather."

HEATHER WATCHES HIM APPROACH, slowly, as if to ensure he doesn't startle Zola. He crouches down and drapes an arm gently across her shoulders.

Zola turns her head to look at him. "Paul." Her voice cracks, and she waits a moment before taking another attempt at speaking. "I never got a chance to thank you."

"Thank me? For what?"

"For listening to me." She runs her sleeve under her nose. "For helping me."

"I was too late. I should have gone sooner." Heather watches Paul's eyes shimmer beneath a sea of tears so close to spilling over.

"It wouldn't have made a difference. She was gone the second Nick took her away from the school."

"I don't know if I can ever forgive myself."

They sit in silence for what feels like hours. Charlie hasn't moved from his spot in front of Heather's gravestone.

"What happens now?" Zola asks.

Paul shrugs. "We leave. Get these kids far away from here and make sure they get the help they need. Things are going to get very ugly before they get better. They need someone on their side. We can do that for them. For Heather."

Zola nods and climbs to her feet before turning to Charlie. "Are you ready, sweetheart?"

Charlie shakes his head. "No! I'm not leaving."

"It's time to go, Charlie. I know it's so hard, but we have to go now."

"No! No! I'm not going!" Charlie screams. "I want my mom! I'm not leaving without her!" He waves his arms wildly, like he has no idea what to do with the pressure of everything threatening to burst from inside him.

Heather wants to run to him and take him in her arms. But it's Zola who comforts him instead.

"Shh. I know, sweetheart. I'm sorry. I am so sorry. Your mom can't come with us." They sink back to the ground, where Zola rocks him back and forth as he cries. "I miss her, too. So much."

Paul moves to Charlie's other side to wrap his arms around his son. Flanking him with people who love him.

Charlie's body goes limp. "What if she can't find me where we're going?"

Zola pulls back for a minute and ducks her head to look into Charlie's eyes. "What do you mean?"

"She came to see me last night. She woke me up and told me she loved me and that she'll always be with me, no matter what." Charlie looks down at his hands as his fingers fidget.

Zola places a gentle finger under his chin to lift his face to her. "She visited you? You mean in a dream?"

Charlie shakes his head. "How will she know where we're going?"

Zola doesn't seem to know how to answer that question. "Charlie, one day, I'm going to tell you all about your mommy, and just how brave she was. How she never once stopped trying to find you. I promise." Zola strokes Charlie's cheek with her thumb. "But right now, we need to leave. Can you be brave, too, and come with me and your grandma and Theo?"

Charlie nods his head and climbs to his feet. Zola follows him, and Heather watches Zola wrap an arm around her son's shoulders as they walk to the car. Paul follows until he breaks off to climb into his own vehicle.

As Charlie and Zola approach the car, Zola steps in front of him to open the door.

Charlie stops and turns back, looking right at where Heather is standing. His eyes connect with hers.

Heather blows him a tiny kiss and watches as Charlie pretends to snatch it out of the air and place the kiss on his heart. He blows a kiss back to her, and Heather grabs it and presses it to her own heart.

Heather smiles, trying to look as happy as she possibly can, and she waves to him.

Charlie doesn't smile, but he waves back at her.

Zola turns to look at him, and Heather watches as Zola looks out across the way. "Who are you waving to, Charlie?"

Charlie doesn't look at Zola as he shrugs a little and climbs into the car.

Zola scans the area once more before climbing into the driver's seat.

Heather watches them disappear into the wooded roads that will take them wherever they plan to go, and then she walks to the headstone.

She traces the petals of the camellias lightly, watching them bow and bend under her touch. "Thank you, Zola."

epilogue

2 MONTHS LATER...

FIRE AT BRONSWOOD

Developing story.

Firefighters were called late last night when a couple out for an evening walk saw flames roaring up to the sky. It appeared they were coming from Bronswood Academy, the site of a gruesome discovery earlier this month when accusations surfaced claiming that former headmistress Anastasia Rosler had been selling select students to an underground ring of affluent bidders under the guise of raising funds for the school's various programs and scholarships.

Police discovered that children were being held in inhumane and horrendous conditions while they awaited illegal placement with adoptive families.

Investigators aren't sure what caused the fire, but it was determined that the fire originated in the basement, where the victims were held hostage.

The fire consumed the entire recreation room and west wing of the school before firefighters were able to extinguish the flames.

No charges are being filed at this time.

She pushes a strand of newly colored chestnut brown hair behind one ear and folds the newspaper in half, laying it gently on top of Heather Hartford's tombstone. She looks up, her pale blue eyes sparkling, and she smiles as she touches the ring on her left hand. "Well done, Heather. Well done." She brushes her hand across the granite and walks away.

acknowledgements

    I believe that the world around you will confirm when you are onto something. The signs will stack up, providing you little bits of confidence and confirmation that what you're doing, is exactly what you should be doing. Bronswood was no exception.

    From the time I announced what my sophomore novel was about and received one of the largest amounts of "yes, I'd absolutely read that" responses on an Instagram poll ever, to the multiple occasions I would stumble upon a tiny door in a room when I'd never knowingly noticed one before, to giving my characters unique names and then finding at least one character in each book I read over the last few months, to my daughter's school hosting its first ever "gala" event after I'd already written about the Bronswood gala. The signs were numerous and my writing partner has my complete log as I'd giddily share each one in real time with her. I felt in my bones that Heather's was exactly the story I was meant to tell in my second novel.

    But none of it would have been written without a slew of help behind the scenes. So here we go…

Thank you to my husband for your unwavering support and willingness to grant every request for added writing time at a moment's notice. Thank you for being one of my earliest readers and cheering on another year of me acting like an author.

Thank you to my writing partner, Jessica Jones, for agreeing to work with me again, for reading countless drafts, for noodling through every plot point. Mostly, thank you for giving me access to your brilliant mind. You made this story so much better.

Thank you to my editors, Jamie Warren, and Tami Renville, for meticulously plucking out every mistake, and providing your insights into plot and character development. My writing is stronger because of you.

Thank you to my sister-in-law, Christina Kiefer, for looking at thousands (which doesn't feel like an exaggeration) of cover designs and thoughtfully adding numerous finishing touches that perfectly encapsulated Bronswood's mood.

Thank you to my sensitivity readers, who helped me develop a credible and layered picture of the trauma that victims of domestic violence suffer.

Thank you to each of my beta readers who provided unflinchingly honest opinions, questions, and perspectives of Heather and Charlie's story.

Thank you to Bridget Klyuchik for always seeing a place for my books on the shelves of every Target aisle and bookstore you walk into, every TV and big screen you watch, every library shelf you scan, and for leaving the search result for my books on every public computer screen you encounter.

Thank you to Miranda at Brood Coffee Shop in Lincoln, for supporting a local author with such enthusiasm and to every barista who fills my cup while I replenish the shelves with my books.

Thank you to Barnes & Noble in Roseville for your support

of local authors and efforts to put the right books in the hands that want them. Thank you for inviting me in to sign books.

Thank you, Samantha Lilly, of Happlilly Homesteading for championing Heather in her love of baking and developing the perfect lemon blueberry loaf for her and her family. What a gift that I get to include one of your delicious creations in the pages of this book.

Thank you to every advanced reader, Bookstagrammer, bookseller, librarian, BookToker, and bloggers who champion my books. They reach the hands they do, because of you and all your incredible work.

Thank you to the Lincoln Public Library for being the first library to stock my books and for inviting me to speak at local events. Libraries have a special place in my heart and your support means the world to me. I'm so honored to have a place on your shelves.

To my friends and family who provide me endless encouragement and excitement. Your joy and enthusiasm when you tell your friends that I'm an author make me feel far cooler than I actually am. Because of you, I keep writing.

Lastly, but far from least, to every single reader who chose this book—thank you. Of all the books in the world, you picked this one. And that is indescribably cool.

Lemon Blueberry Loaf

by Samantha Lilly, Happlilly Homesteading
www.happlillyhomesteading.com
Instagram @ourenglishfarmhouse

INGREDIENTS

Lemon Blueberry Loaf :

1/4 cup Sourdough Discard
1 cup Butter
2 Tsp Baking Powder
1 1/4 cup Self Rising Flour
1 cup Sugar
4 Eggs
3 Tbsp Milk
3 Tbsp Lemon Rind, grated
1 cup Blueberries

Topping:

1/2 cup Powdered Sugar
1/4 -1/2 cup Lemon Juice (to desired tartness)

DIRECTIONS

Preheat oven to 350° f

Beat sugar & butter together making sure to cream the two. This will take about 5 minutes. You don't want it to be gritty.

Slowly add your eggs and your sourdough discard.

Add your flour and baking powder together.

On low speed add your milk, lemon rind and lemon juice.

Stop your mixer and fold in your blueberries gently.

Line a loaf pan with parchment paper or make sure to coat it with flour so nothing sticks and place your batter into your pan. And place into the oven at 350° for 40-50 minutes. Check fineness by placing a toothpick in the middle. If it comes out without sticky batter it's done.

To make your topping you will combine your powder sugar and your lemon juice over low heat making sure to continually stir as to not let the mixture stick to the bottom of the pan.

Once your cake is done you can pour your topping over your cake and let cool for 30 minutes.

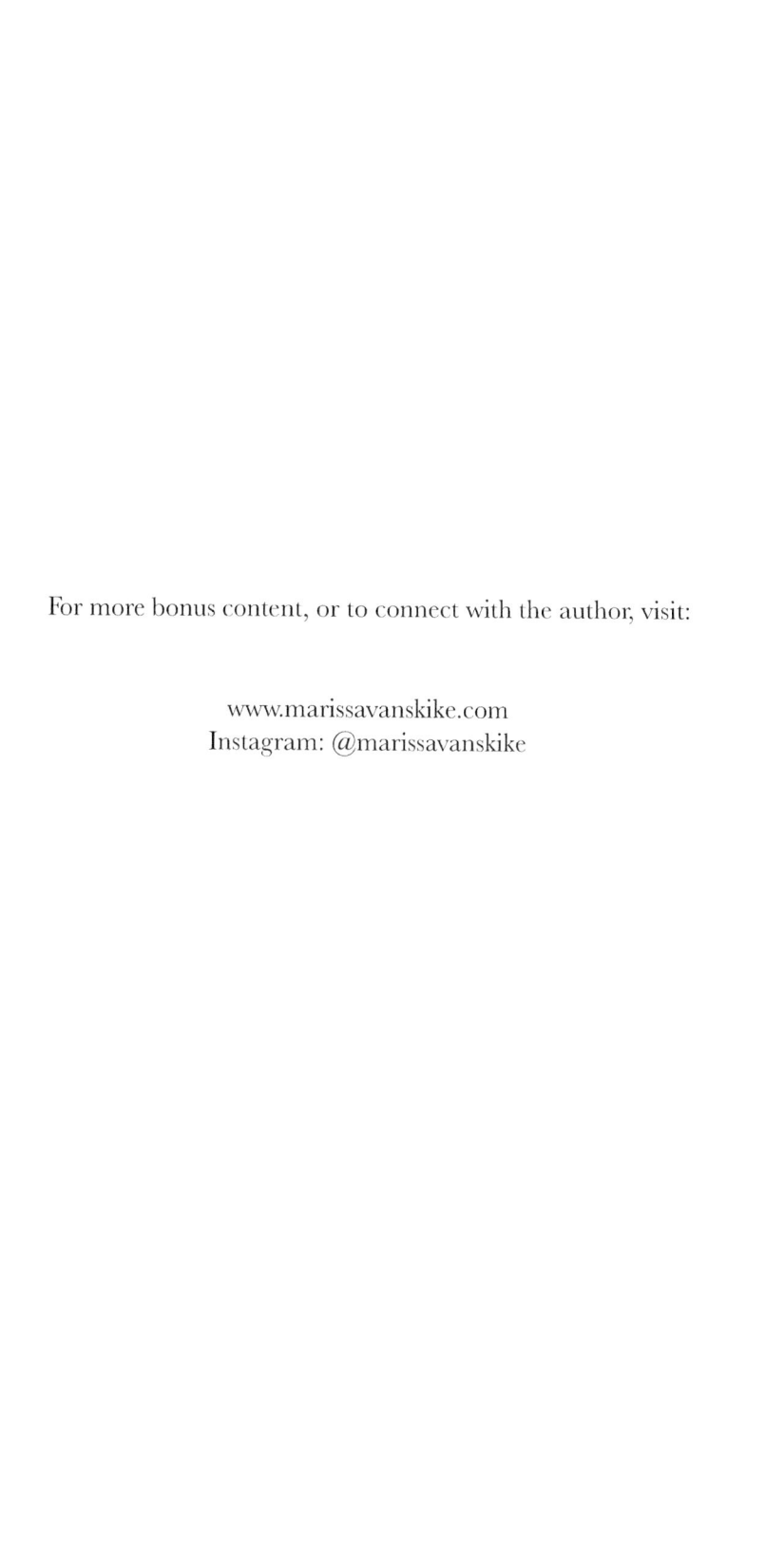

For more bonus content, or to connect with the author, visit:

www.marissavanskike.com
Instagram: @marissavanskike

ABOUT THE AUTHOR

MARISSA VANSKIKE is the author of *How It Had To Be*. When she isn't busy shuttling her children to their various activities, you can find her outside with her family or caffeinating herself with a book in her hand. She resides in Northern California with her husband and three children.

Printed in Great Britain
by Amazon